Swan Song
a novel by Susanne Perry

SWAN SONG

First edition. February 3, 2023.

ISBN: 979-8215323106

Written by Susanne Perry.

For Dave ...

... for his love, his belief in me, and his constant encouragement. He served as my advisor and research consultant for this book on aspects of chemistry and lab operations. From the first draft, the help and experience he shared made the story happen on each page. Dave liked the story and gave it his seal of approval. I wish we'd been able to share this moment.

Chapter 1

I sat frozen, immobilized in the driver's seat of my gray, ten-year-old Toyota Prius. My hands gripped the steering wheel although the little hybrid wasn't running. I didn't know whether I could start the damned car much less drive it from the parking lot of the medical office. I tried to review my conversation with Dr. Edmunds, the conversation that had ended minutes earlier, but the mundane, less-important details had scurried to the periphery of my consciousness. Doctors are trained to have such conversations with clarity, with sensitivity, and Dr. Edmunds had done her best I had no doubt of that. Unfortunately, there is no easy way to share news of this kind with another human being and as far as I know, there's no way to train a person to receive it either.

Whether I like Dr. Edmunds as a person doesn't really matter, but I do like her, based on two appointments after a referral by my primary care physician. Concerns about symptoms and irregularities in bloodwork led to the referral. More important than my liking her, I trust Dr. Edmunds as a physician. Aside from her qualifications and my opinion of her, the truth according to Dr. Edmunds is that I am going to die.

I had arrived at her office an hour earlier, on time for an eleven o'clock appointment. I took the elevator up to the second floor of the medium beige office building and walked to the midpoint of the lighter beige corridor. I stopped at the slightly darker beige door designated as the place of business of Dr. Kathryn Edmunds, M.D, F.A.C.S, Oncology. I dislike beige. I find it a boring color. I suppose oncologists lean toward boring in their choice of décor, keeping excitement to a minimum for the sake of their patients.

Entering the small, modestly decorated waiting area, I checked in with the receptionist who mentioned that I wouldn't have long to wait and found a place to sit. I had scarcely settled into my chair when I heard my name called by the nurse and was asked to follow her to the doctor's office—not to an examination room, but to her office.

Dr. Edmunds was seated at the desk studying the computer screen. Upon seeing me, she rose and took my hand in greeting. "Hello, Mara," she said in that comforting voice that sounded so natural. "Come in and sit down, please. How are you today?" It was polite of Dr. Edmunds to ask about my current state and her interest seemed genuine. When she asked the question, as she had at our first appointment, I was encouraged to share details beyond the medical scope. At least that was my take on our interactions and was likely her intent.

"Hello," I responded as I released her hand, relieved to take one of two upholstered chairs facing the desk. The fatigue had returned although I hadn't exerted myself beyond getting myself out of bed and to the appointment. Some days it didn't take much. *I'm not a morning person* had been my mantra for years. "I'm good," I answered through an exhale. In casual conversation, I usually responded with *I'm good* when asked how I was doing. No one really wanted to know anyway, and *I'm good* avoided a lot of worthless conversation.

This was not a casual conversation, however, and the truth was that the trek from the parking lot had left me a bit out of breath and I was relieved to sit. "I slept well which makes it so much easier the following day," I added. *Slept well,* in my case, meant that I managed to get four hours of light sleep between four and eight that morning.

"That does help, doesn't it?" the doctor responded. "Did you work last night?"

"I did. It was busy—the last evening of a conference," I recalled with a sigh. "The hordes were letting off steam while out of town on business, buying expensive drinks. We were hammered behind the bar for hours. I must have gone through a ton of ice. We didn't get out of there until three. I usually work on Thursday but I'm looking forward to this evening off. I need it." I needed it because I was tired—but then I was always tired.

"You work at Anasazi Resort, is that right?" asked Dr. Edmunds. The bar where I work is part of a posh resort complex in Scottsdale, a winter retreat for wealthy retirees where the local businesses work awfully hard at helping them spend their money.

"Yes," I confirmed, but Dr. Edmunds knew this. We had talked of it before. "If you tend bar, it's a good place to do it," I said. Situated just far enough away from downtown Phoenix, Scottsdale provides a well-manicured bedroom community and an escape for golfers and visiting executives with overflowing corporate expense accounts.

"It's a big place," she added, keeping the small talk going.

"It's huge," I agreed. The resort features a five-star hotel and convention center with all the amenities, including a casino and golf courses. I had tended bar for a branch of the management corporation in Los Angeles while I was in grad school. When I needed a job, I was lucky to have the in with HR.

Supporting myself bartending had become a good fit, or so I told myself on a regular basis. The job is good money for the hours and although it is challenging work, harder than most bar patrons knew, I rarely put in forty hours in any given week. Except for a few regulars, I talk to people, feign genuine interest for a brief time, then rarely ever see them again.

Dr. Edmunds responded with a closed-mouth smile, her lips a straight line. I detected a slight nod before she rested her chin in the palm of one hand. She broke eye contact for a moment and glanced briefly to her left at the PC monitor.

"So," she began, her gaze returning to my face. "I have results from the lab and from the MRIs. The tests have confirmed what I suspected: you have is a disease of the bone marrow. It is called multiple myeloma." Dr. Edmunds paused, reading my expression which invited her to continue. "This is a strain of cancer. The disease eliminates healthy blood cells by producing abnormal proteins. This is what is causing your symptoms—the back pain, the fatigue, the loss of appetite—the problems that concerned you enough to see Dr. Frye."

"I have cancer?"

Dr. Edmunds nodded slightly and said, "Yes. I'm afraid you do.

I felt a sharp intake of breath that was more of a spasm and my fingers squeezed the arms of my chair. My heart rate spiked. My stomach plunged. The moments of silence seemed to stretch uncomfortably. I wanted her to keep talking with that calming voice, conveying the mundane details so I wouldn't have to think past them.

"The cancer began as what we call an M.G.U.S.," she continued. "At the beginning stage, the level of proteins is lower and no damage to the body occurs."

Absorbing what Dr. Edmunds was telling me, certain words struck hard—*cancer, abnormal* and *beginning stage.*

"Wait," I begged as a thought made its way to the surface. "Am I to understand that I've had this for a long time?" I wished tears had welled, but there was no such reaction. My heart thumped and my throat constricted, making it hard for me to speak. Each syllable resounded through my chest.

"Not exactly. Multiple myeloma is connected to a benign condition, the one I mentioned. It is called M.G.U.S., or monoclonal gammopathy of undetermined significance. It is the MGUS that you've had for years. It has progressed to the present condition."

My eyes traveled from the doctor's face to the back of the monitor she had been studying. I realized that before I entered her office, Dr. Edmunds had been perusing intimate details about my condition, but I hardly cared. I managed to inhale deeply and felt my eyes open widely as I looked at her. Then I uttered a strange statement, sounding quite like the scientist I used to be. "I gather that its significance is now determined."

The doctor nodded. "The cancer is in the bone marrow. It is inoperable. And Mara, I'm sorry to tell you, it is aggressive."

Words flooded my brain again. *Cancer, bone marrow. Inoperable? Aggressive?* Shock consumed me, but I hid the emotion which was my usual practice. My emotions, reactions, even thoughts rarely are displayed on my face. A professor in college once commented on my *flat affect.* Her comment didn't bother me much because she was an insufferable bitch on her best days.

"My belief is that you've developed related symptoms for quite some time," Dr. Edmunds told me. "The lethargy, sleep problems. Depression."

For years, I had chastised myself for becoming a lazy lump of shit. No motivation. Little or no effort to exercise. No desire to excel at anything and it worsened as time passed. I engaged in a minimum of activity, just enough to function. Depression made me stay in bed, in the dark, wallowing. I had little use for interpersonal relationships outside of my roommates, Lulu and Amir. Friends were exhausting. There was my older brother, Joe, a graphic artist. Joe and I rarely spoke because I felt like a fool compared to him which added to the depression.

I inhaled, exhaled, and took a tissue from the box which Dr. Edmunds discreetly moved closer to me. Still, there were no tears, but I wiped my eyes and nose as if by autonomic response and fumbled with the tissue because my hands were shaking. I looked up at the ceiling and noticed large, brown spots as if a shaken cola had been allowed to spew above my head.

"You think that I developed a condition—this M...G...US thing." I repeated it back to the doctor stumbling over the acronym. "And you believe it might have been lurking in the shadows for years?"

"That's usually the scenario, yes," answered Dr. Edmunds.

"Do you know for how long? How long has this nuclear warhead been inside me?" I heard myself ask the questions and tried to absorb the answers.

"I can only estimate, Mara, but between five and ten years."

I could feel myself collapse from the inside. I had to cover my face with my hands for a moment before I could continue. "And now this MGUS condition has turned into inoperable bone marrow cancer called ... what was it again?" The palms of my hands pressed into my temples.

"Multiple myeloma," the doctor repeated slowly. "I have information for you about the disease and what to expect. The onset of newer symptoms, your back pain and loss of appetite, even the change in your bloodwork, has been rapid. The severity of your long-term issues—the tiredness, the apathy, the depression you've experienced—these issues also have increased, am I right?"

I nodded. "I would say there has been a slow, steady decline from bad to worse."

"We can discuss treatment options and I will honor your wishes, whatever you decide. The information I'm sending with you will outline those possibilities." Dr. Edmunds looked away for a split second, long enough to tell me that she did not relish what she needed to say next. "I would be remiss if I didn't share that at the stage of your disease, the available treatments—chemotherapy, radiation—offer very limited, if any improvement and might cause you additional concerns. In a nutshell, treatment may detract from instead of adding to the time you have. Treatment could cause you more pain and discomfort and alter the prognosis for the worse."

"In your opinion, my condition is not only inoperable and aggressive—it is also untreatable."

"Conventional treatments might do more harm than good. As I said, I will respect your wishes and try. It is your decision. After you read the information, we will discuss it. As for the symptoms you experience, we will do what we can, especially where your comfort is concerned."

"How much time do I have?" As I asked the question, I pictured my hand turning the knob on an old-fashioned parking meter, hoping I had deposited enough change.

"We can only guess but based on the rate of progression, a few months. It could be weeks."

Slam! I felt as if a blow had been rendered to the side of my head. I stared, wide-eyed for a moment. I think I may have nodded before I put my head back and stared at the spotted ceiling. When I returned my gaze to Dr. Edmunds, she looked thoughtful.

"I'm going to recommend that you speak with a colleague of mine. We work in tandem quite often with certain patients," she explained. His name is Henry Maloney and he's a psychologist. Would you be open to that?"

"Why?" I asked.

"Because what you are going to experience is as much about your mind as it is your body. Talking with Henry, or any mental health professional, can be beneficial. If you'd rather talk with someone else, or not at all, I will understand. But I know Henry and I respect him—and his manner of therapy."

"How could he be helpful to ..." the words stuck like peanut butter in my craw, "... to someone who is ... dying?" I inhaled deeply after I said the word. As I exhaled, the sweet simplicity of breathing was not lost on me and I lingered in the moment, savoring it. "But if you think talking with him will help in some way, I will."

"I do think it will help, Mara. This is Henry's contact info." She extended her hand, and I accepted the business card from between outstretched fingers. I accepted the card without thinking about it. I was doing many things without really thinking and it was uncharacteristic of me.

Dr. Edmunds clasped her hands together and placed them on her desk. "Whether you talk with Henry or choose another therapist, I'm going to recommend counseling as part of your treatment. Do you know if your insurance covers mental health services?"

Insurance coverage. Cost. Hearing the doctor's question, I realized I had no answer. Therapy wasn't cheap as far as I knew and it wasn't something I would have ever considered, instead shoving the practice into a corner as a pseudo-science. As a response, I shrugged.

"We will see each other in a few days so I can answer all your questions, talk about options, and go from there. The treatment I suggest would be largely palliative—to help you rest, manage pain, relax. Take time to process your situation and read the information specific to your condition."

The doctor handed me a thin, pocket folder containing sheets of paper. "For now, Mara, do you have other questions for me? Anything else I can help with?"

"No, no, I don't think so," I answered. In truth, I had many questions, but none I wanted to say aloud right then. "We'll talk next week then?"

"Yes. Lynn will step in and make an appointment with you before you leave. Call any time if you have a question before I see you again."

Dr. Edmunds stood and walked around the side of the desk. She placed her hand on my shoulder. "You and I will be together every step down this road, Mara." I felt her concern and appreciated her kindness. As I got to my feet a thought entered my head, but I kept it to myself. *You won't be there for the last step, Doctor. I'll be taking that step on my own.*

Lynn, the appointment scheduler, entered the office and we arranged a follow-up appointment. I felt her study me closely and she asked if I wanted to arrange other transportation. I shook my head and told her I would drive myself home. I left Dr. Edmunds' office

through a rear exit that I had not known existed and a few brief minutes later, here I am sitting in my Prius clutching the steering wheel.

Chapter 2

It took a few minutes, but I pulled myself together enough to drive out of the parking lot. A block away a shade spot at the curb called to me and I pulled over. I left the engine running with the AC on and sipped iced water from my thermos container. After a couple of deep breaths, I thought about the fact that I'd been issued a death sentence. I was going to die and not in the abstract way we think about our deaths as happening on an unknown day in the distant future. No, my death would occur relatively soon, and it sounded like it was going to involve pain. A great deal of pain.

How could this be? The truth was that I had been unmotivated, unhappy for most of my adult life and Dr. Edmunds claimed that I may have *acquired* those attributes. They might not have been personality traits, but symptoms of a disease, an ailment. Was it possible that I was not cursed with the personality of a zombie, but had it inflicted upon me? My thoughts did not drift but came down hard on a past that I had ignored.

With two degrees in chemistry, I worked in a laboratory for a company in Phoenix for many years. The job brought me to Arizona after I earned my M.S. It was unsettling for me to think about that period in my life, a time when I felt accomplished, when I had achieved a long-sought goal. A great deal of time had passed. The memory caused tears to finally reach my eyes.

My former position had been with Presson-Hagee, the industrial chemical company. I had worked there for five years when the company abruptly closed the lab. Employees were told that it was expensive to keep the lab on site and the company planned to outsource. The decision had been sudden but at the time I wasn't too bothered by it. The severance I received was generous, providing time to decide what to do, where to go next. The truth was that during the last year I was employed at P-H, I was not handling the hours, the stress, the demand to produce, as well as I had in the years prior.

When the lab closed, I was glad to take a couple of months off and I did nothing until I took the job bartending at Anasazi. I needed the change and the hours appealed to me because I was barely sleeping, struggling to wake up and get to work each day that last year in the lab. But when I took the job at the resort, I hadn't expected I'd still be working there so many years later. I was disgusted by my situation, but did not have the need, the energy, or the motivation to attempt a change.

Heading home, I wanted to curl up on my huge bed with Avo, my blond lab, in the dark of my air-conditioned bedroom. Informing my friends was something that would happen. Maybe. Soon. I supposed it would have to happen. I would have a conversation with Joe, but off the top of my muddled brain I wasn't sure when we had last spoken together. Maybe over the holidays, but that was months back. My brother always told me my luck sucked. Once again, he was right.

The noon-hour traffic was flying on the 10. I made my way to the 202 and made it home in forty minutes. My three-bedroom, one-story adobe house with an enclosed courtyard had been home for a long time. I had gone out on a financial limb by buying the house in my third year of employment at Presson-Hagee. I fell in love with the traditional southwest courtyard enclosed by a stucco wall and the living room offered the perfect corner for the baby grand piano I had inherited from my grandmother. When I bought the house, I still played piano occasionally, but I hadn't felt inclined to enjoy the beautiful instrument in a long time. When the job ended, I had considered selling the place to recoup my investment. Fortunately, selling the house had not been in the cards.

Soon after I began tending bar at Anasazi, I met Lulu and Amir. Lulu, whose full name is Luisa, is a petite Latina who deals blackjack in the casino. Growing up in East LA with gang-affiliated brothers taught Lulu two things: to take care of herself and to get the hell out of East LA. Amir manages the front desk at the hotel. He loves the Arizona climate. It reminds him of his native Iran. Amir's parents are Baha'is, and he was raised in the tradition. He doubts any of them will ever return to their homeland.

Lulu and Amir were dating when I met them—or more precisely, they were *trying* to date. When they had time off work together, they began to gravitate to the bar. Conversation was easy between us and when I wasn't terribly busy and with no one listening, the three of us would solve the problems of the world. Their visits were good for me because on most topics, we were like-minded, and our discussions were usually spirited and often hilarious and I had little spirit or hilarity in my life.

A few years older, I became the sage elder sister neither of them was blessed to have. It was a new role and I enjoyed it. It was none of my business but while it was obvious to me that they enjoyed each other's company, they carried on more like siblings or coworkers than lovers. Neither of them seemed to place any heart or much effort into a deeper relationship, but it was clear they loved each other as friends. Anyway, who the hell was I to judge?

After a few weeks, they each began to visit my bar when the other was working and sought my counsel on how to break it off without being the bad guy. The support sessions at the bar continued for weeks until they announced that they were, forever and always, just friends. To this day, they credit me with saving the friendship when I did nothing more than offer a smile and a nod, that same smile and nod for which bartenders are famous.

As it turned out, my car was in the shop overnight for new brakes and Amir offered to ferry me to and from the resort for my shift. With Lulu along as always, the three of us arrived at my house. They knew I considered selling the house and that I dreaded the idea. They accepted my offer of a cold beer and when Lulu and Amir saw the house and met Avo, they begged me to rent rooms to them. I figured the arrangement would last a few months, but years later, here we all are.

I unlocked and opened the front gate and waited in the shade of the Palo Verde, assessing my emotional state. I couldn't remember if I had told Lulu or Amir that I had a doctor's appointment, but neither of them would think it odd if I made a beeline to my room. We got on well because we afforded each other a wide berth and at this time of the day, it was not unusual for one or both to still be sleeping depending on their schedules the night before.

Avo was in his usual spot, spread out on the cool tile of the entry. He had taken to lying there whenever I was not at home. My dog greeted me by thwapping his tail and raising his head half off the floor. Lulu sat on the couch in the living room. The piano was behind the couch, the keys facing the room giving a view of the backyard when seated at the bench.

Lulu's legs were folded under her, and her thick, black hair was wound in a precarious pile on her head. She looked to have awakened recently and held a large mug of a steaming beverage. Knowing Lulu, the mug held her daily dose of strong, black tea. I was relieved to see Lulu sitting there and my reaction surprised me. I was so glad to see Avo, so glad to be home. The sensation was close to overwhelming.

"Hey," said Lulu. "I just got up. Avo wanted to go outside." She looked at the big dog and said in a baby-talk voice, "Didn't you, honey? Didn't Auntie Lu let you out?"

"Oh, I'm sorry. He peed after I fed him before I left," I said as I knelt and caressed his furry head with my free hand. "I thought he'd be okay until I returned."

"It's okay, Mara," she told me with a sleepy grin. Lulu looked at Avo and returned to baby-talk. "He's just our sweet boy, aren't you, Av?" Lulu sipped her tea and continued in her normal, Lulu voice. "Besides, I wanted to be up when you came in. How was the doctor? Does he know yet why your back hurts all the time?" I had mentioned my appointment, it appeared, and Lulu's question provided an opener.

I stood up, tossed my purse and keys on the entry table, walked over to the couch, and plopped down next to Lulu. Avo followed. He sat next to me with his head on my lap. I could swear that Avo's big brown eyes told me that he knew the news already, that he loved me, and that he was so deeply sorry.

"Well, yes. The doctor is a she and *she* knows why my back hurts." I looked toward the hallway leading to the bedrooms. "Where's Amir? Is he sleeping?" *Might as well tell them both,* I thought. They would know soon enough.

"He's at work. He told me last night that he had to go into the office for a few hours today. End of quarter," she explained with sarcasm and a wave of her hand like it was the dumbest of reasons. "All those numbers and reports. Yuck, but he'll be home soon. We were hoping to have dinner out together. It is rare when we all three have the same night off."

Amir wasn't home, but I felt like talking. Talking about what I'd learned. I wanted to tell someone, and Lulu and Amir were the only people I could imagine telling. "The water in the pot is still hot. Do you want tea?" asked Lulu, taking a sip. The steam had stopped rolling from the mug.

"No, I think I'll pour myself a glass of wine," I answered without bothering to check the time of day. "Then I'll tell you about the doctor."

Ten minutes later Lulu put her tea aside, deciding wine was a good idea. My friend asked every imaginable question, she hoped it was all a mistake, and she kept telling me that she was sorry. I was glad I had Lulu there to tell and doing so hadn't made me feel especially selfish. Selfish or not, it was the truth, and I would have to get used to talking about it.

A memory struck me when I looked at Lulu's face as I shared the news that I had terminal cancer. The memory was of my Aunt Rina—or at least it was of Aunt Rina's eyes. When I was sixteen years old and my brother Joe was eighteen, Rina had to inform us that our parents had died from injuries in a car accident. The look I saw in Lulu's eyes mirrored what I had seen in Rina's that sad day: sorrow at the pain of another.

I remembered the information Dr. Edmunds had given me and realized I had left the folder in my car when I arrived home. "I left something in my car," I told Lulu. I stood up and Avo roused to attention, his eyes on me.

"We'll come with you. Come on, Av." We walked out into the heat and over to my car. While I retrieved the folder of paperwork from the car, Avo took the opportunity to pee, leaving a dark, wet stain on the soft, green trunk of the Palo Verde.

Sitting down on the living room floor, Lulu and I drank another glass of wine while we read through pages of information about MGUS, multiple myeloma, and cancer of the bone marrow. The information said I should be able to maintain my daily routine until the protein levels reached a certain point. A regular schedule of bloodwork would alert Dr. Edmunds to the progression of my disease. I would gradually become weaker and experience a greater level of *discomfort*. Discomfort is the polite word for pain that makes you want to rip your hair out. After that I could expect a fast decline. The rate of the protein increase was individual, of course. We read about options for pain management, medications to help me sleep, et cetera.

We read through the information advising about the limited options for treatment. The data was convoluted and confusing and was dependent on various numbers related to lab results and thresholds, but the gist was clear: my condition was too advanced to risk it. My prognosis was not likely to lengthen, and the *discomfort* was predicted to be intense with or without the intervention. Palliative measures it would be.

I saw the business card for Dr. Henry Maloney and picked it up. I was staring at the card when Lulu asked, "What's that?" I explained about Dr. Edmunds suggesting a therapist. "Oh please, consider it, Mar. I know you're not one to believe in therapy, but it can help. It will be good for you if you like the guy. If you don't like him, we'll find someone else." Lulu used the word *we*. It warmed my heart.

"I'll talk to him," I answered.

Two hours had passed when the front door opened and in walked Amir. He glanced at the open bottle of wine on the coffee table. "Well, this is nice, the two of you starting the party without me," he said with sarcasm. I wanted to stay strong, aided by the wine, but I became emotional as I recounted the sad news for Amir.

Chapter 3

I woke up the next morning and looked at the clock. It was after nine and I was hungry. Hunger pangs were rare because my appetite had decreased severely over the past couple of months. The pangs caught me off guard until I remembered that dinner the evening before consisted of crackers, popcorn, handfuls of mixed nuts and more wine. Avo was patiently panting, staring at me, no doubt needing a trip outside.

Turning over in bed, I thought about being hungry and then I remembered: *I have terminal cancer.* The recollection created a huge lump in my gut and the hunger pangs disappeared. Is this how I was destined to start my mornings from now on, for however long my body managed to hold out?

I ruined the previous evening for Lulu and Amir. *Maybe I should have waited to share,* I wondered. I rarely wanted to go anywhere on my night off, but my two friends usually cajoled until I allowed them to drag me out of my house. No one felt like going out after receiving my news.

Slowly, I struggled out of bed and made my way to the kitchen. I let Avo out, filled his food and water bowls and made coffee. For years I considered coffee to be the elixir of life. Funny, huh? Not funny anymore.

A couple of years ago, I had a dog door installed for Avo, but he rarely uses it. Unless he needs to take an emergency pee or poop, he prefers to have one of us let him in and out. Maybe Avo feels we need a purpose and assumes it is his job to provide us with one. None of us mind and my sweet boy never has accidents.

I sipped my coffee and watched Avo sniff around the backyard. He prefers to do his business near the wall that surrounds the small plot of property. When he came over to the door and peered into the glass, I opened the door, and he trotted in. Avo headed for his breakfast and I headed to my bedroom, coffee in hand, thinking about last evening.

The three of us went over the information from Dr. Edmunds while drinking more wine and eating snacks from communal bowls. Throughout the evening, we periodically hugged Avo. Neither of my roommates are very devout in their respective faiths, but at times of conflict or sadness they had those foundations under their feet. I had not been schooled in any religious tradition whatsoever and as a scientist, my belief system was more entwined with the laws of nature and the world of things I could touch, see, investigate, and define. For a chemist, the atom is the divine.

The three of us sat on the floor and Amir asked about the therapy referral. "This psychologist, the one your doctor wants you to talk to—you're going to do it, aren't you?"

"Yes, I think I am. Let's face it, at this point talking to a therapist can't do any harm," I said, oozing sarcasm. I looked at Lulu. "I know you think it is a good idea."

"It was helpful to talk out my feelings with a neutral person, a professional listener, when my father died," Lulu said. "The priest tried to be helpful, but I needed to feel comfortable. The therapist helped me realize that I felt guilty, that I thought I had disappointed my family, and I felt that way because I loved them. She helped me see that it wasn't only my fault that things happened the way they did when I left home. I wasn't given a choice." Lulu stopped abruptly and put her hands over her face. "Oh shit," she said. "Sorry, Mara. I shouldn't have brought any of that up."

"It's okay, Lulu. Really. It was a rough time."

"But this therapy, it should be for you, not your doctor," Amir said with empathy in his dark eyes. "Mara, this is about you. You didn't have a choice about getting sick. This cancer sucks and you did nothing to make this happen to you. You always blame yourself when bad things happen."

"I know you've just received this news, Mara, but have you thought about contacting Joe?" Lulu asked. Her tone was tentative because she knew I avoided talking with my brother at the best of times.

"Honestly," I answered, brushing my hair from my face, "I don't know yet. I will need to tell him. He's the only family I have."

"No, no, he's not. Your family is right here," Amir said, as he gripped my hand. When I looked over at Amir, I watched as his expression of concern turned thoughtful. "I can't help but wonder about your job with the lab. It was a long time ago, Mara, but it feels like an elephant in the room."

"I know," I answered with a sigh. "My job at P-H did involve production of dangerous substances —solvents used in the computer hardware industry." I shrugged knowing there was nothing I could do about it now. "When you train in the discipline, you become well-versed in the risks. Safety is primary. For everyone."

Amir hesitated before he asked, "You remember no accidents? Anything odd?"

"Honestly, Amir, not that I recall." As I said this, I knew it was a stretch of the truth. I had thought about it earlier, but I simply could not remember because the last year I worked there I was in such a fog. "The industry follows the required protocols," I said. "They take necessary precautions." I knew this to be true and I could recall no incidents nor accidents that had occurred.

I shook my head. I wasn't stupid. The multiple myeloma and the precursor condition, the MGUS, were likely the result of exposure to carcinogens. Even in my state of shock and confusion there was no denying the possibility. I started working at P-H when I was twenty-five. I worked in that damned lab for five years. Eight years had passed since the lab closed. According to Dr. Edmunds' guess, the period made sense for the progression of the disease. The scenario was possible, even probable, but I had enough reality to think about now.

Anger, or something like it, filled my chest and made it hurt. I took a deep breath and looked at Dr. Maloney's card. "I'll call this therapist in the morning."

***

"You've reached Dr. Henry Maloney. If you're calling during regular business hours, I'm with a patient. Please leave a message and I will return your call as soon as possible. If you are calling after regular business hours, please call my service. The number is 602-555-7200."

The voice was of a man, older than me. Calm and pleasant, his speech flavored with inflections of New England. There was no final r-sound articulated in *regular, after,* or *hours.* The greeting was followed by the expected beep. "My name is Mara Cordovan," I explained in my message. "Dr. Kathryn Edmunds gave me your card and ..."

"Hello, Ms. Cordovan," said the same pleasant voice as I was interrupted. "This is Henry Maloney. I was hoping to hear from you this morning. I spoke with Kathryn. She mentioned that you might call."

"Oh, um ... hello," I managed to utter. I was taken by surprise when Dr. Maloney answered. He hadn't picked up until he heard my name, making me feel mildly important. Then I remembered that I'm not important as much as I have a short shelf life.

"I don't want to presume, but I hope you are calling to make an appointment. Is that right?" There it was again, the accent. Dr. Maloney's accent made me smile, not because it was particularly amusing, but because I liked the sound of it. He sounded friendly.

"Yes, I'd like to make an appointment," I answered, and it was true. "Do you have a time open in the afternoon over the next few days? Mornings aren't good for me. I work nights."

"My appointments start at ten. I keep an hour open each morning for charting, but I rarely pick up a call. I had a cancellation for today at one p.m. When I heard your name, I wanted to offer you the hour. Is today too soon?"

"Today at one is good. Thanks." I waited a second and then asked him, "Did Dr. Edmunds tell you about my case? Uh ... my situation? My diagnosis?"

"Kathryn mentioned you are a patient of hers, that she had referred you. That's all I need to know for now. You and I will cover the rest together," Maloney said.

"I have an odd question, Dr. Maloney. I don't mean to sound rude, but do I need to commit to more than one session? Or can I make that decision after I see you today?"

"You don't need to commit to anything, Ms. Cordovan. You call the shots—one session or dozens, it will be up to you. I take it you have my office address?"

"I do," I told him and recited the address from his card. "I will be there at one this afternoon. Thank you, Dr. Maloney."

"Call me Henry and I'll see you at one. May I call you Mara?"

"Please do," I answered, and we ended the call.

Avo had finished eating and joined me in my bedroom, reclining into his favorite relaxed position. I picked up my cell phone again and sighed. I found Joe's name in the contact list and made the call, knowing he never picked up while he was working. As I expected, the call went to voice mail.

"Joe, it's Mara calling. Call me when you have a minute. I'm up and anytime is fine except this afternoon. I have a doctor's appointment at one and I work at six. Talk soon." I took a deep breath, relieved to put that conversation off to a later time.

Chapter 4

I arrived at Maloney's office a few minutes before my one o'clock appointment. A web search that morning confirmed for me that my insurance would cover fifty percent of Henry's fee. This meant I would incur out-of-pocket expenses for something in which I wasn't totally invested. I reminded myself that the choice to use therapy and for how long was my own.

From the street, the row of office suites looked like single-story apartments. There was limited signage to indicate that the address housed professional services. Tall, expansive mesquite trees sheltered the building, and I was struck by the difference between this property and Dr. Edmunds' office. The building had been painted bright, desert colors. Maybe therapists resist boredom as oncologists resist excitement. I entered through a large, iron gate which I assumed was secured after hours. Beside each doorway, a wooden plaque offered the provider's name and specialty.

The third door to my right was marked as the office of Dr. Henry Maloney, Ph.D. The words Licensed Clinical Psychologist were etched under his name. I entered and stepped into a small waiting area with a bronze-colored leather loveseat and chair. The walls were a sage green and a woven Navaho rug covered most of the floor. A heavy, wooden table was positioned to one side and held several magazines. A small water cooler sat in the corner near the loveseat with paper cups hanging in a sleeve nearby. The only wall adornment was a pamphlet holder featuring a variety of social and health assistance services.

I heard a door open down a short hallway. As I turned, a man with longish, dark hair and a bushy mustache approached and extended his hand to me. As he came closer, I saw the salt and pepper in both his hair and mustache and glasses hanging by a cord around his neck. He wore khaki slacks and a short-sleeved, cotton button-down accented by a vague stripe. His shirt was untucked. On his feet were leather sandals.

"You must be Mara," he said, as I shook his hand which was cool to the touch. "Henry Maloney. It is nice to meet you. You found the office alright, I take it?"

"I did. No problem at all." Henry's office was only twenty minutes from my house. It had been a nice drive even in the heat.

"Would you like water?" Henry pointed to the water cooler. I declined the offer.

"We'll talk in my office," Henry said. I followed to an open doorway. There were two other doors in the short hallway, one designated as a restroom. The other door was not graced with a sign and featured a deadbolt that told me it was probably locked.

Henry's office was spacious compared to the waiting area. The room was furnished with a large desk across the room under a horizontal window, the light from outside diffused by a sunscreen. Two soft, comfy-looking chairs were positioned with their backs to the desk. Near the doorway we had just entered, a single chair faced the other two. Henry closed the door and offered me a seat in one of the comfy-looking chairs and his body language said that the single chair near the door was to be occupied by Henry. The view from his chair was of the desk, the window, and a clock to keep his eye on the time during appointments.

As we took our seats, I noticed that the view from the comfy chairs was of Henry, the closed door, and a small table on which a spiral note pad and a pen had been placed. On the wall above the small table hung two framed items: a diploma from University of Portland conferring a Doctor of Philosophy in Psychology to Henry Leland Maloney and a smaller sign that read, *If you want someone to listen to you, start the conversation with 'I shouldn't be telling you this.* I liked knowing that Henry Maloney had a sense of humor. I felt at ease which was probably the goal of the item on the wall.

Henry and I discussed the news I received from Dr. Edmunds the day before. He expressed sadness, asked questions, nodded as I answered, and jotted notes. We covered family, that there was just Joe, and that my circle of close friends was miniscule, only Lulu and Amir—and Avo.

"Avo? The dog's name is Avo?"

"Yes, short for Avogadro."

"Like the scientist? The Italian? As in Avogadro's Number?"

"Yes," I told Henry with a slight smile. Few people in my current sphere knew anything of Amedeo Avogadro or his famous number, the constant that begins 6.02. "Avo's birthday is June the second."

"Atomic theory, if I remember correctly?" Henry asked with a grin.

"That's the common belief, but more accurately his interest was molecules, moles," I answered, explaining my background in chemistry "His famous number, known as a constant, states that equal volumes of gases under the same conditions of temperature and pressure will contain equal numbers of molecules."

"I enjoyed chemistry!" Henry exclaimed. "I took only limited courses, but it was fascinating. You must be very bright, Mara and I don't mean to sound patronizing, but that's a tough specialty." Talking about chem led our discussion to Presson-Hagee, my background with processing solvents, and that I hadn't worked in the field for several years. Henry displayed a level of interest befitting his profession. We didn't touch on possible exposure that likely caused my cancer. I was glad for not going there because, denial or not, I didn't want to talk about it.

"Your diagnosis is recent news for you, Mara," Henry said, guiding the conversation back to the reason I was in his office. "Very recent. I want you to believe me when I say that, as with all shocks to our systems, you might look differently at your diagnosis in a week, and differently still in a month. This is one of the reasons people with a terminal disease are referred for therapy. Sometimes patients need help arriving at that point where the news can be accepted."

"One of the reasons?" I asked.

"Yes. Another reason is that you are grieving as you would grieve any loss, but the object of your loss is your future. There are stages to grief, as you might already be aware. They are a bit like steps that one must climb and often we cycle amongst them. One of the other reasons this is difficult is that we spend the first half of our lives growing, maturing, and planning how we want our lives to unfold. Then if we're fortunate, we spend the second half of our lives enjoying what we planned for—deciding how we choose to spend the time we have left. If we aren't quite so fortunate, we learn as you did, that the ending to that second half is going to occur much sooner than we would have suspected. It is my belief that the truly unfortunate ones are those who lose their lives suddenly. They are not afforded the time you've been given to decide how to spend the precious time they have left."

I thought through what Henry was telling me. Yes, my situation sucked, and it sucked badly, but might it be worse to not know the difference? To abruptly slam the door shut. I wasn't sure.

"I understand what you're saying, but I guess it is a matter of perspective," I told Henry. "I can see someone disagreeing with your assessment. In a case like this, like mine, I can see a person choosing to ... opt out early, taking all unknowns out of the equation." I could see someone choosing to slam that door shut of their own volition while they still were able.

Henry looked in my eyes then at the pad of paper he held but he did not make a note. "It is known to happen. Usually under extreme circumstances. Tell me this: could you dare to feel fortunate that you have been given time to make plans for what you want to get out of the time you have left?"

"Well, I can say that yesterday after I was told I was going to die, I realized how amazing it felt just to breathe, as if I'd taken the simple activity for granted for so long. I was comforted by friends who felt badly for me. I felt sorry I had to tell them."

Emotion hit and I fumbled in my bag for a tissue as Henry silently placed a box of them near me. Dr. Edmunds had made the same gesture in her office. I wiped my eyes and tried to explain. "I've never felt like a very fortunate person. I really haven't enjoyed my life, I guess. As the philosophical statement goes, I've just existed. I've not been motivated to really live."

"Then within this terrible turn of events, Mara, you've been given a great gift. You have a chance to do things, make changes, heal old wounds and if you want, flip your middle finger to fate. Some call it a bucket list. You can accept things in your past that you've let bother you because now you might truly understand that they don't matter in your grand scheme, or that they never really did matter."

At this point, I nodded and stared at him. I was astounded at what I was hearing, this new perspective. I was dying, but Henry was encouraging me to define the rest of my life, no matter how brief, as I wished it to be.

"How are you doing physically, Mara? You mentioned you work nights. What line of work are you in?"

"I tend bar at Anasazi. When the lab closed, I went back to bartending, thinking it would be temporary." I explained my work situation as briefly as possible, not making excuses. "My roommates work there as well, in other positions. Physically, I fight fatigue and it has become more noticeable. I don't sleep well but that's not a new issue for me. I started having intermittent back pain and a loss of appetite. Those were the concerns that led me to Dr. Edmunds."

"Do you work long shifts behind the bar?" Henry asked. "Can you take breaks when you need to?" Dr. Edmunds had asked similar questions.

"Typically, I work about six hours a night, five nights a week. I rarely work until closing, but occasionally it happens. Breaks are taken when we fit them in after the early-evening crunch time. I try to rest during the day and control the back pain. I haven't had to miss a shift, at least not yet." I took a moment to think about how to explain it further. "I've tended bar for so long, the job is second nature in many ways, like muscle memory, and I'm not expected to be vivacious at the crack of dawn, which is an added plus."

Henry grinned. "Yes, it sounds like it. If you like the work, keep working. It is up to you. When the job doesn't work for you anymore—maybe because you aren't feeling up to it, or you decide you'd rather spend your time doing other things—quit. If you need it, Kathryn and I can help you with alternate sources of income through social services."

"That's not an issue," I told Henry. "I don't have a lot of expenses, so financially, I'm in good shape."

Henry looked at me over peaked fingertips for a moment, then he said, "As for your finances, your property, even your belongings, you'll want to make decisions about your estate and certain bequests. Don't dwell on these decisions for too long at this point. We can discuss it another time, or not discuss it at all, it's up to you. I have found, however, that many people like to talk about bequests. They find it reassuring and ...," Henry said, as he placed his hands on the arms of his chair and moved forward slightly, "... our time for today has ended, I'm afraid. You are welcome to think about our conversation and call to make an appointment, if you would like to talk again."

"I don't need time to think about it. I would like to talk with you again."

"I'm glad to hear it. I would suggest once a week." Henry stood and walked over to the desk behind me. I stood and turned to find that he was sitting at his desk, having pulled up on a laptop what looked to be a scheduling calendar. "You can have one p.m. every Friday."

When I agreed to the therapy schedule, Henry made a quick notation in the calendar then closed the laptop. He reached for a handful of papers, folded them, and placed them in an envelope, then handed them to me. I provided Henry with my insurance information and signed a consent to authorize billing.

"This paperwork explains my policies and expectations. My afterhours contact number is included." I took the envelope from Henry's hand and stared at it, thinking that I had left Dr. Edmunds' office with a similar item. Henry extended his hand to me. "It is a pleasure to have met you, Mara. I'll see you next Friday at one." He showed me out through a back exit that opened to the parking lot. It seemed that he and Dr. Edmunds were like-minded about patients needing privacy.

The sun glared and the mid-day heat soared as I climbed into the Prius and cranked up the AC. I had never thought about making a Bucket List. At thirty-eight, I wasn't a kid, but I always thought I'd have plenty of time and would get around to it. My guess is that's what we all say until we're headed to Machu Picchu or scheduling a sky-dive.

What did I want to do, see, accomplish before I was finished here? How did I want to leave this earthly plane? How would I leave my affairs, as they say? In order? In utter disarray? My thoughts drifted to swans. Folklore says they sing beautiful songs before they die, sort of a last hurrah. I wanted to sing a song too, my own last hurrah—but I didn't yet have a vision of it. My head was buzzing from the conversation with Henry, but my body needed rest. I looked at the time and was glad I would soon be home. I wanted nothing more than a nap before I headed to my shift behind the bar. I took a moment to check my phone. No call back and no message from Joe.

Chapter 5

When I walked into work that evening it was the first time since my appointment with Dr. Edmunds that I was occupied by something that felt normal. I was glad for the chance to interact with coworkers and serve patrons who had no idea that I was one of the walking dead. The bar is linked to both the dining room of the hotel and its lobby, making it a popular place to meet for cocktails. On the rare occasion that I walked through the casino, I thanked my lucky stars that I didn't spend my evenings serving ticket drinks and draft beers to greasy gamblers.

The trip from the employee parking area to the bar took me directly past the hotel reservations desk. Often when I arrived for work, I would see Amir behind the wide desk speaking with a guest of the hotel or talking with one of his staff. As the manager, he spent most of his time working in his office unless called to the front. As I passed, I looked for him but didn't see my tall, dark-haired friend. Rarely did I see Lulu at the resort when we were working because I avoided the casino. It was even less likely that our shifts would allow us to share the ride to work together, but it happened a few times.

The evening began with a bang: a wedding party of twelve with a seven o'clock reservation for their rehearsal dinner were enjoying our happy hour to the fullest. A pharmaceutical company sent their management team of a dozen executives and their assistants down from Denver for a staff retreat, or so their name tags indicated. Aside from that, there was a forty-five-minute wait for a table in the dining room. Guests at my section of the bar were ordering from the top shelf, behaving themselves, and leaving me nice gratuities. We all hustled our asses off, especially the servers and the bar backs, and when I next saw the time, it was almost nine. Guests began to look a little less heat struck as they came in.

I heard someone call my name and when I looked in the direction of the voice, I saw Joe standing at the end of the bar. Taken by surprise, I forgot what drink I was making and had to check the order a second time. Again, I tried to remember the last time I had seen my brother, but it couldn't have been terribly long because he looked the same. My expert opinion told me that Joe had had a few, as had the guy with him whom I was sure I had never met.

"Hey, how are you?" I asked as I walked over. "Or is that a silly question?"

"Mara! I got your message, so I knew you'd be here," Joe explained. He didn't sound drunk, just more excited than he usually sounded when he talked to me. "This is Ed, my buddy from work. Ed, this is my sister, Mara." Ed and I exchanged smiles and nods. "We are celebrating, and I told Ed we needed to come and have my sis make us each one of her killer Manhattans."

"I can do that. What are we celebrating, guys?"

"You are looking at the newest project manager at Gregson Graphics," he said as he took an exaggerated bow. "There was a little party at the office after the announcement, but Ed and I got out of there as soon as we could."

"Not soon enough by the looks of things," I said with a grin, my brows lifted. Dean, my bar back for the shift, laughed at my joke.

"You know how it is, the beverage selection left a lot to be desired," Joe told me, shaking his head. "Anyway, we're calling an Uber. No driving tonight."

"Cool. The bar is full though," I told them, surveying the occupied barstools. "You and Ed find a table. I'll serve your drinks myself. Up or on the rocks?"

"On the rocks," Joe answered, pointing to a small table. "We'll be over there. Is that okay?"

"Sure," I answered, waving them in the direction of the table.

Since I was due for a short break, I let the crew behind the bar know I'd be back in ten. I delivered the drinks on a tray, told the guys they were on the house, and removed my bib apron. Staff did not normally take breaks at a table in the bar, mingling with guests, but bartenders could sometimes bend the rules and get away with it. Joe's table was off to the side of the expansive, dimly lit lounge and no one cared anyway. The guests in the lounge were into their own alcohol-fueled conversations.

"Congrats, Joe. That's great news about your position," I told him, taking a seat at the small table. I had an iced water for myself.

"Thank you," Joe answered between sips. "This is great, Mara. You have a gift. You're a true Potions Master. What did I tell you, Ed?"

"You mean Potions Mistress, dumbass," said Ed, enjoying sips of his own drink. He grinned at me and rolled his eyes. I liked him already.

"Yeah, yeah. You're right, whatever," Joe said, absorbed in his cocktail. My brother looked up at me and asked, "What's going on with you, Mara? You're kind of thin."

"I'm okay. Tired." I sipped water slowly. My back had begun to bother me.

"What did you want to talk to me about? When you called."

I turned my head as a host stepped over to speak to a table of bar patrons sitting near us, telling them that their table was ready in the dining room. The host gathered their drinks on a tray, having offered to carry them to their table. As the party of four walked away, I took a breath and looked at Joe. It hadn't occurred to him that I might wish to speak with him privately, but it was rare that I would even call or leave a message so what else could I expect?

"It can wait," I said. *If it isn't too long a wait,* I thought. "Are you free at all this weekend?" I asked. "Maybe you can stop by. Avo would like to see you."

"Avo! Yeah, that sounds fun. I'll stop by tomorrow or Sunday," he said, making the plan without giving me a say in it. "Mara has a cool dog, Ed. Avo's a big, mellow, blond lab. He's great." Ed nodded, sipping his Manhattan.

"I work tomorrow night. Sunday will be better for me, Joe. Come by about two, okay?" He looked me in the eye for a moment, as if surprised that I had narrowed his options.

"Okay, yeah. Two o'clock Sunday."

"I'll call tomorrow and remind you. Tomorrow morning you might not remember being here." It was a joke, but I had seen it happen. "It was nice meeting you, Ed, and thanks for partying with this character. I should get back to it." I stood up. The ache in my back lessened when I wasn't sitting. "Can I send over two more? They're on me. My part of the celebration." They weren't really on me. Lead bar staff were allowed to comp drinks as they saw fit, usually to appease irritated guests.

"Sure," they both said in unison.

"As long as you make them, Mara." Ed winked. "This was great," he told me as he held up his nearly empty glass.

Nice guy. Maybe I'll see him again one of these days. As the possibility of seeing Ed again occurred to me, I realized that such considerations were now poignant. Walking away, I waved goodbye and made a mental note to remind Joe about Sunday and that it would be best if he visited alone. I sent two more Manhattans to Joe and Ed, compliments of the Anasazi Resort.

***

My shift ended at midnight and by then, the pain in my lower back was hard to ignore. If I took something for the pain as I left work, it would kick in about the time I got home. I just needed to get to my car. The rather long walk to the employee lot was onerous after any evening shift and I admitted to myself that the trek had become more difficult. Fatigue after my shifts had increased and now, I had to contend with the back pain. It wasn't the work *behind* the bar as much as getting myself *to and from* the bar that was taxing for me. Henry said it was up to me if I continued to work. I didn't want to stop working and didn't yet feel the need, but at some point, my employment would end.

I sat in my little car and took deep breaths. I reached in my bag for the bottle of Vicodin that I had held on to after a root canal last winter. I shook a tablet into my hand, downed it with a sip of water then headed for home. The temperature was still hot as hell, but the sun was down, and the stars were shining. It was a beautiful desert evening.

When I pulled into the driveway, I saw no cars. No one was home except for Avo. I went into the house and Avo greeted me from his usual spot near the door, thumping his tail.

"Come on, Avo. Time to pee." I walked to the living room door that led to the patio, turned on the exterior lights at the rear of the house, and took a quick look around the backyard. No obvious desert creatures hanging around, so I let Avo out. I changed from my work attire into loose cotton shorts and a tank, grabbed a cold bottle of Dos Equis Amber, and sat on the couch. The pain in my back had eased and the beer was tasty. I rubbed the icy bottle across my forehead.

Within a few minutes Avo was ready to join me in the house. Closing the door after he trotted in, I turned off the bright outside lights, leaving the small multi-colored accents burning. The neglected piano sat in the corner of the room. I walked over and sat on the bench that faced the back patio area. How long had it been since I sat at the piano? I couldn't remember because it had been so long. So much time had passed. All those days looking at that piano and telling myself that I'd have plenty of time to play music.

I raised the hinged cover that protected the keys and placed my thumbs near Middle C. The index finger of my right hand struck the first note of the melody, the left hand found the notes to the broken minor chords. Before I was aware that I was playing the instrument, a Beethoven composition was flowing from me.

As a piano student so long ago, the compositions of Beethoven had been my favorites. I loved the Minuet in C and Für Elise, in particular. In my fourth year of lessons, my piano teacher had asked me to practice the Piano Sonata No. 14 in C-Sharp minor, better known as Moonlight Sonata, for my recital piece. The lulling melancholy of the composition demands quick and definite alternating between loud and soft, *forte* and *piano*. My teacher was convinced I could deliver a remarkable performance of the Sonata and because of his encouragement, it became the first performance that gave me that sense of *ownership*—as if I had infused the piece with *my own style*. The notes of Beethoven's composition delivered by my heart and through my fingers—had come forth as my own interpretation.

Sitting at my piano all these years later, I played the first movement from memory with few mistakes, the notes firmly imbedded into my mind and my fingers. My tears made it impossible to continue and I should have expected to be hit hard by that sad, mournful composition. My intent hadn't been to put myself through the emotional ordeal, but playing the opus was a natural reaction as I sat at the piano and the anguish gripped before I could back away. Calming myself, I wiped my face with the lower half of my tank top. Avo was stretched out asleep behind me. I grabbed another beer from the refrigerator and returned to the living room. Now past the emotional distress, I was astounded to have remembered the Sonata after so much time.

My thoughts turned to my diagnosis, Presson-Hagee, and my coworkers. Other than management positions, most of the fifty or so employees had worked in production. The lab team was not a huge group—two chemists and two assistants at any given period—and the assistant positions were usually filled by grad students, often fulfilling internship requirements. One coworker named Evan had been on my mind over the last couple of days. I had no plan or desire to explain to someone, especially someone whom I had not talked with for a long time, that I was dying. *Yeah, hey Evan. We haven't talked in years, but guess what? I'm gonna die soon.* I liked Evan, liked his family, and wanted to connect with him. Who was I kidding? I wanted to ask Evan if he had any memory of regs violations, malfunctions with ventilation hoods, anything. I picked up my phone and scrolled through my contact list. I still had an email address for him.

Evan Rowen was middle-aged when I started with the company in my twenties. He had been an exemplary chemist and I learned much by working alongside him. We got along well. He was a decent guy with a family, and he enjoyed the work. Months before the lab closure was announced, Evan abruptly ended his employ with Presson-Hagee. He did not tell me the reason he left the company and I assumed he had secured a position with another lab. We remained in contact for several years, but it had been a while, probably four years since we had spoken.

I decided to try the email I had for him and hoped it still worked. I opened an email app on my phone and wrote the following:

Hello Evan: Long time, no see. Mara from P-H here. I hope you are doing well, and the family is good. I don't know whether this email is still a good one to use, but I hope this reaches you. You might be able to answer a couple of questions about the lab. I realized recently that you and I had not talked very much about our experiences working there. Email back if you're interested in meeting up sometime. Mara

Chapter 6

I awoke with pain in my lower back. I wasn't sure what time it was or how long I had been sleeping. The clock said five-thirty, so I had slept well for over three hours. It might have been the meds, the two beers, the quiet house, or a combination of those things. Avo and I had turned in around two a.m. after I sent the email to Evan Rowan. I heard neither Lulu nor Amir come in—assuming they had both come home after work. We didn't keep tabs on each other and certainly did not expect to answer to each other for how we spent our time. Maybe home was depressing for them now that they were living with a dying roommate.

Slowly, I got up out of bed, trying not to disturb Avo but not accomplishing it. He rousted as soon as I moved away from where he was lying on what had become his side of the bed. I had not taken a Vicodin since midnight, so I was probably okay to have another. *Probably?* I asked myself if I really needed to think in those terms anymore. If I wasn't driving, or putting another person at risk, why worry about it? Reaching for my bag, I found the bottle of pain meds. As I shook out a tablet and counted, I saw that there were only three more. I would call Dr. Edmunds before my appointment next week and discuss another option because I needed pain relief more often.

It was unlikely I would get more sleep and naps in the afternoon before work had become part of my routine. I drew up the blackout shade, just enough to see out. It was almost full light already on this late spring Saturday morning. I checked the outside temperature on the display I keep by my bed. It had cooled to below eighty degrees, cool enough to enjoy sitting outside for a short while. Being outside in the cooler temperature of the early morning was hard to pass up because I was not usually awake before it was too damned hot out.

Avo and I could enjoy ourselves out on the patio. Maybe when the meds hit, I'd fall back to sleep.

After I let Avo out, I made coffee and took a mug with me to the patio. Birds were enjoying the cool as much as I was and Avo was having a fun time sniffing around and taking care of his business. I sat down to listen to the birds and sip my coffee. Sitting and savoring the morning was an odd experience. Not odd, I guess, but unusual in that I hadn't done this in a long time. I simply had not taken the time or made the effort. It was like playing my piano the night before but enjoying the morning was different than how I felt at the piano. I was neither sad nor emotional. I was just *being*.

I took deep breaths and stretched, then went inside to refill my coffee. I retrieved my phone and the contact info to reach Dr. Edmunds after hours. It was early on Saturday morning, but I could leave a message. I returned to the patio.

My call was answered by a woman named Philippa. She listened to the reason for my call, what I needed, and why. Philippa was very pleasant and thorough and made a note that the Vicodin had been working. She asked if a short-term prescription of that medication might be acceptable until I could see the doctor at my appointment next week and asked which pharmacy I preferred. Philippa made it clear that I might receive a call back either from her, a colleague, or from Dr. Edmunds herself if the physician had further questions at this time. If I did not hear from the doctor or her service by that afternoon to please call again. Philippa doubted I would need to make a second call, but she wanted me to know what to do in the event.

I ended the call, glad to have that chore out of that way. Despite the coffee, fatigue had set in, and it was starting to become warm outside. Avo followed me into the house. We went to my bedroom to lie down. The next thing I knew it was after eleven.

***

Amir was washing his car, a ritual that he followed most Saturday mornings. He wore old, baggy shorts, no shirt and tattered slip-on deck shoes as he waved from the other side of his SUV. The driveway was shaded just enough from the Palo Verde to make the chore bearable in the heat. Amir stayed wet from the hose, which was the main idea.

Lulu had started laundry and was hanging items to dry in the laundry room. "Hey, good morning," she said. "I peeked in on you last night when I got home. Both you and Avo were sleeping. I was glad I didn't disturb you. Did you sleep all night?"

"Oh no," I said, "no chance of that. I was up for an hour, hour and a half maybe. Early. I didn't hear you last night. I must have been in deep sleep at that point. I went back to sleep about seven."

Lulu listened as I told her I'd talked with Joe and had asked him to come over on Sunday. Lulu's expression turned sad as she thought about the reason for my invitation. "You two should be alone tomorrow. Have you mentioned this to Amir? Not that he won't understand. We can run errands or something."

"Thanks, Lulu."

"No problem," she said. "Well, ... there is a problem, a big problem. What I meant to say was it's not a problem for us to be out of the house."

"I know what you meant," I told her. "Would it be okay if I text you when to come home tomorrow? After I tell Joe? I might want you to come home for support, for both of us."

"Of course," she said. "Let's talk to Amir."

Amir was acquainted with Joe. They didn't see each other often, but they got along and could maintain a conversation. While Amir took a break inside to chug down cold water, we talked about the plan for Sunday afternoon. He understood my request to have him around for moral support after I gave Joe the news. As we discussed the plan, I saw sadness and discomfort creep into Amir's face before he went back outside.

While I was thinking about it, I called Joe to deliver the promised reminder call. I sat in the living room with coffee as the call went to voice mail. I wondered if my brother had been celebrating his promotion into the wee hours and was still sleeping it off. I left Joe a message that Avo was excited to see him and reminded him that we had agreed on two p.m. I mentioned that I had enjoyed meeting his friend, Ed, and that maybe we could get together another time. I made it clear to Joe that I needed to talk with him privately tomorrow.

When I got off the phone, I had a message of my own. It was Dr. Edmunds' office confirming that a prescription had been called in for me and I could have it filled anytime. Then I saw the notification of an email reply from Evan Rowen. I opened the email and read the following:

Hello Mara: It was nice hearing from you. This is Evan's son, Cameron. I'm sorry to tell you that my father passed away four months ago. He had battled a rare form of cancer for several months. I've kept his email to respond to estate issues as well as other loose ends and I smiled when I saw your name pop up. You mentioned questions about P-H. I doubt I can help you, but I'm willing to try. Cameron Rowen

As I read the email from Cameron, I was gripped by shock and sorrow. My gut clinched and I leaned forward, my shoulders slackened and the hand that was not holding my phone instinctively covered my mouth as if to contain a cry. *No, no,* I thought. I had liked and respected Evan, I liked his family, and I was sad for them.

Over the next few minutes, I re-read Cameron's email, processing the news. Anger set in and my heart began to race. I felt perspiration form on my face and neck. According to his son, Evan had been diagnosed with a rare form of cancer only months before his death.

There were too many parallels. Our shared diagnoses could not be a coincidence.

After a few deep breaths I calmed enough to trust myself to walk to my bedroom. Avo trotted after me. Closing the bedroom door, I sat on the foot of my unmade bed. Amir was still outside, and Lulu was busy in another room, which was fortunate. There was shock and anger on my face and explaining myself or sharing the news about Evan would be too difficult.

I sat there thinking about Evan, his family, his death, and about how quickly Cameron had returned my email. My thoughts landed at my own cancer diagnosis and the longer they swirled in my head, I became dizzy, close to hyperventilating. Should I call Henry Maloney? But what could Henry do? Express his sorrow that my former coworker had met the same fate that I would soon face?

Sharing the news about Evan's death with anyone would not be helpful to me. What would be helpful was to reach out to Cameron and if he was truly willing, as he had sounded in the email, have him tell me as much as possible about his father's death and his decision to leave Presson-Hagee. Whether I would share with him about my own diagnosis was undecided. I sent another email:

Cameron: I am so sorry to hear about your father. He was a wonderful man and I had great respect for him. Please offer your family my condolences. I would like to speak to you, in person or by phone, whenever you are available. My number is 602-555-5206. Mara

Chapter 7

The rest of my afternoon was spent trying to keep my mind from dwelling on upsetting topics. I read, straightened up the kitchen and my bedroom, and ran a couple of errands with Lulu. She insisted on driving, and it felt good to be out. We made a slight detour for coffee frappes and Lulu talked me into a blueberry muffin. We picked up my prescription of pain meds at the pharmacy. Dr. Edmunds had provided just enough Vicodin for two doses per day until my next appointment. The instructions were to take one with food around noon and another at bedtime and since Dr. Edmunds was aware of my weird schedule, she knew this would work for me.

I was ready to rest when we returned home so Avo and I napped. When I woke up, I had a long shower and a small veggie omelet, courtesy of Amir, then I got myself ready for work. By five o'clock we were each headed to work for a busy Saturday evening.

A few minutes into the drive, the Bluetooth signaled an incoming call from a number I didn't recognize so I didn't bother to answer. Sitting at a light near the resort, I realized I had a voice mail and hit the option to listen. The message was from Joe's friend Ed, but he identified himself as Ed Mancuso. Joe had given him my number. Ed wanted me to know that he enjoyed meeting me last night, apologized for his semi-drunken state, and complimented my Manhattans. He said he would like to have dinner on one of my nights off and if I didn't find the invitation too forward, I could call him back and discuss a plan.

I had not lived the life of a celibate. I had been involved in relationships in the past, but not lately. The truth was I had not dated at all for a couple of years. The notion required more effort than I was willing to invest. Having said that, I was charmed by the message, by the humor and the courtesy in Ed's voice. I remembered him calling Joe a dumbass at the bar the night before. I felt like laughing and it felt good to want to laugh, but as for meeting a man I liked, and having him like me enough to ask me out, once again, the timing sucked.

When we were younger, before our parents were killed when our lives were still normal, Joe occasionally introduced me to friends of his. I dated a few of them. Nothing serious or physical ever happened, but my friends at the time were envious. My good-looking older brother had cute friends, they said. Did I know how lucky I was? After our folks died, Joe and I struggled to support each other emotionally. We struggled with it, I suppose, because we both needed emotional support and we had none to provide to each other. We became distant. I wasn't included in much of his life and stopped meeting his friends. To be fair, I didn't try to include Joe in my mundane activities either.

Joe was eighteen when our parents died. He had just finished high school, but he was a legal adult. I was all of sixteen. Our only support system other than each other, was our mother's sister, our Aunt Rina. When I shared with Lulu about my cancer, I remembered Rina face as she broke the news to us about our parents' accident. Rina and her husband, our Uncle Fred, were named executors of our parents' estate, including legal guardianship of me, as directed in my parents' wills.

Joe and I loved and trusted Rina, but we never liked Fred, partly because he mowed over Rina with no regard for her opinions. Fred was at best, condescending toward Rina and at worst, ridiculing. I once overheard a conversation, an argument really, between Rina and Fred. The argument was about me.

After our parents were killed, Rina stayed with me at our home in San Bernadino, trying to maintain a sense of normalcy for me until the end of the school term. Fred showed up one weekend and I didn't know it at the time, but he was there to ready the house for sale. Rina told Fred she knew it was inevitable, the sale of the house, because their home was in Nevada and neither Joe nor I were old enough to keep a house. I was at the top of the stairs about to come down and stopped short when I heard my name.

"My biggest concern is for Mara," I heard my aunt say. "It will be a huge adjustment for her to move to Vegas with us. She's lost so much already."

"What the hell are you talking about?" bellowed Fred.

"Fred, be quiet," pleaded Rina. "Mara is right upstairs. She might hear you."

"That kid is not moving to Vegas with us," he laughed. "Absolutely not."

"Well, of course she is. Where else would she go?" asked Rina. "We're the only family she has!"

"It's decided," he told her. "She's going to live with her coach. The rent is cheap. You can see her on semester breaks."

"Fred, she needs to be with her family, with people who love her." I had never heard Aunt Rina use a defiant tone with Fred. It was out of character. I loved her for trying, but it made no difference.

"Listen to me—that moody bitch of a niece of yours is not living with us." Fred stormed off. Rina's *moody bitch of a niece* returned to her bedroom and closed the door.

My part-time basketball coach was a young elementary school teacher named Mrs. Lattanzi. She and her husband were nice people, but I hardly knew them, had never visited their home, and we certainly weren't close. They had two little boys, for whom I would spend a lot of time caring over the next year and a half. After months in their home, I learned that Fred told them a concocted story about how I hated to leave my school and my friends. I was devastated at the idea, he told them. He played to their sympathy and offered babysitting in exchange for room and board. Fred told the Lattanzis the arrangement was my idea and they never thought to doubt him. Why should they, right?

I missed Rina, but the last thing I wanted was to live in the same house with Fred. Even after learning of Fred's deception, I lived with the arrangement although I didn't see a choice. I never admitted to the Lattanzis that I hadn't been consulted nor did I talk with Aunt Rina or Joe about Fred's deceit. At the end of the next summer, I moved into my dorm at UCLA.

Rina and Fred—or more precisely, Fred—had total control of the money left to us by our parents in a trust for our support. Minus our expenses and a suitable administrative stipend to Fred and Rina, Joe and I were each to receive half of the estate on our twenty-fifth birthdays.

Fred was extremely frugal with funds. Joe and I worked our way through school and did without things, necessities that Fred said were frivolous. Fred claimed that he wanted to ensure a decent nest egg for each of us. Aunt Rina died when I was in college. It was around this time that we discovered Fred was a gambler and that he had frittered away mine and Joe's inheritance, a little at a time. By the time Joe was twenty-five there was little left. We pursued legal action, but Fred had covered his tracks and the effort went nowhere. Our beloved uncle lives comfortably near Las Vegas where he still gambles away survivor benefits from Rina's pension.

I wasn't sure what brought Poor Rina and her asshole husband to my mind. Maybe it was thinking about high school and college and how those times were unhappy. Although Joe and I had no one else, no other family, the circumstances made us grow apart instead of becoming closer. For whatever reason, the memories were significant as I pulled into the employee parking area.

***

The evening moved along at a brisk pace. During a lull following the dinner rush, the in-house phone line behind the bar rang and I saw that it was the hotel front desk. "205," I answered, indicating the extension so the caller would know they had reached the main bar. "This is Mara," I added as required by any staff answering the phone.

"Mara, it's Amir. How are you doing?"

"I'm doing okay. It's been an okay night. What's up?"

"I'm swamped over here with late check ins, and they will probably be coming your way."

"Thanks for the warning," I answered, with a smile.

"There's something else. A guy, an exec type, just checked in. On an expense account."

"Okay, are you trying to fix me up with some corporate slave? I guess we better hurry, huh?"

"No, smart ass, I'm not trying to get you a date," said Amir. He was rushing to get it out, whatever it was, but relieved that I was in a fair mood given the circumstances. "The guy is an exec from Presson-Hagee. His name is Davisson, Paul Davisson. Do you know the name?"

I did indeed. Paul Davisson was my former boss.

After closing the lab, the corporate office of the company moved to San Diego. There were operations still housed in Phoenix, but I had no clue what services they provided. I was dumbstruck at hearing the name, but the timing was even more uncanny. So, Davisson was still with P-H. It had been none other than Paul Davisson who had insisted I sign a Non-Disclosure Agreement upon my hire.

"Yeah," I managed to respond. "I know the name."

"His card says he's the CEO of the company now, Mara."

I heard a voice behind me. A customer at the bar wanted my attention. "Excuse me," they said. I turned around to see Paul Davisson in the flesh, standing at my bar.

"Thanks for the call," I told Amir. "We'll talk later."

Chapter 8

As far as I could tell, Davisson didn't recognize me. I was glad for this and insulted at the same time, but so much time had passed. I stared at him, fortunate to recover my senses within a reasonable amount of time and asked, "Yes, Sir, what can I get for you?" His eye didn't take in my name tag.

"Johnny Walker Red. A double on the rocks. I'm in ...," Davisson looked at the small folder holding his room key card. "... 418. Charge it to my room." He surveyed the lounge, pointed to a table, then turned halfway in my direction, as if his forced interaction with the likes of a lowly barkeep had been satisfied. "I'll be over there," he said.

"Very good. I'll have it brought over, Sir," I answered. He walked away without giving me half a glance. No please, no thank you, no smile. Minimal eye contact. Some things don't change.

I filled a double rocks tumbler with ice and reached for the JW Red, poured a generous amount into the tumbler until the ice cubes were covered. I directed a server named Debbie—a part time dancer, tall and almost all legs—to deliver the drink. I watched as Davisson tried to flirt with the woman half his age. Other things never change either.

Paul Davisson was older than me, mid-thirties when I had worked for him in the lab at Presson-Hagee and now he had to be close to fifty. He was a big guy with that build often described as *stocky* to avoid calling the guy fat and out of shape. He was even more *stocky* now by an added thirty or so pounds. His hair was still light, and as is the case with blond hair, he had no visible gray. The pockmarked face, the result of rampant adolescent acne, was the same only older, and Davisson had grown a huge moustache that covered his lips and the sides of his chin.

As I prepared orders at the bar, I kept my eye on Davisson without being obvious. No one had joined him, and he wasn't interested in talking with anyone except Debbie, who smiled and walked away as quickly as politely possible each time he tried to chat her up. The server had put in an order for a second double JW Red on the rocks and the point-of-sale system told me that the drink was again charged to his room.

I watched Davisson from behind the bar for a while longer until I stepped away to take a break. I sat in the back, thinking about what Amir had said on the phone. Davisson was now the CEO of Presson-Hagee. That hadn't taken long. I reviewed the organizational chart in my head, remembering the management structure. In eight years, he'd have had to climb three rungs on the old corporate ladder and been deemed better equipped to run things than at least four colleagues in lateral positions. I had no doubt there had been a lot of what my father had called brown-nosing as well as some screw your buddy.

With Paul Davisson sitting in the bar enjoying a drink, my thoughts returned to the email from Cameron and the news that his father had died from a rare form of cancer. I was outraged for Evan and for myself. The exposures that had caused our illnesses were likely related. Had we been placed at risk while doing our jobs? I could only speculate.

I reached for the phone in the back room and dialed the hotel front desk. It was answered by a desk clerk who asked me to hold briefly while she rang Amir.

"This is Amir. How may I help you?" he asked when he came on the line.

"Guess who stepped up to my bar a mere second after you mentioned his name?"

"No shit. He did have that 'knock one back' look about him. Sorry, Mara. I didn't mean to bother you. For good or bad, I just thought you'd like to know. Sorry I couldn't warn you sooner."

"I'm glad you did, Amir. Thank you for the heads up. He didn't even recognize me." I paused for a moment before I asked, "How long is he with us?"

I heard the click of keyboard strokes. "Mr. Davisson is our guest through the end of next week, so a full seven nights."

I sighed, trying to sound slightly worried at the prospect of having Davisson in proximity. "Okay. Maybe we won't run into each other again." I said this knowing as well as Amir that over a week's time, I was likely to see Davisson in the bar again.

Amir moved on. "What time are you off?" he asked me.

"In a couple of hours," I answered. "I'm first out of here after the rest of the crew has breaks."

"Good. Try to take it easy, Mara. I will see you later tonight or in the morning."

We ended our call, and I went back to work to give another bartender a break from the action. Paul Davisson was gone, his table empty. I watched a young couple walk over and take seats where Davisson had sat a short time earlier. He was nowhere in sight, but he could be in the restaurant, the casino, up in his room, or anywhere at the resort. With his taste for double whiskey on the rocks, it was likely I would see Davisson again before his stay with us ended.

***

The last two hours of my shift came and went with no surprises, but I was exhausted when I made it to my car and my back ached badly. I popped a pill for the pain. That practice was part of my new routine as well. Traffic was light except for a slowdown due to a fender-bender, and I was home in time to enjoy a few minutes outside with Avo before we went to bed. The pain in my back had eased and once more, I went to sleep without hearing either Lulu or Amir come in.

I awoke in the morning realizing that I had slept reasonably well, at least for me, which was a bonus as I had the next two days off from work. Then I remembered a dream about Paul Davisson. The dream did not amount to anything significant, except that he was in my home, sitting at my table asking for a refill of his double JW Red on the rocks. Oddly, in my dream Davisson wanted to review call order, the old system cocktail servers relied on to request orders from the bartender. *Remember, Mara, neats, rocks, marts, then mans,* he said. Verbally calling drink orders to bartenders was commonplace before point-of-sale computers made the practice obsolete.

Call order was intended to make the process faster because it was based on a hierarchy of glassware and how the drink was made, simple to complex. A neat is a shot, rocks, a shot over ice. Marts are for martinis, mans, a Manhattan, et cetera, all the way through blends, mixed drinks, and combinations, never ignoring the top shelf requests. The only reason I could fathom that call order would filter into my dream was that Davisson had appeared in my bar, and like call order, he loomed from my past.

Remembering the dream made me feel vulnerable, unprotected. Had I felt vulnerable when he stood at my bar? I might have been taken by surprise and not aware of feeling vulnerable, but I knew I didn't want him in my home, not even in a dream. The call order was a reference to my current area of expertise, however, and given the circumstances, I decided to consider it a good omen.

Avo hadn't stirred so I stared at the ceiling over my bed for a few minutes thinking of more pleasant things. I thought of the message left by Ed Mancuso, and I smiled before my reality set in. It would be nice to have dinner with Ed and I told myself that he had called me without knowing my situation. At least I could tell myself it wasn't a pity call.

I would return Ed's call today and after spending time with him, I would tell him that I was dying. But hold on—I had only just met Ed. Was it that important to share my ominous news with someone I barely knew? No, of course not. It was my news to share or not share.

Besides, my failing health would soon be too obvious to hide. If I saw Ed only one time, which was a depressing thought, I'd never tell him anything and a decision would be moot. If a friendship developed, I might want to tell him for the sake of honesty but doing so would still be my choice.

I decided to play it by ear, an interesting metaphor for a musician. The metaphor implies winging it, following the mood, the moment. But for a musician, the ability to *play by ear* was a feat of conscious thought and execution. Someday soon, I would share with Henry that Ed had called and offer up my revelation about decision-making and disclosure. I wondered what Henry might have to say.

Chapter 9

Avo and I hung out around the house, which was usual for a Sunday. I kept looking at the time. Joe was due to arrive around two o'clock and by one-thirty, Lulu and Amir had taken off together. Each of them assured me that they would be watching for my request for them to return home.

At ten minutes after two, I heard Joe's car in the driveway and so did Avo. We greeted him together at the front door. In his hand was a six-pack of chilled Pacifico which Joe promptly handed to me. Joe sat on the floor to play with Avo, much to the dog's delight.

"Hey, Buddy," he said to Avo as he stroked and petted the dog. Avo had landed in Joe's lap, his tail wagged. "You look so good, you big fella." Joe directed his attention to me long enough to ask, "You don't work later, right? And you like Pacifico?"

"I don't and I do," I answered. "Thanks for bringing it, Joe. I'll open a couple and put the others in the refrigerator." Carrying the six-pack toward the kitchen, I repeated my scenario with Lulu when I told her I was dying, except in that instance, it had been wine. *Oh, to hell with it,* I thought. If you can't drink while you tell your friends or your only living relative that you have terminal cancer, then when the hell can you?

Joe and Avo had moved to the living room floor, still playing together but settling in. I placed one bottle of Pacifico on the coffee table near Joe, held the other in my hand and sat on the couch.

"I saw Lulu's car outside. Is she here? Maybe she would like one," Joe said as he reached for the beer. "I'm guessing Amir isn't around, am I right?" he asked, taking a long pull.

"They took off together, but they'll be back soon. We can save them each a beer."

Joe and I chatted, making small talk for a bit. I told him that Ed had called me. Joe wasn't surprised and hoped I was okay with his sharing my number. I was fine with that, I answered. "Ed's a nice guy," he said, nodding. "He's a good friend."

I took a deep breath and started the tale. "There's something I need to tell you. It is important and it's kind of sad."

"Oh yeah? What's that?" Joe asked, taking a drink of beer between the questions. Avo had settled down, recovered from the excitement of having Joe visit and was now sprawled on the cool tile.

It was surprisingly easy for me to continue, and my calmness, odd as it seemed, was welcomed. It wasn't that I didn't care about Joe's reaction or relished imposing my bad news on him. I assumed it was easier to tell him because I had already told two friends and had had conversations with both Dr. Edmunds and with Henry.

"I saw a doctor a few weeks ago because I had been even more tired than normal, and I'd started having pain in my back. Then I lost my appetite and was sleeping even less."

"You are thin, Mara. I asked you about it the other night at the bar."

"Yes, you did. It wasn't a good time to talk about it. You were celebrating, Ed was there. That's why I wanted to talk to you today. Privately."

"That's why we're alone." Joe sat very still with a look of alarm on his face, his eyes on me.

I nodded. "The doctor started doing tests, asking me all sorts of questions, then referred me to another doctor. A specialist."

"So, what is it? Can they help you?"

At that question, I responded with a shake of my head. "Joe, the truth is that I have terminal cancer. It is aggressive and there's no treatment."

Shock and sadness registered on my brother's face. He placed his beer on the coffee table and put his hands to the sides of his head and stared at me.

"Oh, my God, Mara. Is the doctor sure?" As Joe asked the question, I saw grief in his eyes, and I felt as I had when Aunt Rina told us that our parents were dead. The difference was that now I was on the other end of the news and while I wasn't dead, I had shared with my brother that my days were decidedly numbered. Dread, emptiness, and sorrow swallowed us. We were siblings, but even though we were not close, it was difficult news to share and hard to hear.

I explained to Joe as much as I could for the time being, keeping in mind that there were details that could wait—at least for now. I told him that I had informed Lulu and Amir about my condition. As my friends and housemates, they needed to know, and I had needed to tell them.

Joe nodded and said, "Of course, I understand." Joe was thoughtful for a moment then said, "When you called me at work the other day, you wanted to tell me."

"I wanted to make plans to tell you. I wouldn't have dropped the news over the phone."

"Then I showed up out of the blue at the bar, drunk and celebrating, with Ed in tow." Joe shook his head and covered his face with his hands. "What a moron I am."

"You had no idea what I was going to tell you. Don't feel badly about the other night." I went on, consoling Joe for feeling insensitive although I had just shared that I had a terminal illness. "Anyway, I like having you stop in at the bar occasionally. I was happy for you and your promotion, Joe. You had every reason to celebrate and besides, it was nice meeting Ed."

"Ed," said Joe. He took a deep breath as he thought of his friend who had asked for the phone number of his dying sister. "Are you going to tell him?"

"I will, when and if the time is right. Right now, I barely know Ed so I can't say. When he needs to know, I'll tell him. Will you be able to keep my secret?"

"Mara, this is about you. Totally. I won't tell anyone."

I nodded. Joe and I were not physically demonstrative siblings, and I was relieved that he hadn't rushed over to hug me. His reaction had been as I expected, and this made it easier still. At least we knew each other to some degree.

"What can I do for you?" asked Joe. "Is there anything you need?" He wanted to help but sounded unsure as he asked the question.

"Honestly," I answered, "there isn't, at least for now, but it's sweet of you to ask. Lulu and Amir are waiting for us to give them the okay to come home. They wanted us to talk privately but thought we might like their support. Do you want more time with just the two of us? They won't mind."

"I'm good either way, Mara. Whatever you want," Joe answered through steepled fingers.

It was an easy decision. "I'll have them come home. I think it will be good for both of us to have them here. I'll text Lulu. Why don't you get us each another beer?"

"Sure," said Joe, rising slowly from the floor. As he walked past me, he laid his hand on my shoulder briefly and gave it a squeeze. As he walked to the kitchen, he said. "I think we're all going to need a few."

***

When Lulu and Amir walked into the house, Lulu gave each of us a hug, something we hadn't needed to share ourselves. Amir gripped Joe's arm with one hand and patted his back with the other, the typical manly gestures that show care, and told him, "You know that we will help Mara with whatever she needs." I love Amir. He lives up to the meaning of his name; he truly is a prince among men.

Joe and Amir made a beer run while Lulu and I sat outside in the shade under the patio fan with Avo. My extraordinary dog napped while Joe and I talked, as if he knew we needed to focus but he was now ready for some outside time.

Watching Avo scurry around the back yard, Lulu and I talked about my conversation with Joe. I shared that it had been easier to tell Joe having had days to get used to the news. It had been harder to tell her and Amir when the shock had been fresh. Lulu thought I was dealing with things extremely well and she was glad I planned to continue seeing Henry. Then I told Lulu about the message from Ed.

"Nice," she said with a hand resting on my shoulder. "You're going to call him, aren't you?" Lulu didn't bother to ask if I would tell Ed that I had a terminal diagnosis. She didn't need to.

"I am," I said with resolve. "I am going to call him. He seems nice, he's attractive in a nerdy kind of way and he has a sense of humor. He even liked my Manhattans. Who knows?" I asked, exhaling into the hot desert air. "Maybe I'll get laid one last time."

"Or a few times," said Lulu with a smile. I felt like the star of a reality show titled, *Sex-capades of the Terminally Ill*. What would Henry think? My guess is that he would cheer me on.

The four of us drank beer and ate a huge amount of chips with guacamole. I shared with Joe the information I had received from Dr. Edmunds. Joe processed the information and asked questions. Other times he sat quietly. My news was more recent for him. He hadn't had the time to absorb it like the rest of us. I told him about Henry and that I would be talking with the therapist on a regular basis, that Dr. Edmunds had suggested it.

By seven o'clock, the beer and chips were gone. Joe said he had to go because tomorrow was a workday for him. I walked Joe out to his car. "Mara, I'm wondering about something, but you don't have to answer."

"Okay," I said, laughing. I wasn't drunk, but I was feeling the beers. "What are you wondering?"

"Are you going to be in touch with Fred?"

"Ugh," I answered with disgust, my hand against my stomach, feinting nausea. "That's a buzz kill—and just when I was feeling so good."

"Oh shit, Mara, I'm sorry ... I didn't mean ...," stammered Joe.

"It's fine. It was a joke," I told him. "Funny that you would mention Fred. I was thinking about that SOB and Aunt Rina yesterday. I'm not sure what brought them to mind, but I thought of them."

"Don't waste your time with him, Mara. He doesn't deserve to see you or even to know what's going on. I really hope that asshole burns in hell. Mom and Dad would have wanted him there, too, if they'd had any idea how he would cheat us."

"Neither of us should waste time our time with thoughts of Fred," I said. "I'm sure he doesn't think of us. I still feel bad for Aunt Rina. She was stuck with that prick for so many years." I reflected on Joe's original question. "No, I doubt I will contact Fred. I hope he dies alone and miserable."

The words were out of my mouth before I knew it. It was a bold statement for someone in my situation and the irony was not wasted on Joe. My brother was shocked and stared at me, his jaw dropped, mouth open. Then he laughed and reached for me, pulling me into his chest with both arms as he continued to laugh, the anxiety level swayed by our alcohol consumption.

"That was great, Mara. Classic," said Joe. I joined in the laughter, and unusual as it was, I welcomed the hug from my big brother.

"Hey, I need to go inside," I said. "I want to call Ed back before it gets any later."

Joe grabbed my chin between his thumb and index finger in a way he hadn't done in twenty-five years. I stopped letting him do that when I was a teenager. He smiled and dropped his hand, turned, and walked to his car. "Cool. Tell him I said hello." Joe stopped at the driver's door and yelled, "I will talk to you soon. I hope you rest." I waved and went inside to call Ed.

Chapter 10

Lying on my bed with Avo, pillows propping my head, and my phone in my hand, I hit the key to return Ed's call. I was sure the call would go to voice mail, but I heard Ed's voice answer with, "Mara, I'm glad you called."

"You recognize my number?" I asked, stifling a laugh.

"I do. It's already saved in my contacts."

"Well, that's confident of you. What if I hadn't called?"

"Then I was going to call you at least two more times before I gave up and if you didn't call me back, I would sadly delete it. Don't worry, I wasn't going to stalk you or anything. "

"I had no concerns in that regard, Ed," I answered with a beer-induced chuckle.

"Anyway, I guess I don't need to call you again since we're talking now, am I right?"

"Yes, and I'm glad you approved of the drinks and yes, I'd like to have dinner."

"Excellent. What's a good evening for you?" Ed sounded genuinely happy at the prospect of dinner with me.

"I'm usually off on Sunday and Monday, um ..."

"How about tomorrow? I'd hate to wait a whole week. Unless you aren't available, that is." Polite. No assumptions and Ed wanted to meet sooner instead of later. Smart, given the circumstances. Nice looking, funny, and considerate. The trifecta.

"That would be nice. Tomorrow will be fine."

"I work with that brother of yours until five. Can I come by for you at six?"

"Yes, that's a good time. You can meet Avo, my dog. My housemates might be here. They will be happy to meet you—and they are harmless."

"Okay, we have a plan. Text me your address, would you? I'll look forward to it."

"I will. Thanks, Ed."

"And Mara?"

"Yes?"

"I really look forward to meeting Avo."

"You should," I laughed. "He's way more exciting than I am."

"Well, he is a dog and I hear he's a keeper. You're merely an attractive woman with an okay older brother and a knack for mixed beverages."

I laughed but zeroed in on the fact that Ed said I was attractive. Nicely done, Ed, sneaking that in. "Right. I will send the address and I will see you at six. Good night, Ed."

"Good night, Mara. See you soon."

***

In the wee hours of Monday morning, I awoke with terrible pain in my back. The clock on the bedside table said it was three twenty-two a.m. Avo was sleeping on the floor which he only resorted to if I disturbed him. I rolled over, slowly got myself into a sitting position, took a couple of deep breaths and made it to my feet. Creeping to the bathroom, the pain lessened when I was on my feet and mobile. I would have to ask Dr. Edmunds about it, but there must be more pressure on the sacral region when I reclined or sat for prolonged periods. Made sense. That's why I could be on my feet for hours at work, but driving was best in short trips. Of course, the time on my feet depleted my already meager reserves of energy and it wasn't like I could sleep standing up.

I walked in silence around the quiet house in the pre-dawn darkness. The pain in my back became less intense as I spent time upright and moving, but I wanted to lie down and go back to sleep. I knew from experience that if I was awake for too long, the insomnia would take over and I'd be up for hours. I took a Vicodin, waited for it to kick in, and went back to bed. I dozed off without bothering Avo.

It was nine o'clock when I woke. My bedroom door was open and Avo wasn't in my room. I made my way to the kitchen and found Amir, dressed for work, sitting at the table reading morning news on his tablet. Avo was close by and when he saw me enter the room, he marched over, his tail wagged a good morning greeting. I took a seat at the table, feeling nearly conscious.

"Good morning," said Amir. I heard the cheer in his voice. He was such a morning person and it baffled me how he managed it. "There's coffee. Can I get you a cup?"

"Hey," I said with as much enthusiasm as possible, but missing the mark. "I'll get it. I need to walk around, but thanks." I walked to the countertop near the sink where we kept the coffeemaker, found a mug, filled it, and walked back to sit. Amir's freshly ground concoction emitted a fabulous aroma and tasted even better.

"Is Lulu still sleeping?"

"Yes, I think so. I haven't heard a peep from her."

"Did Avo wake you? Sorry. I was out."

"I was up anyway. He wandered out of your room about an hour ago. I'm glad your door was open so you could sleep."

"Thanks, Amir. I don't know that I would have heard him." I explained about the pain and the added pain meds. I felt neglectful of Avo, but grateful the door was ajar.

"Maybe you should leave your door slightly open when you sleep, Mara. Avo can find Lulu or me or use his door. You should sleep when you can." It was sweet of Amir to mention, but I couldn't respond.

I nodded, complimented his coffee, and thanked him for making it. I finished my coffee, refilled my cup, and turned to Amir. "You're right. I should leave my door slightly open for Avo. It is only fair to him. I don't want him to bother you."

"You know he's no bother."

I left Amir with his news reports and headed to my room, coffee mug in hand. As I stepped into the doorway, I saw the silenced phone was glowing, signaling an incoming call. I recognized the number. It was Cameron Rowen calling.

"Hello," I answered

"Hi, Mara. This is Cameron, Cameron Rowen. I wasn't sure when to call so I took a chance. Is this a good time?"

"It's fine for me, Cameron. Thanks for calling. How are you doing?"

"Doing okay. There's so much to deal with. I had no idea. So many decisions to make on top of the grief. It was overwhelming for a while, but we're making progress." I noticed that Cameron's voice was very like his father's.

"I'm sure that's all true. I am so sorry, Cameron." I thought back to the details of my own parents' estate and being a teenager, I was not involved in the decisions.

"Well, enough of that. How are you, Mara?"

"I'm doing well," I lied.

"You had given up lab work, I believe. Are you working in another role in the industry?"

"Uh, no." I explained that when the lab closed, I took time off and had been working elsewhere. I didn't offer much else in the way of information.

"Oh, I see, okay," said Cameron, although there wasn't much to either see or agree with.

"If I remember correctly, you were with the IT department at the *Arizona Republic*," I asked Cameron. The *Republic* is the largest newspaper in Arizona. "Are you still with them?"

"I am. You have a good memory, Mara," answered Cameron. "You said in your email that you had some questions."

"Yes. I wondered about conditions at the lab. I've had health questions pop up, things that are exclusive to women of my age." I marveled at the quickness of my prevarication, pretending to have a gynecological problem, not terminal cancer. "Not to get too specific, but a specialist I'm seeing was asking about my exposure to substances. Of course, my work in the lab came into our conversation. Did your dad ever mention anything hazardous? Out of the ordinary? Anything that wasn't addressed appropriately?"

I heard a distinct sigh, but Cameron didn't say a word. I started to continue, hoping to spur him on with chatter about the fabricated reason behind my query, but I thought better of it. Maybe he needed time to think of how to respond. My patience was rewarded.

"There were circumstances that prompted Dad to leave P-H. Did the two of you ever have a chance to discuss his departure?"

"No. He told me of his decision to leave, but he didn't share a reason. Cameron, can you share those circumstances now? Might it be to my advantage to know of them?"

"There are things you should know. To begin, Dad had concerns about ventilation equipment, the fume hoods. He brought the issues to Management's attention on a regular basis. The response was always the same, that inspections were completed on the required schedule and the hoods were found to meet the industry standard."

My memory kicked in with details I had forgotten. "I do remember that there were frequent inspections while your dad was still there. I had no idea that he had requested them." The inspections always caused a delay of production because the chemists in the lab had to shut down the process until the tests were completed.

"There was a great deal of back and forth. Dad was very frustrated, but he refused to relent. One day, he was called to a meeting. Basically, he was told to shut up or get out. He was told he was creating too many delays and the company could no longer afford to satisfy his needless concerns."

Needless concerns?! I started to sweat and grew sick to my stomach. It was hard to fathom that P-H considered properly ventilating fume hoods to be a needless concern. There were few more important pieces of equipment in the lab to protect chemists other than well-operating fume hoods. They were tantamount to tamper-resistant medicines or speed limits on the interstate to protect the public.

"They forced him out," I said. It wasn't a question.

"In a way, yes, although officially it was his decision. He felt he couldn't stay in their employ. Dad was told if he discussed the issues, he would never work in the industry again. They would ruin his reputation. They reminded Dad that he had been part of the team that verified inspection standards had been met and documented."

"Who was at this meeting?"

"Three people and Dad. There was Davisson, the lab supervisor at the time, another lackey for the company, and the inspector that signed off on the inspections. His name was Carling."

I had no idea who the lackey was, but I knew Carling and I told Cameron as much. Richard Carling had worked for an oversight agency responsible for, among other things, the safety of commercial chem labs. Of course, I knew Davisson. The man was currently a business class guest of the Anasazi Resort. I did not share that information with Cameron.

"The ventilation became more of a concern when my father discovered another piece of information. He suspected that a compound used in the lab, an industrial de-greaser, was not the same one that the company was claiming to use. Dad was familiar with a product that had been restricted years earlier and he was versed in its physical properties. He suspected P-H was using it unlawfully. He investigated on his own and found out he was correct."

"Did your dad happen to mention the name, Cameron? Of this substance?" I asked but was certain that I already knew the answer and why Evan had been concerned.

"I'm not sure, Mara. I think it was tri-something."

I wanted to vomit at what I was hearing. Trichloroethylene. TCE. The compound had been used widely in a variety of industries as a cleaning and degreasing solvent. TCE was found to be so toxic that it was banned forty years ago.

"How did your father confirm this?" I managed to ask.

"He approached a former colleague; someone he'd known for many years. The man was able to analyze it. Dad's suspicions were confirmed."

The sick feeling in my gut was not alleviated as I considered the scenario Cameron described. Evan's contact had conducted a VOC—volatile organic compound—analysis using an instrument called a mass spectrophotometer. Only an experienced industrial chemist could access the equipment and they would not make a mistake. In addition, I knew that the only way to obtain TCE was illegally. The only reason for Davisson to substitute it for an approved solvent was to save a lot of money—and he would need help to make the scam work.

"Mara, here's the worst of it: Davisson had insisted on a non-disclosure agreement and held that NDA against a generous severance deal. He threatened my dad with the NDA he had on file. Mara, Davisson didn't know Dad had discovered the solvent scam which made my dad even more suspicious. When he was diagnosed last year with cancer, he never said so, but we were sure he attributed it to exposure at P-H." An NDA. Like mine. Imagine that.

"I'm sure that it was, Cameron," I offered, about his father's cancer being connected to the lab. "It's a wonder he didn't tell you all this straight out. Did your father mention legal action against P-H? I would imagine such a scenario would be considered a reasonable exception to any NDA."

"Well, ... I can't prove it, Mara, but my belief is that he was threatened. I think our safety was threatened. His family's safety."

"Are you kidding me?" I couldn't stop myself from exclaiming in disgust. "After forcing him out they threatened his family?"

"I overheard a private conversation he had with my mother right before he died. I wasn't trying to eavesdrop, but it was quite upsetting. Mara, Carling had been paid to falsify his reports. Dad was telling my mother that there was nothing they could do now, that he had to look out for her—and for my sister and me."

"Do you know where he got the information? About the false inspections reports?"

"Dad was smart. He put two and two together between the chemical analysis he managed to have conducted in secret and what he knew of the parties involved. Dad never cared for Davisson, and he never trusted Carling, who owns a company now in Tucson that contracts with the city to complete inspections. My dad contacted Carling after he found out he had cancer. Carling let it slip that P-H had compensated them both and that Carling owed P-H for his good fortune. He must have thought Dad already knew or else he just didn't care since he felt protected."

It had been Carling that supplied the backup Davisson needed. I was speechless. I wanted to say something, but I had no words.

"My dad wanted to do the right thing, the honorable thing, Mara. But he became so sick, so quickly. His priority became looking out for us. For my mom. In the end that's all he could think about. He was obsessed with it."

I found my voice, and answered, "Of course he was, Cameron. Considering the risks, why are you telling me all this? Aren't you afraid of threats, of reprisals?"

"I thought about this hard, about whether I should tell you, some, or all of it. I've been thinking about it since I received your first email. My dad is dead. Nothing will change that. Carling doesn't know he told my mother anything or that I overheard. I decided Dad would want you to know. If he had been thinking clearly, before the fear set in, he would have said you deserved to know. If he hadn't been so ill at the end, he would have made sure everyone knew, but he didn't have the strength, or the time left for a fight."

"I don't know what to say except that I thought the world of your dad. I don't begrudge him his decisions. Again, I'm so sorry."

"Me too. Thanks, Mara."

"It's too sad. I'll let you go now, Cameron. Give my condolences to your mom and your sister."

"I will and thank you. Dad enjoyed working with you. He said you were a highly competent chemist. Take care of yourself, Mara. Goodbye."

Chapter 11

I sat on my bed, stunned. I forced myself to snap out of it. My coffee was cold. I took my coffee cup and walked to the kitchen. Amir was gone and Lulu was still sleeping. I made a small pot of coffee and after it brewed, I poured a cup and Avo followed me out to the covered patio.

It was still early and there was a decent breeze. I sat sipping my coffee, thinking about myself, my life and all I had been confronted with lately. I never considered myself to be special, but not worthless either. I am not beautiful, but I'm not unattractive. My complexion is medium, not olive and not fair, scattered freckles. I wear little make-up, only a small amount of enhancement. I am of average height and slender, but no longer athletic as I had been in my youth, and I was becoming thinner by the day due to having little appetite. I wear my dark, wavy hair shoulder-length, easy to clip back, rarely doing anything else with it. My eyes are large and brown. My appearance was always secondary to me because it was my intellect and my strength that had carried me through even when nothing could motivate me.

Depression, lack of energy, and little interest in my own life had plagued me for years. My habit was to let things happen to me instead of pursuing anything or actively enjoying my life. Now I learned there was a time bomb in my bones, dormant for a long time and it might have been due to the greed of the people who paid me for my expertise. But when I trusted them, when Evan trusted them, they let us down. What if Dr. Edmunds was correct and the time bomb, the MGUS that became a multiple myeloma, was responsible for my years of disinterest in my own life?

Henry had encouraged me to make decisions about how I wanted to spend the time I had left. I remembered my conversation with Cameron, the sorrow we shared about his father. I thought of the revulsion that hit me about the deception at P-H. As I sat on my patio with my coffee, watching Avo nap, I decided I'd be damned if I would accept what I had learned. Besides, I was damned anyway. Cameron had told me to take care of myself, not knowing that in my case, self-care was futile. Or was it? I owed it to myself, and to a future I wouldn't live to see, to act on the information I had received. I could choose to go out with a bang instead of a whimper. I had mentioned to Cameron that his father might have had legal steps at his disposal over and above the NDA. The same was probably true for me, but the actions I was considering did not involve a legal arena. No. What I considered was more eternal and my swan song would be lethal.

I don't remember where I read it, but a philosopher once said that we often have an epiphany when faced with our own mortality. Well, I was decidedly faced with mine and I felt a fervor I had not experienced in years. Henry is right—accepting that you have nothing to lose is a feeling of unlimited freedom.

Chapter 12

The rest of my Monday was consumed by an assortment of thoughts and pursuits, some commonplace, some decidedly odd. Amir was at work and Lulu slept until mid-afternoon and the solitary time was put to good use. I picked up around the house without over-doing it, spent more time with Avo in the back yard, and tried to rest as much as possible in between. I was determined to keep the back pain under control and wanted to keep the meds to a minimum. Sitting had become the worst position for my back so I consciously tried to spend my time either on my feet or reclined.

I found myself looking forward to visiting with Ed and this surprised me. I hardly knew him, but for some weird reason, it didn't feel that way. I wanted Lulu and Amir to meet him and was oddly okay with a new person approaching our inner circle. I thought about dinner and tried to recall how long it had been since I had enjoyed a man's company other than hanging out with Amir or an occasional visit with Joe. My dinner plans with Ed were different. Sadly, I wondered if this evening might be one of my last such occasions. I wondered about our dinner conversation. *How was your day off, Mara? Did you do anything interesting? Oh, you know, the usual—I tried to manage the pain caused by untreatable cancer and I contemplated revenge on the people I blame for causing it. Ordinary stuff.* I shook the scenario from my mind, deciding not to let morbid thoughts about death, mine, or anyone else's, take over the day.

By early afternoon, Lulu was up and after a couple of hours, she left for the gym, promising to return before six. She wasn't going to miss meeting Ed.

I spent a good deal of time musing about Davisson and how odd it was that he, of all people, had turned up at my bar ordering a drink. When I stepped back to consider that I had only recently learned of my diagnosis and the news about Evan plus the information about P-

H, the timing of Davisson's appearance was uncanny. If I was a spiritual person, I might even think it was providence, a blessing, except that since I was contemplating harm, that should negate thinking of the coincidence in those terms. *But why should it,* I asked myself? Why couldn't I consider the timing a desperately needed break? *For me,* I thought. Didn't I deserve to have something work to my advantage? Finally? If I was going to avenge my fate, then the circumstances were about me, not Davisson. But how to do it?

My mind flashed on a bottle of Johnny Walker Red, and in my mind's eye, I saw my hands pour whiskey into double rocks glasses.

***

I had never been one to waste time primping or fluffing and it would be futile to start now, wouldn't it? I rarely left the house in the evening when not headed to work, but when I did, comfort in the heat was always the bottom line. I showered and investigated my available items of apparel.

It alarmed me to learn that several pieces hanging in my closet no longer fit me. They were much too large and hung from my body. I tossed them aside, realizing that it was unlikely I'd gain weight and have the occasion to wear them ever again. In the back of the closet, hidden away, was a light-weight skirt made of a gauzy cotton. Putting it on, I was able to adjust the gathered waist to fit. I had not worn the skirt for so long I had forgotten about that feature. The soft fabric was comfortable and had just enough weight to fall lightly around my knees, and I rather liked the tie-dyed pattern in black, gray, and white. I pulled on a pale gray, sleeveless sheath. The top was intended to fit snug, but it was comfortably loose, and I liked that it was long enough to cover my thinning hips. I decided the pieces worked together.

After I dressed, I stood in the bathroom and studied my reflection in the vanity mirror. Dark eyes fringed by natural lashes stared back at me from under brows that were neither too thick nor too thin. My dark hair had dried in the afternoon heat which had caused the loose curls to draw up in length, not quite reaching my shoulders as it had when it was damp from the shower. Usually, my hair was neatly clipped up behind my head, keeping it out of the way and off my neck for comfort especially when I was working. I ran my fingers through it and decided to leave it loose.

I checked the time and saw that it was five-forty. I heard the front door open, followed by Lulu shouting, "Mara! I'm home!" Avo had been snoozing on my bed while I dressed. Hearing Lulu, he roused slowly and began his stretching routine.

"I'm in here," I responded, calling out from my bedroom. In my hand were small, silver hoop earrings. I placed one of the hoops through the piercing in my left ear.

"I left the gate unlocked. I want to jump in the shower," said Lulu, as she bounded down the hallway to my open bedroom doorway. When she saw me, she stopped short, eyes wide. "Mara," she said. "You look lovely. You're looking forward to this evening?"

I smiled. "Thank you. I think I am," I said, as I inserted the other earring.

"I'm glad for you. I think it is good for you to get out. No, I *know* it is good for you. Give me five minutes in the shower and I'll be presentable enough to meet Ed," she said, as she turned down the hallway to the shower, stripping off her workout togs as she went.

Phone in hand, I grabbed a small, black shoulder bag to carry the few items I might need—keys, phone, sunglasses case. I headed into the living room with Avo at my heels and placed the black bag on the entry table. Avo followed to the back door which I opened for him and watched him head out to find a spot to pee. I heard my phone alert me to a new message. It was from Ed:

On my way. Travel app says ten minutes out. See you soon.

I answered: Sounds good. Would you like a beer before we head out?

Ed's quick response was a smiley face emoji. I turned my phone to silent mode and heard Lulu finish her shower. I checked the refrigerator and was relieved to see bottles of brew, standing at attention in the door, chilled and ready to be called to service. I reached for a lime, sliced it into wedges, and placed them in a tiny glass bowl. I filled Avo's bowls with fresh food and water and walked to the door to let him in. When I opened the door, the heat hit me as it does this time of year, and I was glad for my covered patio.

At this point of the early evening, the sun was making its way west, casting the back yard in warm shade. I loved my home's orientation at this time of year—partial morning shade in the front of the house and full shade in the backyard in the evening. Avo came in the door, accepted a welcome pat from me, licked my hand, and trotted to the kitchen. After slurping fresh water, he went for his food bowl.

The doorbell sounded as Lulu walked from the hallway and approached the living room near the foyer. Hearing the bell, she stopped abruptly at the door and looked in my direction. A tiny woman anyway, Lulu looked like a teenager in her shorts and tank, a towel on her head.

"That's Ed," I said. "Could you let him in? And join us for a beer, okay?"

"That would be great," said Lulu, as she opened the front door.

When I glanced up, the first thing I noticed was that Ed seemed taller than he had at the bar, but that might have been because he stood next to Lulu. The next thing that struck me was that he was dressed casually, of which I was glad. His expression was relaxed, and I was taken by how handsome he was. He offered his hand to Lulu.

"Hello, you must be Ed," said Lulu, with a pleasant smile as she shook his hand. "Please, come in. I'm Lulu, Mara's roommate. Mara's over in the kitchen with Avo. Our boy is having his dinner."

"It is a pleasure to meet you," said Ed, stepping inside the doorway. Lulu closed the door behind him and pointed toward the kitchen.

"If you'll excuse me for a minute," said Lulu, with her hands patting the towel on her head, "I'll get rid of this." She padded down the hallway on bare feet.

As Ed walked toward the kitchen, I studied him. He wore a polo shirt, untucked and khaki shorts that hit him at his knees. He seemed comfortable and at ease, and although he was freshly shaved, I was relieved to see that he hadn't gone to any outlandish lengths with his appearance. Apparently, we were on the same comfort-priority wavelength. On his feet were slip-on deck shoes, no socks.

When Ed saw me, his face erupted into a grin that warmed my heart. "Hey, there," he said as he walked over to me. "It is good to see you again. How are you?"

"Nice to see you. I'm okay," I answered with a smile. It was true. I was okay. I was more okay since Ed had arrived at my door than I had been in a very long time. "This is Avo," I told him, as my dog snarfed up the last remaining tidbits of his food and licked his jowls. Finished, Avo assessed Ed, figured he was an approved visitor, and thrust his head in Ed's direction for a pat. As Lulu returned to the kitchen, Avo belched and the three of us shared a laugh at his expense.

"Nice, Avo. I'm glad you enjoyed your dinner. I think that calls for a drink." Ed followed me to the living room, our bottles of Dos Equis with lime in hand. Lulu took the chair while Ed and I sat on the couch. The slight scent of something pleasant wafted from him. It was a clean fragrance, like an herbal-scented soap—faint, barely detectable. I liked the scent. The blue of his polo made his eyes almost electric, and I liked that too. Avo sat near Ed, enjoying that this new person would rub his head and ears. Finally satisfied, Avo stretched out on the floor.

"You passed that all-important test, Ed," I told him, nodding toward the relaxed dog.

"Cool," answered Ed, with a laugh. "So, what's your preference for dinner, Mara? We hadn't talked about it."

Smiling, I held an open palm out to Ed, signaling that I wanted to hear his thoughts.

"I'm open to almost anything," he said. "It's Monday and most places aren't busy, but I'm sure you know that. Maybe Thai? Indian? I know an Ethiopian place."

As I thought about the possibilities, I knew I wouldn't have much appetite and wondered how I could explain that away. I took a drink of my beer. "I like to eat light when it's warm out—and it is always warm out," I said. "Vegetarian is nice, but that doesn't mean meat is not an option, if you'd like."

Ed nodded, after he swallowed a sip of beer, "I asked Joe what you liked. He said Italian is your favorite."

"Joe said Italian was my favorite cuisine?" I asked with a flat expression.

"He did," answered Ed, nodding, his lips sucked in.

"Italian is Joe's favorite," I laughed. "But your last name is Mancuso. Do you like Italian?"

"It is and I do. But I don't eat Italian very often, at least not pasta," Ed confessed. "Too heavy for me."

I looked at Lulu who wore a huge grin. She looked me in the eye, raised her brows and said, "Well, I'm sure you two will enjoy dinner, whatever you decide." Lulu stood up, extended her hand to Ed, and said, "Very nice meeting you." She turned to me and said, "I'll make sure Avo gets outside again later."

"Thanks, Lulu." I turned to Ed. "Ready?" I asked.

"Sure, let's go."

Chapter 13

We climbed into Ed's Jeep and after he got the AC going, making the evening heat more tolerable, he drove out of the neighborhood. "Lulu is very nice," remarked Ed. "I believe you have a second roommate, right?"

"I do. His name is Amir. Did I mention that the three of us met at work?"

"Really? Do Lulu and Amir tend bar?"

"No," I said, shaking my head, imagining fastidious Amir behind the bar. It would take an hour for him to make a drink. "Amir works in reservations. He manages the office and he and Lulu have been friends for a long time. Lulu deals Blackjack in the casino."

"Interesting! I can only imagine the stories she can tell."

"I wish you had met Amir. He's a great person."

Ed's eyes were peeled on traffic as he drove, but he glanced in my direction often, trying to be attentive. "I hope to have a chance to meet Amir in the future."

Future. There it was. There were words that stung like a slap in the face when I heard them, and *future* was one of them. Others were *plans, someday, later,* and phrases like *at some point.* I can make plans, but what if I don't have a later for them to occur in? If someday is predicted, what if it arrives too late for me? My thoughts returned to my cancer and its ominous prognosis. Then I thought of Davisson and my thoughts turned even darker.

"Mara, where did you go?" asked Ed with concern. "Are you alright?"

The tone in Ed's voice startled me and I realized I had slipped into a mental funk. I pulled myself out of it but remained alarmed that my consciousness was so quickly hijacked. "Oh, I apologize. That was rude of me. I was thinking about how long I've known Lulu and

Amir. I guess my thoughts drifted." *It wasn't totally a lie*, I told my-self. Shit. Maybe this dinner date wasn't such a good idea.

My hand rested on the edge of the seat, and I felt Ed place his hand over mine. "No need to apologize. I was afraid I'd said the wrong thing in hoping to meet Amir, like it might be an issue."

"Definitely not an issue," I said with a smile, determined to light-en the mood, however, Ed was over the top in that regard.

"You did say that Amir is a great person and, after all, I'm a great person too, so we have so much in common, he and I."

"Yes, you are, and yes, you do," I agreed with a laugh. "And amus-ing. I loved it when you called Joe a dumbass."

Ed's face broke into a big smile, and he said, "Oh yeah, that's me, Mr. Amusing. That's right, folks, I'm here all week."

We were enjoying the joke as Ed pulled into a parking spot. I looked out the window to my right and my jaw dropped when I saw that we were sitting near the entrance of Jhankar Mahal. I turned back to Ed, and told him with complete honesty, "You are amusing and brilliant! I love this place. I haven't been here in years. I didn't know it was still here."

"When you said you liked lighter fare and possibly veggie, I thought it had to be Indian tonight. Hungry?" I gave Ed a smile, my dark mood vastly improved, and I did feel like I could eat something.

***

As soon as we entered the restaurant, the scent of spices in the air whet my appetite. Although parties were waiting, an attractive host asked with a gracious smile to please follow her to our table. Ed may have called in advance, but it was a mystery as to when he'd been able to manage it. We hadn't discussed food until we sat at my place. He must have called earlier.

The woman leading us through the dining room had jet-black hair secured at the back, covered by the sheer drape of her sari. I saw a bindi, reddish in hue, had been placed between her arched, dark eyebrows. Large eyes behind round, wire-rimmed glasses were heavily lined by thick lashes. She led us to a table situated at a window in the back of the dining room. Between the aroma, the polished wood, the sitar music and our attentive host, the ambiance was perfect. Ed asked if the table was to my liking before he committed to sitting down. I smiled and said that it was lovely. It was nice having someone so attuned to my comfort. We were told that Anand, our server, would be with us shortly.

Perusing the menu took but a few minutes. We decided to start with yoghurt cakes—dahi kabab. The starter had been a favorite of mine and I was happy to see that it was still offered. We decided to share tandoori bharwan aloo, a grilled dish made of marinated, stuffed potatoes. When Ed asked for Malai Saag, spinach in a rich, heavy cream sauce and served with flat bread, Anand smiled, nodding his approval. Ed spoke with Anand about their white wines and when they selected one, our order was complete.

Over dinner, we discussed our families. Ed began by asking about my last name. "Cordovan is Spanish," I said, "originating from the Andalusia region, but the connection goes back so many generations I never think much about it. The name had something to do with leather craft, but that's all I know, except that Seneca, the Roman philosopher was from the area."

"Interesting," said Ed. "It's a beautiful name."

"Why, thank you. I like yours too, Mr. Mancuso."

Ed's father was still living, his mother had died five years ago. His parents divorced when he was young. He had an older brother named Andrew who lived and taught school in a suburb of Atlanta. We discussed friends, Ed said that he lived alone, and had no pets. He wanted a dog but wouldn't inflict apartment life on an innocent dog. I reminded him that Avo had already approved of him, and he could feel free to visit often and get his fix.

"Tell me about school. Did you play sports?" I asked.

Ed laughed. "I did not. I was an art class geek. Picture a tall, lanky kid that rode his ten-speed everywhere, took vocal lessons, and helped the drama department with set design."

I smiled at Ed's description of his younger self. "Did you enjoy school? What about science classes?"

"I enjoyed my classes, but high school was a means to the next phase—admission to an arts college. I passed Science by drawing a large and fully accurate representation of the solar system."

Joe had shared with Ed that we'd lost our parents in an accident and that I wasn't yet seventeen at the time. He couldn't imagine it, he said, and when I reminded him that he'd lost his mother, he shook his head. Ed agreed it had been a loss, but he had been an adult when his mother died and in Ed's mind, the circumstances were quite different. His empathy was heartfelt, and I told him so. Ed was concerned that no one had made that distinction before.

"Did Joe mention that I hold degrees in chemistry? That I used to work as a chemist?"

"He did, but not with a lot of detail. I know that's why he called you the Potions Master."

"Or Mistress."

"Right," said Ed with a laugh. "Joe said the company you worked for closed. He said you enjoy tending bar."

If it was only that simple, I thought. *Don't go there,* I warned myself. Don't let angry thoughts ruin this lovely evening.

I explained about the job at Presson-Hagee and that the lab closed in my sixth year with them. I told him I went back to bartending as a backup and had stayed. It was a simple story because it was true—it just wasn't complete. I explained about Avo's name. Ed had not heard of Avogadro or his number and although he was as interested as Henry had been, Ed waved his hands in surrender, saying he was happy that there were people smart enough to understand such things.

I mentioned that the world needs graphic artists, as well, and that I could not draw a suitable stick person. "My parents were proud of Joe, of his talent. It was like a gift they had given each other," I shared.

"I'm sure they were proud of you too, Mara."

"I'd like to think they were. I did well in school while my parents were alive, but my focus at that age was sports. I played basketball and softball. Then there was piano."

"I saw the baby grand. It's yours? You play then?" asked Ed.

I nodded. "I took lessons for years as a child and even as a teenager. I haven't played much in the last few years." In truth, I had stopped studying music shortly after my parents were killed. Remembering my experience with Beethoven at the piano a few evenings ago, I looked down at the table.

"I'm sure it was time-intensive," said Ed. "And you had other subjects to study. I don't play an instrument, but as I said, I took voice lessons and sang in choir." He looked embarrassed, but I was impressed.

"I should have figured as much with the beautiful tone of your voice. You've been trained," I said. "I could tell when we talked on the phone."

Ed looked pleased by my comment. "I can even read music," he added with pride. "Vocalists call it sight singing."

"Nice," I answered. "Then you know how much effort is involved. I didn't have the science bug then. Not until my parents were gone and Joe was away at college."

"Speaking of Joe, he's concerned about you."

"He is my older brother," I said with a shrug but avoided his eyes. "Did he mention anything specific?" I asked the question with a small amount of fear although Joe had promised he wouldn't tell Ed my secret.

"Joe said he doesn't see you often. He thinks you're too thin." Ed paused before he added, "I told him you looked fine to me."

Yes, I thought. *The multiple myeloma diet—enormous success.* I smiled and thanked Ed for the compliment.

"We don't see each other often," I said. I kept to myself that this was because neither of us make it a priority and because my successful brother makes me feel like a shmuck. "It might seem odd, but we haven't been close since we were teens."

"You both went through a lot." I looked at Ed. What he said was true and Joe and I would have more sadness to get through. Especially me, and Joe because of me. Ed seemed to read my mind because he said, "Okay, I'm not going to be a bummer anymore. No more bringing up the past, I promise." Ed held his hand up as if taking an oath.

I offered Ed a smile. I wanted him to know that I appreciated his thoughtfulness, that he was easy to talk with. I agreed to move on to a happier subject and I wasn't ready to tell Ed that it was hard to leave the past behind when you had no future.

Finishing our dinner, Ed asked if I wanted to order something else. I enjoyed several delicious bites of each of the dishes we'd ordered but couldn't have eaten more. We took our time with our food, the wine, and especially with our conversation.

Jhankar Mahal featured live Indian music each evening. We listened to the quiet strains throughout our meal and now other instruments, a tabla, and a flute, joined the solitary sitar. We listened as the exotic melody took us to another time and place that didn't involve cancer, pain, or deceit from the past. My lower back was starting to ache, not terribly yet, but I felt as though I needed to walk a bit and as much as I was enjoying this perfect evening, I felt my energy fading.

The check came. Ed paid the bill, and we left the restaurant.

***

I nearly dozed off on the drive to my house. I explained to Ed that I don't sleep well, and that my relaxed state was a sign that I'd had a great dinner in the company of a lovely new friend.

"I can't say I've been called lovely before," remarked Ed, with a laugh, "but I'm happy you see me that way. I think."

"Lovely is one of my favorite words," I said, "and to be honest, I feel very lovely right now. Just very tired too."

We pulled into my driveway. We didn't see Lulu's car, but Amir was at home. Ed parked and turned off the ignition. He turned to me and said, "You should feel lovely, Mara. You are a lovely person, and I had a fun time tonight. Being with you is so relaxing. I didn't have to entertain you or engage in conversation constantly. I enjoyed that so much. Do you know what I mean?"

"I do. Like pausing to appreciate the Indian music together. A lull in conversation doesn't mean you have nothing to say. It can be soothing, calming, but people become nervous." I was so tired that the most activity I could manage was to turn my head to speak.

A second later, Ed and I shared a kiss. His lips were close to my chin when he whispered, "It was great getting to know you. I hope to see you again soon." We kissed a second time then I whispered back that I'd like that too.

Walking up to the gate, I asked Ed to come in to meet Amir. "That would be nice," he agreed, "but only for a moment. I know you're tired."

I opened the door to see Avo stretched out in his usual place. His head popped up when he heard us come in, but other than thumping his tail, he did not move. Ed squatted to pet him which is what Avo wanted anyway.

Amir was in the living room sprawled on the couch. He turned as we entered the house, then reached for the remote to mute the television. "Hey," he said, as he rose from the couch. Amir looked half asleep as he took steps toward the foyer.

"Hey, yourself," I said. "I'm glad you're up. Amir, this is Ed. Ed, this is my friend, Amir." Ed left Avo and stood to offer his hand to Amir. The two men shook hands and exchanged greetings. *Nice to meet you, you work with Joe, yes, and you work with Mara, well, yes sort of, and you met Lulu and Avo earlier,* and so on.

Amir looked at me with a level of concern that I hoped Ed didn't notice. "How are you doing, Mara?" Amir asked me. It was nice of him to ask, and I appreciated Amir's concern—I just didn't want to make an issue of it at that moment.

"I'm fine, just tired," I answered with a sleepy smile. "We had a nice evening."

Ed and I looked at each other and Ed replied, "Yes, we did," as our eyes locked. After a moment, he turned to Amir and said, "I need to get going or I'll be asleep on your couch soon. This one needs her rest, too. Great to meet you, Amir."

"Likewise," he answered. Then Amir said to me, "I can put Avo out, if you want Mara." I could see that he was worried. *Did I look that fragile?* I asked myself.

"No, we're okay. He can go out front with me while I say good-night. Avo wants to say goodnight too, don't you Av?" Ed and I stepped to the door and as I opened it, Avo trotted straight out. Ed waved and I assured Amir I'd be right back.

Avo headed to find a spot to pee and sniffed around the front yard. Ed and I said goodnight, shared another kiss, this one deeper and lingering, and I felt myself give in to sensations that had been ne-glected for a long time.

When Avo and I made it back inside, Amir was on the couch, and I flopped next to him. "Nice guy," said Amir, turning in my di-rection. "I can tell you like him, but are you sure you're alright?"

I nodded. "I do like him, Amir, and honestly, I'm about as well as I could hope to be."

"You didn't tell him, I'm guessing."

I shook my head, "No. But if I see him again, I will. I'll have to. It would be unkind not to tell him."

Amir reached over and took my hand. "I'm glad you enjoyed your evening." He leaned over and kissed the top of my head. I was exhausted. I made myself get up from the couch and headed down the hallway to my bedroom with Avo at my heels. Within minutes Avo and I were both asleep in my bed.

***

I woke at midnight to the sound of Avo's snores, but soon I fell back to sleep. I woke again at three a.m. and knew instantly that I needed pain meds. My bedroom was warm as is usually the case when I wake to find Avo on the floor instead of beside me. I sat up slowly and checked the outside temperature. It had cooled and there might be a breeze, so I opened a window. I found the prescription bottle and took a dose. Lying back down, I moved the light blanket I slept under away from my body. I sighed deeply to relax myself while I waited for the meds to kick in. I was about to go back to sleep when I saw an alert on my silenced phone. It was a text message from Ed:

Must tell you again—great evening. Hope you have sweet dreams. I know I will.

Chapter 14

On Tuesday, I rested with Avo close by. I had slept on and off during the night and felt reasonably well when I got up at ten o'clock. I received a reminder call about my Wednesday appointment with Dr. Edmunds. I texted Ed a smiley face and told him Avo said hello.

My evening at work started out slow and I had time to consider a plan. I checked Davisson's room charges and saw that he had run up quite a bill since Saturday evening. He appeared to be having all his meals in his room and by his menu choices, he wasn't worried about calories or cholesterol in his diet. According to the charges, his nightly routine was to have drinks in the bar before he headed up to his room. He would then order room service—a sandwich or a burger—and two or three more doubles before he called it a night. Johnny Walker Red was a daily staple for the man and confirming that helped me formulate my plan.

The resort had at one time employed a food runner and bar back named Vincent, who went by Vinnie. He wasn't a bad worker, but the kid had no idea how to keep a job and could not help but antagonize the managers. He had never been taught any respect for authority nor did he understand the importance of faking it. Vinnie liked me and we got along okay because I tipped the kid well and because I always made sure he ate on his breaks. With so many of the young kids working for tips, break food might be their only meal that day.

Vinnie's employment with the resort was a means to facilitate his other enterprise which was dealing ecstasy, hallucinogens, synthetic opiates, and methamphetamine. Apparently, he was gifted at acquisition and distribution of said items. Certain people enlisted Vinnie to fill requests for guests thought worthy of clandestine considerations. Eventually, his activities would have seen him fired, or worse, thrown in jail, and one day he saw the writing on the wall and quit. I'm sure such practices were still operating without Vinnie because where there is demand, there is supply. That supply chain was one thing I'd be counting on.

On a break, I called Vinnie from the liquor storeroom. He was thrilled to hear from me. "Hey, Girl. How the heck are you? Still making that bar look good?"

"I'm trying, Vinnie. How are you?"

"Can't complain. Doing okay," I sensed a slow, relaxed demeanor. Vinnie was enjoying the fruits of his labors.

"Hey, I miss you. How's business?" I asked.

"Good," he answered. I heard a quick, unmistakable inhale. "How they treatin' you?" Vinnie asked above stifled, held breath, followed by an audible exhale.

"Same as ever. Can't complain. I'm working tonight but I'm on a break. Thought I'd try to catch you. The deal is, I hurt my back a few weeks ago. I was thinking you might be able to help."

"Sure," said Vinnie. "I got just the thing for you, girl. How about oxy?"

"The pain meds work fine. I just can't get myself going the next day."

"Then you're talking meth," he decided. "Sure, a little meth and you'll be flyin'."

Vinnie read my mind. The conversation progressed exactly as I'd planned. I was familiar with the chemical properties of methamphetamine hydrochloride, originally developed for use in nasal decongestants and bronchial inhalers. Prescribed by physicians as Desoxyn, it's still used to treat attention-deficit/hyperactivity disorder because, in small, controlled doses with closely monitored administration, it can improve attention and lower impulsive and hyperactive behaviors. Of course, that's not why Vinnie's customers want meth. No. They crave bigger quantities for that brief, over-the-top euphoria caused by the release of very high levels of dopamine. Any substance abuse counselor will tell you that meth is highly addictive because it teaches the brain to repeat the pleasurable activity of taking the drug. The addiction to that euphoria is what the Mexican cartels are counting on when they smuggle it just a few hundred miles north to Phoenix. The best way to obtain enough to reach that euphoria is on the street and only if you know the right person. Apparently, I do.

With access to a lab, I could have produced a suitable derivative in a sufficient quantity, but I didn't have a lab, personal protection equipment, or the necessary chemicals. Besides, why bother when Vinnie was a phone call away? More important, I didn't have time. I only had until Friday.

"Sounds really good," I told Vinnie. "Can I have enough for a week to try it out?"

"Sure, sure," he said as we agreed on a cash amount. "You be careful though. This is strong stuff, you know. Try a little at first, to get used to it."

"Yeah, yeah. I'm not stupid," I answered, sounding insulted. "I should be out of here by eleven."

"You still park in the same spot?" asked Vinnie. "Still driving that little electric thing?"

"Still got the car, and yeah, I park in the same area," I assured him.

"Text me when ya' outta there. I'll see you in the parking garage. I'll park my ride around the corner. I can sneak in on foot."

"Got it, but Vinnie, you'll be alone, right? I don't trust anyone else."

"No worries, girl. I'll be totally by myself," he chuckled a laugh only a stoner can produce. I had to wonder if Vinnie would remember to show.

"Thanks. I'll look for you," I said as I ended the call and went back to the bar.

***

The employee parking garage was accessible only with a key card, but a character with Vinnie's skills would know a foot route in. He was waiting near the elevator, but off to one side, avoiding the security camera. Vinnie told me how great I looked which was just polite bullshit, and he gave me a hug. I felt him reach for my hand, but instead of grasping it, he placed a small packet there, closing my fingers around it. I mimicked the same gesture with the money I held in my hand. Vinnie wouldn't let me drive him to his car, preferring to exit the way he'd come in.

I sat in the car considering the situation. I was holding a small packet containing a dangerous, controlled substance which I had obtained through illegal means. I had decided as I formulated the plan that the risks, at least for me, were minimal compared to what I was facing already. If I were caught with the drug in my possession, so what? I was dying. The opinion of others, the stigma to my reputation, even possible imprisonment, did not concern me. The way I saw it, I had nothing to lose. I looked at the clear plastic packet. Vinnie had supplied me with enough of the crystal to wake me up each day for the next seven days. Davisson would ingest it all, in graduated doses, over three days. On the way home, I stopped and bought a bottle of Johnny Walker Red.

Cadence: in music, a beat or measure.

Chapter 15

My follow up appointment with Dr. Edmunds was on Wednesday at eleven o'clock. After the same drive I'd taken the week before, I returned to her office, the place where my life had changed irrevocably. I walked down the same beige hallway, past those beige doors, but today, for some inexplicable reason, the light, the very air in the building seemed different. I had learned a great deal in the past few days, about myself and about my poor friend Evan. I was dying of cancer, but I felt oddly purposeful. There was a lightness in my step due to the attentions of Ed Mancuso.

We were in an examination room this time and we discussed the notes in my record that were added after my call over the weekend. The nurse had taken vitals and Dr. Edmunds felt around my lower back, palpating here and there. She had me move in certain ways and strike odd poses. She was pleased that the Vicodin was working but said that I might need something stronger soon and she mentioned Fentanyl, coupled with an anti-emetic, because Fentanyl can cause nausea.

We discussed my reservations about Fentanyl. I was alarmed by news reports that concerned high incidences of overdose. Dr. Edmunds explained that medical grade Fentanyl was much different, much purer than the recreational rainbow stuff peddled illegally on the street, and the dosage was better controlled.

She asked me about work, wanted me to know that she applauded my continued effort. If I felt strong enough, I should continue, adding that I should try to get as much rest as possible on the days I worked. Dr. Edmunds was pleased to hear about my appointment with Henry and was equally pleased that I planned to see him each Friday. I thought the conversation was ending when Dr. Edmunds asked one last question and her expression grew serious. "Have you shared the news of your diagnosis with anyone?"

Sitting on the exam table, wearing the softly textured paper cape, my legs dangling, I nodded. "Yes," I replied, with a resigned sigh. "I've talked with my roommates. They are really the only people I spend time with, outside of work." I paused for a thoughtful moment, looking at my hands, then continued. "I told my brother. He's my only family, except for an elderly uncle that I really don't care for." I thought of Fred and his machinations. "I haven't seen our uncle in years." If the doctor saw the look of hate that clouded my eyes, she didn't mention it.

"You seem to be dealing with things well, Mara," said Dr. Edmunds. I agreed. I wanted to tell Dr. Edmunds that planning revenge on the person whom you hold responsible for your condition can help your outlook more than you would think possible. But of course, I couldn't tell her that. Instead, I told her that talking to Henry had been beneficial and that he had encouraged me to take control of the time I had left.

Dr. Edmunds smiled slightly, full of understanding and placed her hand on my upper arm. She squeezed my arm lightly and said, "I'm glad, Mara." Then she stepped toward the door and said, "We'll talk after the next round of lab work, which I will order today. You don't need an appointment for the lab and anytime in the next two weeks will be fine." The doctor looked me in the eye, her hand on the doorknob. "Call me if you need anything." I nodded and offered a cautious smile as the doctor left me. I sat there, legs dangling and continued to smile, thinking about how well, indeed, I was handing things.

While at my appointment, I'd missed a call from Ed. I listened to his message in the car while waiting for the AC to cool the vehicle. Ed said that he was thinking of me, hoped to see me soon, and wished me a nice evening at work. Also, Ed said that Joe had questioned him for two days for details of our evening, but Ed had only offered him a smile and told Joe that he was proud to have passed

Avo's approval test. When I returned Ed's call it went to voice mail. I left a message that I hoped we could talk soon and joked that he should hold his ground because Joe needed to mind his own business.

It was a nice message. Ed's attentions had lifted my spirits. He was a nice person and deserved to know the truth. I would think about how and when to tell him about my cancer, but now I had to prepare for a different task.

Avo greeted me when I let myself in the house and other than the dog, the house was empty of occupants. Perfect. I changed into comfy clothes and let Avo out the back door. From the kitchen, I collected a shot glass then reached for a long-forgotten pint bottle of vodka from the top shelf of the pantry. I took the items into my bathroom and retrieved the bottle of whiskey I'd purchased the previous night.

I needed to conduct a taste test. I opened the bottle, filled the small shot glass with JW Red and tossed it back. I grimaced as the cheap scotch assaulted my taste buds. I poured whiskey down the vanity drain, keeping about half the bottle. I poured a short shot, topped it off with vodka and drank it. I was unable to discern a difference in taste between the two shots.

I took the packet of crystal I'd bought from Vinnie and poured two-thirds into the bottle of scotch. A light shake was all it took to dissolve it. The crystal disappeared before my eyes. I drained all but the last few ounces of vodka down the sink and added the remaining crystal to the bottle. A light shake did the trick once more. Potions Mistress, Extraordinaire.

Returning to the kitchen, I rinsed the shot glass and placed it in the dishwasher. I let Avo in, fed him and filled his water bowl. Back in my bedroom, I checked that the JW Red was tightly capped and placed the bottle on the floor of my closet then placed the vodka bottle in my bag. I flushed the tiny packet that had contained the meth.

The small vodka bottle would travel to work with me the next two evenings. If Davisson was predictable—and according to his room charges, he was—I would prepare his Johnny Walker doubles on the rocks with a little spiked vodka. If the scenario developed as I hoped, he'd have drinks in the bar and not notice the slight difference in the taste. It was likely that Davisson would notice if I had used water to dissolve the drug. The smarter choice was alcohol. Vodka would do nicely, and the pint bottle was easy to conceal. I planned to lace his drinks over the next two evenings with small doses to prime the pump, so to speak. The hidden bottle of Johnny Walker would appear on Friday—as my coup de gras.

The plan in place, Avo and I settled in for a nap. I avoided taking any pain meds as I had just knocked back two shots and was unusually relaxed, especially considering what I was planning to do. Before I fell asleep, aided by the alcohol, I thought over my plan. No, it was not fool proof. Success depended on the expected routine of my target and on my ability to execute my plan without getting caught. There was no guarantee on either count. Plus, if I decided against putting the plot into action, for whatever reason, it was doubtful I'd have an opportunity to implement a Plan B. Davisson was in my wheelhouse only through Friday night and then I might never see him again. Even if he continued to patronize the resort on business trips for the next decade, my days were numbered. This was my only chance at revenge.

There were a couple of possibilities that poked at my conscience: I would need to be certain that Davisson would be the only one to drink the spiked beverages. I could not let my vengeance place an innocent person in harm's way. I still possessed that much humanity. It was Davisson that I intended to harm and only myself who would be responsible if my plan succeeded. I would back off if I detected otherwise.

A second possible scenario loomed in my imagination: what if I was discovered before I could complete the mission? If I were discovered, so be it. Even if Davisson survived my plan, the exposure of what he had done at Presson-Hagee would ruin him. But that wasn't enough. I wanted him to pay for his indifference, his greed. I had to try. The way I saw things, I had nothing to lose.

When I woke from my nap, I realized that Davisson had visited me in my subconscious for a second time as I vividly recalled the dream. I dreamt we were in the employee parking garage. Davisson recognized me and cautiously approached. He was pointing at me, asking me questions. In my dream, I turned my attention from Davisson and saw Vinnie laughing hysterically. When I turned back to Davisson, he was gone. I decided the dream was as close to prophetic as I could hope.

I saw that I had missed another call from Ed. Since he had tried to call only minutes prior, I hit the recall choice, hoping to catch him. He answered on the first ring.

"Mara. How are you?"

"I'm fine," I answered, with an escaping yawn. "I was napping before work. Avo and I nap in the afternoons most days." *Naps were part of our routine even before I knew I had terminal cancer,* I thought.

"That sounds like a sweet interlude, but I hope your phone was silent. The call didn't wake you?"

"My phone is always silent, unless I expect to hear from someone special and yes, if you were wondering, you do qualify. You rate un-silent mode, Ed."

"That's great news for me," said Ed laughing. "I called to ask if you'd like to plan something for this weekend, but that's days away. If you aren't busy, maybe we could meet for lunch tomorrow or Friday? Either day is good for me." Men who work banker's hours would have no interest trying to date someone with my schedule. It was nice that Ed had considered alternatives.

"I would like that," I answered. *I can fit in a lunch date around my plotting,* I thought to myself. "Tomorrow is better for me," I said, remembering my appointment with Henry on Friday afternoon. "I'll meet you. What's close to your office?"

"There's a decent café a few blocks down. It's called Bountiful. They have great salads. Have you been there?"

"I haven't but it sounds fine. Is Joe still being a pest?" I asked, attempting rare humor. "Actually," I said, thinking of my brother, "I should call him."

"It's been busy around here. I haven't seen much of him so, no, he hasn't badgered me."

"In that case, taking his good behavior into account, we could invite him to lunch, but only to be nice, and only if we make another plan for the weekend. It *is* only fair. He *did* introduce us." Ed laughed and said he thought it was a generous offer, but was I sure? Including my brother in our lunch plans was not his intention and he wanted me to know that.

"I guess I feel like being nice to Joe. It would be good karma and besides, we can make up for it." The suggestion in my statement hung comfortably between us. Before he could say anything, I told Ed, "I can't quite believe I said that, but I don't care, Ed. That's how I feel."

"Mara, I promise you that we'll make up for it. I hope you have a nice evening at work. I envy the Manhattan drinkers. I'll see you tomorrow and I'll message you later."

Ed and I decided that I would be the one to ask Joe about joining us for lunch. I smiled to myself, thinking of Ed's wish that I have a nice evening at work. I hoped it was nice, as well. Nice and successful.

Chapter 16

I thought about calling Joe with an invitation to lunch, but I opted for a text message instead. I wasn't panicked about my ensuing plan or wavering in my resolve, but I wasn't going to take my eye off the proverbial ball. Causing pain and suffering, even when deserved, was a new endeavor for me and I needed to have my wits about me. My conversation with Ed had been pleasant, very much so, in fact, but until I put the plot into play, I felt compelled to limit my interactions with others. I wanted to listen to my own counsel and not be dissuaded even by accident. In all honesty, I was concerned that I'd give myself away.

By text message, I explained that Ed and I would be at Bountiful tomorrow and that he was welcome to join us if he could fit us into his schedule now that he was so important. Joe responded that he would like to but had a meeting. If things changed, he'd be there. He even thanked me for the invite. A few minutes later, Joe messaged again:

So, you like Ed?

I responded: I do. He's nice. Funny.

Joe: Are you going to tell him? You don't have to. You don't even need to tell me.

Me: I am. He should know. Planning to see each other this weekend.

Joe: If I don't make lunch tomorrow let's talk soon.

Joe added heart emojis. I had never known him to use heart emojis, at least not in messages to me.

***

As things turned out, Davisson was already in the bar by the time I arrived. He was trying to make conversation with any young woman within a short distance, whether she be staff or patron. Chris, the day bartender, was eager for me to relieve him. He said the guest drinking Johnny Walker Red was on his first double. This was good news for me, as was the fact that he was drinking JW Red, but then drinkers are true to their labels. It was also to my advantage that Davisson wasn't sitting at the bar where it was more likely he might recognize me, but I asked myself if it would really make a difference? I took my bag to the storeroom, removed the vodka bottle, and placed it carefully behind a case of liquor knowing that I would likely be the only one in the storeroom that evening.

I relieved Chris of his duty behind the bar and wished him a good evening. He noticed I wasn't wearing my name tag as required by the resort. This was by design, but when I acted surprised, he offered to loan me his. It didn't matter what name was on the name tag, only that I wore it. I thanked him and promised to leave it near the till. Chris gathered his belongings and left.

There was a slight lull in orders, so I moved fast, stepping into the storeroom with two double rocks glasses. It took me about thirty seconds to pour a small amount of spiked vodka into each glass, return the pint bottle to its hiding spot, and walk back to the well behind the bar. I placed the glassware under the service counter near my workstation at the well. They appeared to hold nothing more than a small amount of melted ice.

Minutes later, Debbie, the server, approached with an order for a double JW Red on the rocks. The order confirmed that the drink was to be charged to Davisson, P, Room 418. I looked at the order. Debbie waited for me, as they do, having made an order from the floor. There was still time to abandon my plan. *Did I really want to do this? Was I sure?* I picked up one of the two glasses and filled it with ice. The watery solution was no longer visible. I placed the glass on the bar and reached for the whiskey, pouring until the ice was covered then placed the glass within Debbie's reach. Off she went with it, straight to Davisson's table. My plot was in motion.

Did I have regrets? On the contrary. I grew keenly interested in how Davisson would react to the methamphetamine. I wanted to observe and note how long it took to notice any effect or any change in his behavior. I wondered if Davisson, knowing that he had effectively poisoned his staff years ago, had reacted in the same way. I thought about his dedication to his profit margin and his pay off to Carling, the crooked inspector.

I filled orders for other patrons, trying to ignore the second rocks glass waiting for me to employ it should I have the chance. After about thirty minutes, I saw another order from Debbie for a double JW Red. As she waited for the drink, I went through the same simple motions as before. Debbie looked at me when the drink was ready to deliver, and I saw her eyes roll.

I glanced over at Davisson, then back at the server, and asked, "Third one, right?"

"Yes," Debbie answered, with discreet annoyance. She was used to dealing with men of a certain ilk and their irritating ploys. Tall and slender, Debbie was a danseuse and part-time ballet instructor with Ballet Arizona. I had seen her perform and she had confided that dance simply didn't pay well enough to support her, so she worked a couple of shifts with us each week.

"Is he a problem?" I asked. "Some guys need help monitoring their intake."

"Some guys need help monitoring several things. This one's liquor intake is the least of his issues," Debbie said quietly with a smile. She took the drink to Davisson. Half an hour later, Davisson had finished the drink and was headed to Room 418 with no discernible effects of having been drugged. I wasn't sure if I was relieved or disappointed by this, but I was glad he was out of my bar.

But it was only Wednesday. I hoped for the exact scenario tomorrow evening, bringing me a step closer to Friday's finale.

Leaving work at the end of my shift, I was in severe pain. I had not taken my first dose of pain meds that afternoon because of the two shots I consumed while perfecting my lethal concoction. I wanted drugs to interact with the alcohol in Davisson's system, but not in my own. Luckily, I remembered to return the pint bottle of spiked vodka to my bag.

After arranging to leave work about an hour earlier than usual, I made it to my Prius. The hike to the parking garage was long and difficult, but soon I was sitting in my car with my open prescription bottle, a pill in one hand and my water container in the other. I noted the time and calculated the exact hour I could have my next dose according to Dr. Edmunds' instructions. The medication was to be taken with food, but I had no appetite. All I wanted was to make it home and stretch out on my bed. With the vodka hidden in the glove compartment, I made it home in record time and was soon asleep with Avo next to me.

****

I woke up when I heard Lulu and Amir talking together. I looked at the clock and saw that the time was three a.m. The pain in my back had eased to a dull, achy stiffness. As I listened, I could hear that they were talking about the resort. I slowly rose to sit on the side of my bed and for once, Avo didn't seem to notice. I saw that my bedroom door was open which explained how I was able to hear the conversation from down the hallway. Amir and I had talked about leaving my door open a few inches for Avo, but I had been in pain and so out of it I couldn't recall if doing so had been my intent. I stood, walked to the doorway and into the hall.

"Hey," I said. "How was work?" I was interrupting their conversation, but as they each turned to look in my direction, I saw regret on both their faces.

"Mara, sorry. We didn't want to wake you," Lulu told me.

Amir was flustered. "I'm so sorry, Mara. I checked on Avo when I came in about an hour ago. He went out to pee and then went right back to sleep next to you. Lulu came home and I forgot to pull your door closed again."

"It's fine. Thanks for checking on him. What were you talking about? Did something happen?"

Amir and Lulu shared a look, then Lulu began. "A drunk came through the casino around eleven o'clock. He was bothering people and running into them. Then he started punching the slot machines, yelling that they were attacking him. We had to call Security."

"Security contacted me to find out if he was a hotel guest. Mara, it was Paul Davisson."

"Huh? That's bizarre." Davisson had become overly excited and aggressive. The meth had affected his behavior. Vinnie was right; it was strong stuff. I pretended to be as surprised by his actions as anyone.

"We checked his room charges," said Amir. "He had stopped drinking hours before but hadn't eaten anything."

I thought for a moment. I wanted to appear half-asleep but tried to participate in the conversation. "Unless he was using cash but that's not likely," I said. I sat on the couch.

"He didn't have his room key card on him, but he had I.D." Amir said, filling in the details. "I would have verified it was him just to get him out of there. Security took him up to his room and left him there. They checked on him later and said he was passed out."

"Amir says this guy was your boss years ago," said Lulu.

I nodded and yawned, hoping to look unconcerned. "He was. He can be an odd guy, but this sounds strange, even for Paul." I shook my head and offered, "I don't know how his tastes run these days, I never really did, but maybe he's into a weird party crowd. It wouldn't surprise me." I forced another yawn, then said, "I need to lie down."

"We all need to call it a night," said Lulu, shaking her head.

I walked back down the hall to my bedroom. Avo stretched and turned over, but seeing that I had returned, went back to sleep. I took a Vicodin and as I stretched out on the bed, Lulu stuck her head in the door. "Really sorry for waking you. It was kind of weird tonight. How was your evening?" she asked.

"It was alright. I left a little early. My back was hurting." I told her I was meeting Ed for lunch and went back to sleep without another thought of Paul Davisson.

Chapter 17

Ed and I planned to meet at one p.m. at the little café called Bountiful. I had looked at the website for an idea of what to expect although I trusted Ed's taste. They specialized in organic and locally grown produce and featured a wide variety of salads and vegetarian dishes. They were open until four in the afternoon, preferring the lunch and early dinner crowds and boasted a huge carry-out following because they delivered.

I found a parking spot close by and met up with Ed on the sidewalk as I walked to the entrance. When he saw me, he smiled, and I smiled in return. "Hello," he said as he bent forward and kissed my cheek. I put my arm through his and we walked inside. Ed had talked briefly with Joe and was told that his lunch hour meeting was still on. We chatted over lunch, and I was able to eat most of a small spinach salad. It was more food than I had consumed since our dinner on Monday. Ed was good for my appetite.

We finished lunch and Ed mentioned that he wanted to cook for me soon. I told him I was hoping to take Saturday night off and asked if that evening worked for him. He was excited at the prospect and quizzed me on what I did and did not like to eat or drink. We decided on paella, and I offered to make special drinks in his honor before dinner. I placed my forearms on the table and leaned forward on my overlapped hands when an urge hit me and before I realized it, I was in the middle of a disclosure.

"I want to tell you something rather personal, Ed. I'm telling you because if you and I are headed where I think we are, you should know. You deserve to know."

Ed was listening, but I could see that he wasn't worried and wanted to make a joke. "You can tell me anything, Mara," he said as he gazed dreamily into my eyes for effect. "I know you're not married because I think Joe would have told me."

"No, I'm not married, nor have I ever been married," I answered with a smile, shaking my head. I looked at Ed, who was waiting patiently. I inhaled and slowly exhaled the breath, then said, "I have some health issues. It is nothing contagious. The diagnosis was recent so I'm still getting used to the idea that my life is going to be changing."

"Mara," he said, as he reached over and took my hand, his expression changing from playful to serious. "I'm so sorry to hear this. Is there anything I can do?"

"You already are, Ed—doing a lot for me, that is. I enjoy your company and I think you know that I'm attracted to you. I just think you have a right to know that the person I am today might be very different before too long." Ed looked into my eyes, his face sad, but thoughtful. "So," I continued, "if you want to rethink our friendship, I will understand."

The look on Ed's face told me he was shocked—or concerned, maybe both. I wasn't sure what he was thinking or feeling, when he said, "Let's get out of here, okay? We can't really talk sitting here."

I insisted on paying for our lunch, telling Ed it was my turn. We left the restaurant and, taking my hand, Ed led me down the block to a small courtyard with a covered patio area and places to sit.

Sitting there together, it all came tumbling out: the cancer that had hidden itself for so long, my employment at Presson-Hagee and the avoidable exposure to carcinogens. I told Ed about my former colleague, Evan, who had died just months ago. I shared that negligence was involved, but that I was not interested in further legal action despite the possibility that my employer's actions might have provided a reasonable reason to counter the NDA.

Ed listened, expressed sorrow, then outrage, and asked questions. Most importantly, he pulled me to him and hugged me, telling me he was so, so sorry. I sensed the level of sadness, and unfortunately, I wasn't finished.

"There's something else," I said to Ed. Our hands were inter-twined. I squeezed his fingers for fortitude. "My prognosis isn't good. The cancer is aggressive and there's no treatment. I only have a few months and there's no guarantee of that."

"Oh, my god," said Ed softly, his words almost under his breath. He wrapped his arms tightly around me for a moment, but it was awkward because we sat next to each other. "You found this out re-cently?" Ed continued to hold my hand as the traffic and pedestrians made their way down the busy street.

"I received the news right before we met. That's why I left Joe a message and then the two of you visited me at the bar."

Joe shook his head. "You had this terrible news on your mind and couldn't tell Joe with me sitting there enjoying a Manhattan."

"I wouldn't have told him at the bar anyway. It's not exactly a conversation to have in a restaurant or a bar. That's why we're sitting out here now, right?"

"Yeah," answered Ed. "You are right about that." He still held my hand. I sensed sadness, disappointment. I wasn't sure how much de-tail Ed could handle now nor was I sure how much I wanted to dis-cuss right then. And I knew I needed to keep my mind on the tasks I planned for myself at work that evening.

"You need to get back to work, Ed. We'll talk when we have more time together." I paused for a moment, not wanting to continue in this vein, but I owed it to Ed. "Unless of course, you want to re-think what's going on between us. I want you to know I would be very sad if you did, but I would totally understand."

Ed was stunned. He nearly looked angry. "You said that before. Tell me if that's what you want but I'm not rethinking anything."

***

I spent the rest of Thursday afternoon obsessed with thoughts about Davisson and the steps I had taken. It wasn't concern for him personally that plagued my mind, or regrets about my course of action; it was more that the plan had gone off so easily. Hotel and casino staff had seen Davisson's erratic behavior in the casino the prior evening, and I needed to get another small dose of the drug into him tonight, to build up the quantity in his system. Also, it was essential that Davisson continue to enjoy his normal amount of JW Red because I was counting on the meth interacting with the alcohol.

As it turned out, the scenario played out nearly the same. I could have no clue as to what happened during the workday, but by the dinner hour, Davisson again installed himself in the bar. He flirted with everyone within earshot and downed two double whiskeys on the rocks. Debbie had the night off, but both drinks were prepared by me using the same method as the evening before and were delivered by another unsuspecting, but equally annoyed server.

Davisson then retired to his room. He did not approach the bar and he never bothered to look my way so the possibility of him recognizing me had become a non-issue. I was careful to wear the borrowed name tag just in case and other than Amir, and Lulu to a lesser degree, no one had a clue that the two of us were linked by a past association.

As I left work that Thursday evening, I was exhausted. I could tell work was starting to take a greater toll on me physically. I sat in my car after the hike from the bar and reviewed how easily I had adulterated Davisson's drinks. I hid the now-empty Vodka bottle in the glove box as I had the evening before, reminding myself to take it into the house with me. I took a Vicodin and wondered why the Fates had continued to smile on me regarding my dangerous intentions, but when I considered my own limited future and the pain I was in at that moment, if anyone had asked me, I would have said with honesty that my conscience was clear.

***

By the time I arrived home on Thursday night, all I wanted to do was lie down. I managed to let Avo out then I changed out of my work clothes. I retrieved the pint bottle, rinsed it thoroughly, and placed it deep in the bin of recyclables. Passing through the living room I looked at the piano. Music was something Ed and I discovered we had in common. A few other essential chores and that one pleasant thought were the extent of what I could manage before I collapsed on the bed with my sweet dog held close for comfort. I told myself it was from the stress of executing my plan, but the stress from it had been minimal and the amount of worry it had caused me was nearly nonexistent.

I thought it likely that my recent activity demanded more of me than I was used to, what with appointments and difficult conversations. Add the enjoyable but extra activity of seeing Ed and I knew I'd been overtaxed. But the truth was that I was fading. I was sleeping better with the use of the pain meds, but my energy level had decreased. I was experiencing more pain and my strength was waning. Just before going to sleep, I remembered my appointment with Henry on Friday.

For hours, I slept well, waking briefly only twice. I walked around the house a bit to ease the pain in my back and then returned to bed. I changed my position and went back to sleep. When I finally got up, it was after nine a.m.

I made fresh coffee and sat down in the living room. My path had not crossed with either Amir's or Lulu's since late Wednesday when I learned of Davisson's odd behavior, but both of my friends had sent messages. Lulu asked about my lunch with Ed to which I responded with a happy emoji. Amir had let Avo out for a few minutes before he left the house earlier that morning. Apparently, I was sleeping too deeply, or the drugs had induced such a stupor, that I did not notice. I had a third message, a voice mail from Ed. He hoped I was doing okay, thanked me again for lunch yesterday, and wanted me to know that he was looking forward to dinner on Sunday.

On the way to Henry's office, I thought about what to discuss with the therapist. In the past week, I had seen Dr. Edmunds and I remembered that I was expected at the lab for another blood draw. I had told my brother of my diagnosis. I had seen Ed twice—dinner on Monday and lunch on Thursday—and wondered about Henry's reaction. Would he encourage me or think I was drawing from a drying well? My guess was that Henry would be happy for me.

Also, I had talked with Cameron and discovered how his father, Evan died of cancer after being so brutally treated. Then Paul Davisson appeared at my place of work. I would tell Henry about Evan's death. Would I share anything about Davisson? I wasn't sure.

Arriving at Henry's office I took a seat in the small, comfortable waiting area. I looked around and saw nothing had changed, but then I had only seen the room once. Ten minutes later, I heard a door open in the short hallway and a moment later, Henry appeared.

"Hello, Mara. Come in. If you need water, help yourself," he offered as before.

I said hello and followed Henry into the private office. "How are you doing today?" he asked after we had taken our seats. Again, Henry assumed the chair near the door with the view of the desk and window and I had the view of Henry.

"I'm okay," I sighed. "It has been a full week," I said and shared with Henry some of what I'd planned to tell him.

"What about work, Mara? How's that going?"

"It's been fine," I answered. "But I don't know how much longer I'll be able to continue." As I related this information to Henry, it occurred to me that this was the first time I'd admitted it to myself. "This was a busy week and I felt especially tired last night. I'm sleeping better," I said as I shook my head, "but don't feel rested."

"You'll want to prioritize your time and energy, and work is a big factor. You will want to decide what you share with your employer about your diagnosis. Can you reduce your hours without sharing more than you want? Kathryn can require a shorter schedule for medical reasons."

I had decided last night that a conversation with Tomas, the bar manager should happen soon. Tomas was older, quite easy to work for—a nice man. He would let me do whatever I wanted, whether I told him I was dying or not. "I can cut back in hours. Or quit whenever I want. That will be up to me. I'm a bartender. My exit from the workforce will hardly register a blip."

Henry responded by nodding then asked, "How have you been spending your time outside of work?"

I hesitated for a moment, then told Henry about Ed. "He's a friend of Joe's. He's cute, he's funny and I enjoy his company, Henry, but I'm not sure it's smart to spend time on a new relationship."

"That's wonderful, Mara. I'm happy for you. Why do you think it's not smart?"

"Because our friendship will be brief."

"That is something you'll both want to deal with, but sharing with another, staying connected, is a good thing. Enjoy being with him if that's what you want to do. Many people in your place don't have this option. They don't engage with someone new as you are doing."

"I've only seen him on two occasions," I paused, thinking of how to continue. "I told Ed yesterday that I have health concerns, that I'm dying. I said that I would be a quite different person soon." I lifted my hands in resignation. "I just felt that he should know."

"I agree. The situation might be especially difficult for Ed should the two of you become close, but honesty will make things easier on both of you. You will enjoy your time together more because you are putting your cards on the table." I inhaled, nodded, and exhaled.

"And he's a friend of Joe's," continued Henry. "You are providing Joe with a support person. He will need one." I hadn't seen it that way and I told Henry as much, and that I was glad of it.

Henry and I talked about Evan, and I shared more about Presson-Hagee. Henry was sorry to hear about my former colleague and alarmed at the parallels between our cancer diagnoses. Information poured from me once I began speaking, as it had when I shared my news with Ed. I told Henry that we'd been exposed to harmful substances on the job. I didn't share that it was likely preventable, nor did I share that my former employer was to blame. I did explain, however, that Evan and I had signed NDAs.

"There's no legal recourse for you?"

"I could pursue legal action, Henry. There are legal exceptions even with an NDA, but what difference would it make? When the lab closed, further risk was eliminated. They chose to use an outside facility from that point. At least I am assured of that." I was stretching the truth but liked the sound of it. "There was something weird that happened at work. Of all people, my former supervisor showed up. Right at my bar."

"Your former supervisor?" Henry was shocked. He placed the pad he's been writing in on his lap and stared at me. "From Presson-Hagee? Did you talk to this person?"

"Only to fill his drink order. He didn't recognize me. He will be staying at the hotel for the next few days apparently." I felt resentment and anger rise. Maybe I shouldn't be telling this to Henry.

"With everything going on in your head, Mara, tell me what happened. How did you react?"

"How did I react? I wanted to kill him, Henry!" As soon as the words were out of my mouth, I regretted saying them. I tried to calm myself, but I felt my blood roil and my fists clinch. I was losing control. I didn't like it, but I couldn't stop. Maybe there was something to the therapeutic model. "Evan is dead, I'm dying, and this asshole doesn't even remember my face!"

"Do you want to confront him, Mara? Letting him know of the cost you've suffered from your tenure with the company could be very cathartic." I didn't answer. My breathing was fast and labored as I looked at my therapist.

Henry took a deep breath. "You have every right to feel anger about what you've described, extreme anger. Anger is not a choice. Your response to anger is where choice comes into play. Much of what you and I will talk about together involves your choices. I encourage you to make choices that will give you peace, choices you can feel good about."

"I understand," I said, looking Henry in the eye as my breathing evened. "I feel quite good about choices I've made lately."

"Do you have unfinished business in this, Mara?" Henry asked. "Are you able to put it aside?"

I took a deep breath and looked up at the ceiling, hoping for something to focus on like the spots on the ceiling in Kathryn's office, but Henry's ceiling was clear and clean with barely a pattern. I wasn't sure what to say but decided on the truth as it stood regardless of my plans. "Nothing I do at this point will change what's going to happen to me."

"But you are angry?"

"Yes," I said, but I wanted to express deeper feelings and motives. "I feel wasted. I've always been the quiet girl, the one who didn't make waves. I did my homework and stayed out of trouble. I wasn't a problem for my family, my teachers."

"You were a rule follower."

"I was—and I trusted others to follow the rules. As an adult, I've dealt with depression, low energy, no motivation. I blamed myself. I thought these were personality flaws, but according to Dr. Edmunds, they might have been festering for years due to my condition."

"And you have a chance to act on that information and seek restitution." If only Henry knew just how definitively I was acting on it.

"But there's no solution, Henry. Why dwell on a past I can't change?"

"I see your point and I respect it. You have the choice to seek damages, and you choose not to do so."

"It would be a struggle, Henry. There's no guarantee of the outcome, and I see no point in pursuing a fight I won't see to the finish."

Henry nodded. "There is another possibility: you could consider contacting your former employer. Officially. Let them know what's happened to you, Go on record. Doing so might make a difference to you. It might certainly make a difference for someone else."

"Yes," I answered, "It could." I thought about what Henry wanted to hear and answered appropriately. "It would be nice to know this won't happen to someone else. Maybe I should share with the company what I've been through." Henry nodded. "I'll consider it," I said, knowing it would never happen, and on that note, my second session with Henry ended.

Chapter 18

Hours later, I arrived at work for a busy Friday evening and was told Tomas wanted to speak with me before my shift. I hid the whiskey bottle in the storeroom and when I walked into Tomas's office, a member of the security team was already there. The man's name escaped me, but I'd seen him around. *Shit*, I thought. *This wasn't good.* One more opportunity was all I needed to complete my plan. I soon realized that I had no reason for concern, because instead of outing me and my deadly process, they shared with me the following information:

At around eleven o'clock on Thursday evening, an agitated man was discovered trying to enter several rooms on the fourth floor. Security reported that the subject had ranted about someone chasing him and they were unable to determine where he might have been prior to the incident or what had led to his behavior in the hallway. The man was identified as Mr. Davisson, the guest in room 418.

Because of events the evening before, the man was known to the security staff and, upon returning him to room 418 a second time, they decided that something needed to be done. After perusing his room charges, Security realized that Mr. Davisson, for whatever reason, was not handling his liquor well. Maybe he was ill, maybe taking medication—they had no way of knowing. At any rate, his bar privileges were suspended for the rest of his stay. Hotel staff, including Security, were relieved that Mr. Davisson was due to check out on Saturday morning.

Things had taken an interesting turn. I responded that I knew of the gentleman in question and that he seemed to enjoy his drink as well as talking with the staff serving cocktails. I assured them that I understood and agreed with the decision, thanked them, and headed to the bar.

My shift began and I was soon pumping out drinks during a busy Happy Hour. I was on autopilot behind the bar, trying to figure out how Davisson, who couldn't order a drink, would manage to consume a large amount of my special blend of whiskey and provide my coup de gras.

Around seven o'clock, an idea occurred to me. I checked Davisson's account for room service orders periodically and finally hit gold at about eight p.m. Davisson ordered a cheeseburger and onion rings to be delivered to him by room service. Taking my first break for the evening, I retrieved the whiskey bottle I'd prepared from its hiding place and placed it in my apron pocket. I draped a large dinner napkin over my arm in the style of a maître d' to conceal the bulky item and headed in the direction of the kitchen.

With perfect timing, a kid came barging out of the kitchen door just as I approached. He held an order on a tray, and I heard him shout over his shoulder to someone in the kitchen, "Right, 418."

Acting as though by sheer coincidence, I stepped forward and asked, "That's going to 418? I'm on my way up to talk to him about his cocktail charges," I said, like it was some onerous chore. "Lucky me."

The kid was caught off guard by my remark. Bar and restaurant staff used the back corridor to access the staff elevators and parking garage, but I doubted this kid often received any communication about their business. Within seconds the surprise was gone, and his feckless demeanor returned. When he realized he was addressing senior bar staff, deference took over his expression.

I kept pace toward the staff elevator and the kid fell into step beside me, headed in the same direction. I used my key card, identical to the one the kid had tethered to his belt, to enter the elevator. As he was about to step in, I said, "I'm headed there. I'll take the order up."

He looked unsure of what to do and I was quickly running out of time. It occurred to me that his indecision was prompted by not wishing to lose his gratuity. "Listen," I said, as I looked at his name tag, "Kyle. I'll make sure you get the tip." I rolled my eyes slightly, letting him know that the least of my concerns were a measly couple of bucks.

"Cool," he said. A man of few words, Kyle placed the tray in my hands and headed back in the direction of the kitchen. I closed the elevator doors. I placed the tray carefully on the elevator floor and removed the whiskey bottle from my apron pocket. I used the dinner napkin to wipe down the bottle one last time to smudge any fingerprints. I positioned the whiskey bottle next to the covered plate on the tray and placed the large, cloth napkin over it. I picked up the tray then hit the button to take me to the fourth floor.

There was no security camera in the staff elevator, but there would be cameras on the fourth floor where guests frequented the area. I had no clue where they might be, and it was too late to try and find them. I would simply have to avoid them and come up with some reasonable explanation, should I need one, as to why I would be there.

As I stepped out on the fourth floor, the corridor was empty, and I hurried to the door of Room 418. It was not common practice in food service for reasons of cleanliness, but I placed the tray on the floor in front of the door and returned the whiskey bottle to an upright position. I knocked on the door and headed around the corner leading to the stairwell to the left, thinking about the location of security cameras. I couldn't risk peeking, but I heard the door open and heard Davisson say, "Yeah," then hesitate. "Huh," he continued. "Hello?" I heard a grunt, assuming the man bent down to pick up the tray then heard the distinct sound of glass clinking against dish ware. A moment later I heard the door of Room 418 close. I walked back to the staff elevator with haste, down to the first floor and into the same back corridor near the kitchen. When I slipped back behind the bar, I saw that my errand had taken me less than twenty minutes.

I found a relief bartender to work my shift on Saturday and left a note for Tomas. I was off work two hours later. On my way to the parking garage, I saw Kyle taking a break near the kitchen. I gave him a fiver and told him it was from the man in Room 418.

***

I made it home to find Lulu, Amir and Avo stretched out in the living room. Avo greeted me with his tail wagging, and I realized how wiped out I was.

"Hey, said Lulu. "How was your night?"

"Busy," I answered. "How did the two of you manage to get home so early on a Friday?"

"I worked a double because of a scheduling mishap. It's the end of the work week and I'm maxed in hours. Can't work more hours until tomorrow," explained Lulu with a grin she couldn't hide.

Amir drained his beer and looked in my direction. "I've been home since early evening. Can I get you one of these?" he asked, showing me the bottle of beer in his hand.

"That would be great, Amir, thank you," I answered. He nodded, took his empty, and headed for the kitchen. "I want to change out of these clothes, but I need a minute first." Instead of plopping on the couch, I opted for the floor where I could stretch out. I closed my eyes and took a deep breath, hoping to release the tightness in my back. More than anything I wanted to relax, but my back was very tight, and my thoughts were on Davisson and the whiskey bottle I'd left for him. As I opened my eyes, I realized Lulu was speaking to me.

"Are you okay?" she asked, and I knew she had asked the question more than once.

"Oh, sorry," I answered, as a rolled to my side. "Trying to shake off my crazy evening," I told her with a tired, half-smile. "I'm okay, just beat."

Amir returned from the kitchen and placed two full bottles on the coffee table. I must have looked fragile to him because he stepped to where I had landed on the floor and knelt next to me, offering a hand to help me up. With Amir's help, I found a somewhat comfortable sitting position with my back against the couch and Amir handed me the beer he'd retrieved for me.

"There's beans, rice, and an enchilada left, if you can eat something," said Amir. "We ordered take out. I can get it for you."

"Maybe after I change. This is perfect for now," I told him, holding up the beer.

Amir resumed his spot on the chair across from me, taking his beer with him. "I guess Davisson had another bad one last night. You must have heard," he said.

"I did. Tomas told me about it before my shift," I confirmed, shaking my head. "So strange. At least the servers don't have to deal with him in the bar any longer."

"Oh yes, your old boss," said Lulu, to which I answered with a nod. "Thankfully, we haven't seen him in the casino again."

"Security is keeping close tabs on him," said Amir. "They'll be glad to see the back of him tomorrow."

"It didn't break my heart not to talk to him," I told them as I slowly got myself up from the floor. Amir started to come to my aid, but I assured him I would manage. "Let me get out of these work clothes. I'll be back in a few minutes." I left my beer on the table and walked down the hallway to change clothes. When I returned, I hoped to avoid any further reference to Davisson.

We sat in the living room for the next hour, chatting together like old times, playing with Avo. I enjoyed the much-needed respite from my grief and revenge. To please my friends, I managed to eat a small portion of rice and a few bites of enchilada. Both Amir and I had the day off on Saturday, but Lulu would work in the evening. I shared that Ed was making dinner for me before I dragged myself to bed with Avo trotting behind. I took a dose of meds and before nodding off, sent a quick message to Ed:

Avo says hello and wants to know if he can join us for dinner. Is that okay?

Chapter 19

I awoke on Saturday morning with the distinct feeling that time had passed while I slumbered. I checked the time and noticed that I had slept a full seven hours. Amazed by this, I stretched, and considered going back to sleep, but I opted for a nice cup of coffee instead. My bedroom door was open and Avo was not in the room. Either Auntie Lulu or Uncle Amir had let him out.

After rising carefully from my bed, I headed down the hallway to the kitchen. Avo was stretched out on the floor near the front door. He thumped his tail in greeting as I approached. I made coffee and picked up my phone. Ed had answered with the following:

Yes, yes. Of course. Unless you'd rather drive, I'll pick you both up at four.

He sent another message a short while later:

I'll pick up doggie cuisine. What's the boy like to eat?

It made me smile that Ed would go to the trouble to have dog food on hand. I responded with the following:

Thanks for driving. Four is good. Avo says thank you for including him and Mom will pack his grub.

I poured a cup of coffee and as I took my first sip, Amir entered the kitchen. He had his phone in hand and was absorbed in whatever he was reading. When he looked up, he seemed shocked to see me. "How long have you been up?" he asked.

"Not long. What is it?" I asked.

Amir sat down at the table and ran his hand through his hair that was already standing on end. "Listen to this, Mara." He read from his phone: *A guest of the Anasazi Resort was found dead in their hotel room on the premises early this morning. The victim has been identified, but the name is being withheld until next of kin are notified. The circumstances surrounding the death are under investigation and the Resort is cooperating fully. Further details will be announced as the story develops.* "Mara, it was Paul Davisson!" he exclaimed, staring back at me.

I stared at Amir. My eyes were wide with shock. "What?" I responded, trying to formulate a coherent thought. I shook my head in disbelief. "How do you know that? The news alert said they hadn't released the victim's name."

"It was Davisson," he said with certainty. "I was notified by management this morning. They contacted all the department heads. It is a mess, Mara." Amir put his phone on the table and poured himself a cup of coffee. "There was a woman in the room with him. They had been partying and to what degree, no one knows. She woke up in the middle of the night, discovered he was dead. At least she didn't just leave him there." *Yeah. A pity,* I thought. That scenario might have been all the better for me.

We sat at the table, sipping coffee, trying to make sense of the news. *He's dead,* I told myself. *You did it. You murdered a human being,* I thought. No, no, I had not! I had killed a man that deserved to die. I had wondered if, when my end game came to fruition, I'd feel any regret, any sorrow. I had a hollow feeling in my gut, but I decided it was due to the surprise.

"Any idea what caused his death?" I asked, more out of curiosity than concern.

"They were drinking, we know that much. We had refused him service and cleared out the mini bar, but he either found his way to a liquor store or the woman brought it with her. They found an empty whiskey bottle and one empty wine bottle. There was no indication of violence and no sign of drugs, but the police will look closer."

"Was she a pro?" I asked, knowing it was possible, but sex workers rarely provide refreshments. I doubted that Davisson stepped out for wine after a bottle of his favorite whiskey miraculously showed up at his door. It was possible the two of them met up somewhere else, or she might have been a business associate.

"I don't know," said Amir shaking his head. "There wasn't a lot more that Security could find out before notifying the police."

This woman, whoever she is, could have contributed the wine. I hadn't considered the possibility of a second person in the room with Davisson. *Had this woman had a drink of the whiskey,* I wondered? If she had, I caused an innocent person to consume a dangerous drug without their knowledge. I wasn't happy at the prospect, but there was no going back.

Chapter 20

Throughout the day I kept myself busy, pausing my activity in the afternoon for a short nap. My thoughts were seldom far from Davisson's death and Amir received no more information from the team at work. We would know no more, officially, until the police released more details and as far as I was concerned, the less they learned, the better.

By half past three, I was rested and showered and in my favorite pair of shorts and a sleeveless top. I gathered the ingredients for the mojitos I had decided to make for Ed. By the time I packed food and treats for Avo, along with two spare bowls for his food and water, the doorbell rang. Avo had been snoozing in the entry and when I walked to the door to answer the bell, he roused happily.

"Who is it, Avo? Is it Ed? Do you remember Ed?" I asked the excited pup as I opened the door. Ed's expression said he was concerned but glad to see me. I returned the sentiment by reaching for him as he stepped inside the doorway.

"Hello," he said with a smile, and we shared an embrace and a kiss. Avo waited patiently for a greeting from Ed. He offered the pup long, loving strokes and told him, "Hey Boy, you're coming to visit my house. Doesn't that sound like fun?"

"He's ready to go," I told Ed.

"Great," said Ed, looking at me with eyes so bright they could ignite a fire. "How are you?"

"I'm okay," I said. "I look forward to watching you cook for me, and I love paella." I hoped to have enough appetite that Ed would know his effort was appreciated.

"It is my specialty," said Ed. "Kind of like those Manhattans you make, but I am looking forward to trying mojitos."

The three of us headed out to the Jeep with the items I'd packed for the evening. I was still curious about the woman involved, but the death of Paul Davisson was not going to put a damper on my evening. I was determined to enjoy myself.

***

Ed lived in a second-floor apartment of an older complex overlooking a golf course. We walked Avo around the grounds next to the building, thinking the dog would like to stretch his legs and sniff at the new surroundings. Yes, he golfed, Ed explained, but that was not why he chose to live here. When we made it upstairs and I saw his home, I understood.

The apartment was small, comfortable, and situated on the corner of the complex opposite the desert course. His kitchen was simple but serviceable. The living room was furnished with a sofa and a large desk, and a bank of shelves filled with books covered an entire wall. The bathroom and a closet were accessed by a short hallway next to the door leading to the bedroom. It was plain to see that the main attraction of Ed's home was the view. North-facing windows centered by sliding glass doors encompassed one entire wall of his living room. I found the same feature in his bedroom.

I stepped through the sliding door in the living room onto a wide, covered deck that ran the length of the apartment. The view from the deck was of rocky desert hills, rich with saguaro, ocotillo, and desert sage. The area was silent, still, and undisturbed. Ed conveyed with obvious pride that the desert expanse was not zoned for development.

"This is incredible," I told Ed, taking in the view. Avo was checking out each corner of the deck and after we set out water for him in one of his bowls I'd brought from home, he was comfortable enough to find a spot and recline, tongue hanging and breath panting.

Ed had furnished one end of the large deck as a second living room and had created a dining area at the other. The wooden bar-height table was rectangular in shape and surrounded by four bar stools. Large fans above the deck supplied a pleasant breeze.

"Paella will take about an hour, and I have everything prepped," he said. "It is early," he said, checking the time. "How about if we just relax for a while?"

"I would love that. I could stare out at the desert all evening," I answered.

"If it gets too warm, I can turn on the misters," Ed offered. "Or we can move inside. The view is okay from the living room too."

"It's fine out here," I said, looking out over the expanse of desert vegetation. "I'm comfortable. The fans really help."

We sat on a heavy, rattan couch fronted by a large, padded ottoman. Avo immediately moved closer to Ed, who began to stroke the dog's head and back. I smiled at the two of them and said, "The only way to make this more perfect is with a cold drink. Can I use that table as a bar?"

His face broke into a grin and Ed said, "You can use whatever you want as a bar. Can I help?"

"You can. I'll need two glasses, high ball if you have them, and a bowl of ice," I said. "And the bag of items I brought with me."

Ed was already on his feet. "I'll bring everything out to you."

While Ed sat next to me watching with interest, I muddled the mint in each glass with lime juice and simple syrup, filled the glasses with ice then added rum and soda and gave them each a slight stir. I placed a small sprig of mint atop each drink and handed a glass to Ed.

"Cheers," I said as I tapped my glass to his.

"Here's to mojitos and paella," offered Ed as his toast. He took a sip of his drink, licked his lips, and said, "You were right, Mara. A drink did make it even more perfect."

The drinks were tasty, I had to admit. "Here's to an amazing desert view and great company." I leaned closer and gave Ed a kiss, lingering in it. Ed responded with tenderness and my enthusiasm made him reluctant to pull away. We sat side by side at Ed's table, sipped our drinks and laughed at Avo as the dog entertained us. I gave no thought to cancer or death. The plot against Davisson that I had devised and acted upon was far from my mind as was the unknown woman who had been in his room when he died. For a little while, my world and all its misfortunes fell away.

It was then my turn to watch as Ed prepared Paella, the traditional rice dish. He asked about adding shrimp and I gave enthusiastic approval. As he had said earlier, the vegetables were chopped and ready. The stock filled the kitchen with a delicious aroma and the saffron threads in the rice produced a bright golden hue.

As Ed finished cooking, I made two more drinks and gave Avo his dinner on the deck. When we were ready to eat, Ed turned on the misters and we sat at the outside table.

Our evening together was more enjoyable than I could have imagined. The paella was outstanding. I managed to eat a fair amount, and our conversation flowed easily. There was a strong connection between us as well as a healthy attraction and soon we couldn't keep our hands off each other. We ended up on Ed's bed and time dissolved into passion. I had not been physically intimate in a long time, and I didn't remember feeling this natural—eager, uninhibited. Ed's lovemaking was tender, slow, and generous and our frolic was full of both laughter and pleasure. Finally, we pulled ourselves away from each other figuring that Avo would appreciate a walk outside.

Evening had set in. The temperature was warm but not oppressive and the darkness was broken by streetlights. I grasped Ed's left arm as he held Avo's leash in his right hand. Before I realized what happened, fatigue consumed me. All my weight leaned against Ed's arm—I couldn't avoid it.

"Are you okay?" asked Ed, although it was obvious that I was not doing well.

"My energy level has tanked. I guess the evening caught up with me." My back had begun to ache, but the pain was not terrible, not like it often was at the end of a work shift.

"What can I do? Should I take you home?"

"What I'd really like is to lie down. Just for a little while."

"Let's take the elevator," said Ed, leading in that direction. "It's used by the maintenance crew, but no one will mind." I was grateful to avoid the flight of stairs.

Within minutes, I was lying near the edge of Ed's bed with Avo on the floor beside me. Ed said he was fine with the dog joining me on his bed, but I drew a firm line. "My dog is clean, but he's still a dog." Ed brushed my hair back from my forehead, his touch soothing. "Sorry," I said. "I just need a minute."

"Don't be sorry. Just rest."

Ed had stepped away briefly then placed a glass of water on the bedside table. He spoke to me, but his words hardly registered as I slipped into a light sleep. I thought he said he would take care of things in the kitchen and return shortly. If he did return, I wasn't aware of it.

Chapter 21

My eyes opened and luckily, I remembered where I was and what had happened. Avo was beside me on the floor sleeping and Ed was lying next to me. I couldn't see him because I was facing the other direction, but I sensed his presence and was comforted by it. I stirred and felt Ed's hand caress my shoulder.

"How are you doing?" he asked.

I turned slightly toward him and placed a hand over his. "Better, I think. How long have I been resting?"

"Only an hour. You don't have to get up, you know. Rest if you'd like."

"I should take Avo home."

"I was hoping you would stay."

"It is tempting," I said with a sigh, "but I'm not really equipped for an overnight."

"Maybe next time," said Ed, as he nuzzled my ear. I responded with a nod.

I sat up, slowly placing my feet on the floor. The bedroom sliding door was open and through the screen I felt the slightest of evening breezes. I could see the outline of the desert hills in the distance, the sky brightly illuminated by stars and a half moon. I loved the desert landscape. Always had. The silence so powerful, the air so electric. Ed was sitting beside me; his hand stroked my back.

"You've been very understanding, very kind," I told Ed.

"It is not hard to be kind to you. I care about you, Mara." Ed took my hand. He lifted it to his mouth and kissed it. I took a deep breath.

"I find myself caring for you too. This was the best evening I've had in a long time."

Ed crouched in front of me as I sat on his bed. "I had a great evening too. I'm glad you felt comfortable enough to rest. You felt safe here, although Avo didn't leave your side."

"I get so tired. I might have to stop working soon."

"Maybe. Whenever you decide. It is your choice." He took my hand.

"That's what Henry says." I told Ed about my therapist and his urging to make choices about how I wanted to spend my time. "I told Henry about you."

"That's nice to know, at least I think it is." Ed paused, looked at our joined hands. He was thinking about something. "The truth is, I suspected something. My mother had ovarian cancer and I noticed similarities—energy level, appetite. But if I didn't want to see you, to spend time with you, I wouldn't have kept calling. Plus, the way I see it, if you didn't want to spend time with me, you would have declined the invitations."

"It's true. I did want to see you."

"And I want to spend more time with you, as much as possible, as much as you'll let me in the time we have. Are you sure you don't want to stay here tonight?"

"I want to, but I can't," I answered. "I need my pain meds, I need a toothbrush," I joked, and the levity got a grin out of Ed. He leaned in and planted a deep kiss, then rested his forehead against mine.

Avo followed us into Ed's kitchen, and I gathered my things. Ed suggested I leave the rum along with the rest of the mojito ingredients for our next round. I agreed and asked about leaving Avo's extra bowls. While I napped, Ed had rinsed the food bowl and brought in Avo's water bowl from the deck and placed it in the kitchen. When he turned to Avo, the dog was slurping water from it. "Good boy, Avo," he said. "Now, I'd better get both of you home."

***

On the drive home I was quiet. Ed noticed and asked me how I was doing. Work was on my mind. I was thinking—again—about how long I could keep doing it. When I told Ed what I was thinking, he reached over and took my hand.

"I won't presume to offer advice, but would you mind if I tell you what I think?" he asked.

"Yes, please do," I answered, turning to look in his direction. I honestly was interested in what he thought.

"If it was me, I would at least cut back to part time. More rest might help you to better enjoy your free time, and it would give you more time at home with Avo and your friends." Ed brought my hand to his lips and gently kissed it. "And with me."

I responded with a tired smile and had to agree that he had a point. "I think a conversation with my boss is in order. Maybe with HR too."

"Do you have plans tomorrow? No shift at the bar, right?"

"No, I don't work Sundays. A thought occurred to me, and I looked at Ed. "I'd like it if you came over in the evening."

"I'd like that—if you rest in the meantime."

When we arrived at my house, Ed walked Avo and me to the door, but although I asked him, he didn't come in. "You need sleep," he insisted. "I'll see you tomorrow," he told me, after a goodnight kiss that made me swoon.

I went inside the house to find an empty living room, but Amir soon came down the hallway from the bedrooms. "Hey," he said with care. "How was your evening?"

"It was lovely. Dinner was great. Ed made paella for me," I sighed. "I just got so tired."

"Go lie down. I'll let Avo out once more for the night." He walked to the back door and called Avo to follow him. I headed to my room.

By the time I had taken meds and was lying in bed, Avo came bounding into the room. Amir stepped to the doorway and rapped his knuckle on the opened door. "The police released details about Davisson's death. It will soon be on news reports."

"What have they said?"

"They named the woman with him. Her name is Rebecca Hardin. She was a friend of Davisson's. She lives in the area. She told police that they often got together when he was here on business."

I shook my head as I repeated the woman's name. "I don't remember anyone by that name, but I wouldn't expect to after all this time."

"According to her, Davisson was sloppy drunk when she got there. But they were able to confirm that the whiskey he was drinking didn't come from our bar."

"We already knew that. We cut him off," I said without looking Amir in the eye. "The man liked to drink. I guess it caught up with him. Who knows what happened? This woman, this friend, she was drinking wine?"

"That's what the report says, and that she brought it with her," said Amir. "Good news, if such a statement can be made. Anyway, I hope you sleep well. Goodnight."

Chapter 22

As it turned out, I did sleep well until the early hours of Sunday morning. When I woke, I rolled over, stretched, and listened to Avo's snores, contemplating whether to try to sleep for a while longer or give up and start my day early. My mind started to drift from one thought to another—the cancer that was killing me, Paul Davisson and my revenge for his callousness, and the woman who was with him when he died. She had been a professional contact, according to the police. Amir had mentioned her name. What was it? Rebecca, that's right. What was her last name? Rebecca ... Rebecca ... Hardin. That's it. Paul was dead and this woman named Rebecca had survived. I was relieved by this because I certainly meant her no harm and perhaps my relief made me curious about her. She had talked with police and given a statement. It was possible she worked in the lab industry in the area, but I did not remember anyone by that name.

I stretched again and looked at the clock. It was nearly six a.m. I sat on the side of the bed, breathing deeply. I soon felt Avo stretch behind me. When I heard his tail thump the wall, I reached over and stroked his side. Apparently, this was taken as a signal because the dog slowly ambled down from the bed, stood wagging his tail, and waited patiently for me to follow to the back door.

By the time I had poured my first cup of strong, black coffee, Avo was in the kitchen with me enjoying his kibble. As I sipped, I thought of my conversation with Evan's son, Cameron. It had been Cameron who had shared with me the details his father had discovered about Davisson. Now Davisson was dead. Richard Carling, however, who had assisted him, was alive and living in Tucson, according to Cameron. Carling owned a company and was still inspecting commercial chem labs for a living, which in my mind, meant he could still falsify inspection records. My eyes narrowed with anger as I considered the possibility. I picked up my phone and started a web search.

The American Society of Chemists is an organization well defined by its name. As with most professional associations, affiliation is by choice. There are often benefits to one's involvement, from networking to boasting additions to one's curriculum vitae. I still paid a nominal yearly fee for inclusion in the rolls of the ASC—one last vestige of professionalism I afforded myself. I scrolled through the ASC website and found Richard Carling and his current information within seconds, complete with photo.

Carling was older of course, but I recognized the man. I was not interested in any of his background information, so it was handy that the details of Carling's current position were listed first. His bio read like an advertisement. He wanted everyone to know that he was the Owner and Chief Operating Officer at Laboratory Solutions PC, located in Tucson. He boasted thirty years of experience inspecting commercial laboratories as required by law. I had to wonder how many bribes Carling had accepted in that thirty-year span.

Doors opened and closed deeper in the house, and I heard the shower in the hall bathroom start to run. Amir was up and getting ready for work. Sunday mornings in his department were often busy with business travelers checking out. I poured myself a second cup of coffee and leaned forward against the kitchen island, relieving pressure on my lower back.

Disgusted, I left the page on the website that listed Carling's details. Names were listed alphabetically, and I found my own listing a few pages back from Carling. Cordovan, Mara. This was part of my life so long ago, a professional life that had derailed abruptly and to which I had not returned. None of the details in my profile had been updated in years. The photo was from the days of my employment with P-H, of course. My hair was longer. The face was a younger, healthier version of myself. I read through the brief bio that I had submitted years ago, feeling pride but also sadness.

I shrugged off the emotion. It took a moment to find the listings for chemists with names beginning with 'H' and there she was: Hardin, Rebecca.

The woman in the photo was older than me, maybe mid-forties. I had no clue as to the age of the photo, but Rebecca Hardin had completed her degree ten years before me. She was blonde in the photo, with a round, carefully made-up face and full cheeks. Rebecca looked to be a pleasant person with one of those smiles that cause the eyes to nearly close in a squint. Her position was listed as Independent Consultant—which could mean anything—and she boasted affiliations with several laboratories, including Presson-Hagee.

I studied the photo. This woman was friendly enough with Davisson to visit him in his hotel room. She brought her own choice of alcohol, and she was with him when he died. *Why did I care?* I asked myself. Was it simple curiosity or the fact that I had caused Davisson's death and unintentionally placed the woman in harm's way? As odd as this sounded, I felt for her and wanted to know she'd been unharmed by my deadly plot. I made a note of Hardin's number and would decide later about using it.

Amir and I talked before he left for work. He was surprised that I was up at that hour, but he took Avo out front with him for a quick stroll before he left for the resort.

I wanted to call Joe. I'd been thinking about something and wanted to ask him about it. It was late enough in the morning, but instead of interrupting his weekend routine with a call, I sent a text message:

Hey. Been thinking about a trip to Vegas to have a chat with Fred. Would you go with?

Joe responded a short while later:

If that's what you want to do, of course I'll go with you.

I thanked Joe in a return text and asked about the following weekend. He was good with whatever I wanted to do. I appreciated his attentiveness. This was a side of my brother that I had not seen since we were children. I was sorry for both of us.

***

Ed and I spent Sunday evening together. Amir was home from work by five but left again, saying something about a poker game. We made a taco salad together and shared our dinner with Lulu before she headed to work at the resort casino. After Lulu left, there was the two of us and Avo. We sat outside in the back yard and let Avo entertain us with his dog antics.

I mentioned to Ed that a guest at the resort had died, and that the death appeared to be an accidental overdose. "The weird part is that he was someone I knew a long time ago, had worked with in the chem industry," I explained. I wasn't sure why I wanted Ed to know of Davisson's death. Guilt? Not likely. Maybe pride or an odd feeling of accomplishment. Whatever the reason, he soon would hear about the man's death and that I had known him.

"Mara, I'm sorry to hear that. Was he a friend?"

"No, someone I had worked with but not a friend. It was so long ago that when I saw him in the bar, we didn't even recognize each other." Not lies, I told myself.

Ed and I talked about the plans I made with Joe to visit our uncle. Ed thought that I wanted to tell Fred about my diagnosis. I made it clear that the visit was more about gaining closure for me than sharing my sad news with Fred. Ed understood that too and was sorry it had to be that way. So was I.

Chapter 23

The blood draw at the lab on Monday morning followed the same routine I had experienced before except it seemed to me that the technician drew an extraordinary amount of my blood, filling several small tubes. I asked about this, but of course he couldn't offer an opinion. The only response I received was that Dr. Edmunds had ordered tests and would receive the results. What could the doctor possibly need to check so closely at this point? She knew I was dying. The only meds I was taking were for pain. I left the lab, walked next door to the pharmacy, and filled my new prescriptions—Fentanyl for pain, and Zofran to keep from throwing up the Fentanyl.

When I made it home, I saw Lulu's car parked in its usual spot. I entered the house as quietly as possible and the silence that greeted me said my friend was sleeping. On the kitchen countertop, I found a note from Lulu complete with hearts and kisses, saying she would see me before she left for work.

I was ready to rest as well, but I sat in the back yard with Avo for a while. I heard an alert on my phone and saw that I had a text from Ed:

How are you? I miss you and Avo.

I responded that we missed him, I was okay, had just come from my blood draw at the medical office. Ed sent back a kiss emoji and said that he would call later.

There were two other calls I had decided to make. I left a message for Tomas, my manager at work. I was facing up to the fact that the job would soon be too strenuous. Ed suggested I work less to enable myself to rest more and enjoy my time. He had a point. The truth was that the resort had become the scene of my revenge, and I doubted I could feel comfortable there anymore. It was a job, that was all. I didn't need the money and I wanted to spend my evenings with my friends, with Avo, and with Ed. Those things that money cannot buy had come into clear focus.

My thoughts drifted to Davisson's friend. Retrieving the paper where I'd written the phone number for Rebecca Hardin, I punched the numbers into my cell phone then stared at the screen. *Did I really want to talk with this woman?* Obviously, she had survived the evening that resulted in Davisson's death. She had given the police a statement. My level of interest won over and I pressed "call" before giving myself a chance to think better of the idea. After three rings, a woman's voice answered.

"Rebecca Hardin," she said plainly.

I hadn't given enough thought as to what to say plus I was taken by surprise that she'd answered, but it was too late now. I could hang up without saying a word but decided to press on.

"Hello," I said trying not to stammer. "My name is Mara. I used to work at Presson-Hagee." I paused my narrative for a moment to let her absorb and to ensure that I sounded as sensitive as possible.

"How can I help you?" she said, sounding pleasant but business-like.

"I hope I'm not being too forward," I explained slowly, "but I knew Paul Davisson. I worked for him at one time, and I heard about his death. I talked with a friend at P-H. They mentioned you were a close friend. I wanted to offer my condolences."

I tried to sound credible, and the lie rolled off my tongue so easily that I was both surprised and grateful. My reason for contacting this woman was not to offer condolences at all. I was curious about her state of mind after what she'd been through. After all, I had unwittingly put her in that position. It crossed my mind that a career criminal might have recommended against the phone call, convinced that taking such action is how amateurs are caught.

Crime dramas would have us believe that the killer may return to the scene of the crime, watch investigators from a distance, or keep mementoes that remind them of their victims. Perhaps that idea is based in truth, I do not know. I tend bar—I don't solve crimes. The man I had killed had been a criminal, although few people knew this. For that reason, I refused to think of Davisson as a victim and did not need to assuage my conscience.

"Oh ...," Hardin said in response, her reply cautious. "That's very kind of you," she said slowly. "Yes, we were friends. You said your name is Mara? Did I catch that right?"

"Yes, yes, you did. I'm sure this is odd for you, hearing from someone you don't even know at a time like this. Really, I just wanted to say I am sorry to hear what happened. I don't mean to keep you."

"No, this is fine. It is good for me to talk with someone who knew Paul. I've not talked with anyone other than the police," she told me. "I'm sorry, I don't know that many people at Presson. Who was it you talked with?"

Be careful, I told myself as I prepared to answer her question. "He's an acquaintance in the office and has been with the company a long time. He contacted me because we go way back." I skated past the contact question which was easy as I hadn't talked with anyone. I mentioned no name, only that it was a male, hoping she wouldn't notice. I had not assigned a name to this fictitious person, nor had I stated my last name. Lies or not, I would try to avoid going there. As it turned out, Hardin didn't ask.

"You worked for Paul you said?"

"Yes, for five years. When P-H still operated the lab in Phoenix. He was my first boss after I finished grad school," I told her, as if I remembered him with fondness, like Davisson had been a mentor who I would miss terribly. "This was years ago," I added.

"Oh, I see," said Hardin.

"The news didn't say much about his death. Had Paul been ill?" I asked, faking concern.

"I honestly don't know what happened and the police are still looking into it. I'm not a relative so I doubt they will give me any details. I know he was under a lot of pressure and had his own ways of dealing with it. I tried to encourage Paul to take better care of himself, but he wasn't interested."

The woman sounded fine, considering what had happened. She needed no encouragement to talk about it and Hardin didn't seem concerned with who I was. I had to wonder what Henry's take would be about this interaction.

What did she mean by Davisson's "way of dealing with pressure"? Was she referring to his drinking? That choice was certainly evident. Did she suspect or was she aware of drug use? If so, had she participated with him? Was she simply talking about a bad diet and no exercise? She might have referred to all the above. I wasn't going to ask.

"It sounds like he was still doing things his own way. He was kind of a rebel when I knew him." I said this with a slight laugh but wondered if the word *rebel* would bait her into saying more.

"You know Paul," she said, assuming I did. Her voice had relaxed, and a bit of grief had slipped in. "He could be a rebel, you're right. We had that in common, I guess." Maybe Hardin's reference had been to the full list of indulgences I had suspected.

"I do remember that he liked Johnny Walker Red," I said. More bait.

"Oh yes, he did. Very much. How anyone can drink whiskey is beyond me. I never developed a taste for anything stronger than wine." Now I knew. She hadn't shared the spiked bottle with him. I felt relief course through my body, but I plundered on.

"Do you know if a service is planned? I might try to pay my respects." I would never attend any service for that man and had no respects to pay, but it seemed like the appropriate last question to ask before I ended this very odd conversation.

Hardin sniffled. Her grief was more apparent now. She hesitated for a moment, then she answered, "I don't know his family. No one will contact me with that information." There was a lot I could read between the lines of that statement. I knew nothing about Davisson's family, but he had not been married or in a relationship when I had worked at Presson. It was possible that she and Davisson only saw each other when he was in Phoenix on business; a friendship of convenience that had been compartmentalized.

"When an obituary is posted, it will include those details, I would think." I paused briefly. Hardin said nothing else, so I continued pushing on to the end. "I do appreciate your time and, again, I'm sorry for your loss. Thank you for speaking with me." I waited half a second then told the woman goodbye.

I didn't want to hurry away but tried to end the call as quickly and naturally as I could. Contacting Hardin had proved to be easier than I would have thought, but I wasn't going to push my luck. I got off the phone before she could ask me any further questions. I was glad to have blocked my caller ID. I had become weary of this woman and disgusted by her relationship with Paul Davisson. But who was I to judge?

Chapter 24

My morning activities had exhausted me, and the afternoon was spent napping with Avo. I woke up feeling rested and the pain in my back had subsided. My first thought was that the new pain meds were serving me better than the Vicodin. Avo led the way to the living room, ready to head out the back door. I let him out, sat down, and saw a message from Joe to please call him. He had left the message more than two hours earlier and assuming he was at the office, he may or may not pick up. I was lucky to hear him answer after a couple of rings.

"Hey, you got my message. How are you?" my brother asked.

"I'm doing okay actually, thanks. Blood work this morning. Avo and I were asleep when you called," I told him, wanting fresh coffee and something light to eat.

"I talked with Fred last night about making a trip to Vegas on Saturday. Will that work with your schedule?"

"I'll make it work," I answered. I would soon talk with Tomas about my work schedule anyway. I could find a sub to cover a shift. Part time bartenders were always willing to pick up more hours.

"Listen Mara, I think we should fly to Vegas. We're talking about a four-hour drive one way, if traffic is good. It is only a little over and hour by air. That will be more comfortable for you."

I hadn't thought about the logistics when I asked Joe to make the trip with me and he was right. If we drove, I would be sitting in the car for hours and I wasn't up to an overnight stay in the city with no clocks. "I'm sorry. I hadn't thought it through, Joe. A road trip would be hard for me."

"I've already checked flights. I will make the arrangements, but I wanted to talk with you first. We can be in Vegas by late morning, grab a rental, go talk with Fred, and be back in Phoenix in the afternoon."

I was touched that Joe would be so considerate of me, and he wanted to spare no expense. His kindness made me tear up, but I was able to swallow the emotion. "That's a clever idea," I said when I was able to speak. "I really appreciate this, Joe."

"It is no problem at all. This trip should be as easy for you as possible. Have you decided what you want to say to Fred?"

"Other than I'm dying of cancer and that he's a selfish SOB who robbed us blind when I was still a teenager? I think that will about cover it."

Joe sighed but it was followed by a snicker. "I'll support you in whatever you decide to say to good old Uncle Rip-off, but I don't want to see you upset by him."

"He won't upset me. I'm beyond Fred's reaction to anything in my life. Besides, I have all week to prepare myself. Let me know about travel plans for Saturday."

"I will. We'll talk soon."

"We will—and Joe? I'm glad you'll be there. Thanks." I had to end the call because I couldn't stop the tears.

***

Lulu was awake. I heard her bedroom door open and her soft steps down the hall to the living room. She saw my tears and was immediately concerned. "What's wrong?" she asked as she sat near me on the couch.

I explained that I had asked Joe to go to Vegas with me to confront Fred and that Joe was planning for us to fly there and back on Saturday. "Are you worried about seeing Fred?" Lulu asked.

"No. I'm not worried about Fred," I answered, shaking my head. "I want to get things off my chest. I am going to confront him—as I should have done years ago. I'm crying because of Joe. He agreed to go with me to see Fred without giving it a thought," I managed to say through the blubbering. "It was Joe's idea to fly so I wouldn't have to make the long road trip." Tears were flowing.

"Come here," said Lulu, pulling me close to her in an embrace.

Our hug ended when my phone buzzed with an incoming call. I picked up my phone and saw that it was Tomas. "It's Tomas calling. I need to take this. I left a message for him earlier."

"Are you sure? I can tell him you'll call back in a few minutes," Lulu offered.

"I'll talk to him now. Really, I'm okay." I knew how busy Tomas's afternoons were before the dinner rush and I didn't want to put off the conversation.

Lulu nodded. "I'll leave you alone then. I'll shower then make coffee for us." Lulu headed back down the hallway, and I answered the call.

"Hey Tomas. Thanks for getting back to me. Do you have a minute?"

"Sure, Mara. What's up?"

As soon as he asked, in his fatherly voice what was up, the sad details poured out. Tomas listened as I shared that I had cancer and that it was terminal. I explained that there was pain, and it was increasing, and that my strength and energy were fading. I had the impression that Tomas had heard news of this sort before and knew what to say. He asked the usual, kind questions like, *when did I find out? Did I have confidence in my doctors?* I tried to answer his questions without revealing more than was comfortable for me to talk about.

"I need to cut back on my shifts, Tomas. I can bring you documentation from the oncologist."

"When it is convenient for you but that's not my concern right now. Whatever you need to do, let me know." Such a kind man. I thought about the stark difference between working for Tomas, with his compassion, and Paul Davisson with his schemes and deceit.

"I can manage two, maybe three shifts a week. I'd like to keep working Saturdays, but I need to be out of town this weekend. My brother and I are going to see our uncle." Tomas said he understood. He must have thought the trip would entail sharing my awful news with an elderly, caring family member. I wasn't going to tell him that the upcoming visit was more complicated and less loving than that. "Can I decide next week about Saturdays?"

"Sure. I've got two or three part-timers that won't mind being on call."

I was about to end the call when Tomas brought up another subject altogether. "So, I know you've heard about the guy in 418, am I right?"

"Y... yes," I said, my words stumbling over my reaction. "Amir told me about it. It was that man we cut off. The guy who drank JW Red."

"It was none other. I don't wish that end for anyone but thank God, we cut him off. At least we know the bottle he was found with wasn't from our inventory. The seal traced it to a store close by. The police have been here, of course, talking to anyone who had contact with him that night."

My mind raced. Davisson had been in his room, as far as I knew, for the entire evening. I hadn't seen the man or talked with him face to face, but I'd intercepted his room service order. I'd orchestrated the interception of Kyle on his way to room 418. Did the police talk to Kyle? Why wouldn't they? The police would talk to whomever delivered his order. They might have been the last person to see Davisson alive. I snapped out of my panic when I realized Tomas was speaking to me.

"They're saying his death was drug related," said Tomas. This wasn't news to me. I already knew his death was drug related.

"Hard to believe a guy like that wasn't more careful," I said, trying to sound like I meant it, but Davisson's death had nothing to do with whether he was careful. His fate was tied to mine—and to his taste for whiskey.

"The man had problems, Mara. His behavior was unacceptable, remember? He couldn't handle his drink plus whatever else he was using. We've seen it before. Anyway, I'm sorry for bringing up that business. Enough of that. You take care and I'll see you tomorrow."

"Sure, tomorrow." I got off the phone and sucked in a deep breath.

Had I been kidding myself that I didn't care about getting caught? I clasped my hand over my mouth. The police talked to staff at the resort and the room service charge was in the system. Did Kyle know who I was? Did he know my name? If not, would he remember my face? Then I remembered the security cameras positioned somewhere in that hallway. If a camera had captured my image, it would take about three seconds to identify me. I had no good reason for being there.

Wait a minute, I told myself. That's not entirely true. I work there. All I had to come up with was a believable work-related task that would take me to the fourth floor of the hotel. I thought back to the story I told Kyle that night, something about beverage charges. If I were asked, and only if asked, I'd stick with the same story and hope they couldn't connect me to that whiskey bottle.

According to Tomas, the police thought drugs were involved. No mystery there. A simple toxicology test would confirm it, but there was no reason to think Davisson hadn't ingested the drug on purpose. I got the distinct impression from Davisson's friend, Rebecca, that partying in that fashion, with dangerous substances, could have been possible without my help. The police took her statement and I doubted she shared more with me than she had with investigators. Not that I cared, but I felt relieved. I was to work a shift tomorrow and again on Thursday. I would try to avoid running into Kyle.

Lulu came through the living room, headed to the kitchen with the scent of bath products wafting after her. "Do you want coffee, Mara?"

"Sounds good," I told her. I stood and walked toward the kitchen.

"How about something to eat? I'm making tuna salad on wheat," she said, and I remembered being hungry.

"That sounds good too," I told Lulu.

Crescendo: build up to a point of great intensity, force, or volume

Chapter 25

When I arrived to work on Tuesday I was asked, once again, to report to Tomas's office before my shift. I found Tomas, the same fellow from our Security staff whose name I didn't know, and a woman of about my age whom I didn't recognize.

"Mara," said Tomas, "please have a seat." Since the three of them were standing, the dynamic was uncomfortable, but I sat anyway. Tomas placed his hand on my shoulder for the slightest of moments as he stepped over to close his office door. A nod from the security guy sufficed as a greeting.

"Ms. Cordovan," said the woman, taking a chair positioned a few feet away. "I'm Detective Leanna Ochoa with the Scottsdale Police." She revealed a badge and handed me a business card which included a tiny photo, assuring me that she was who she claimed. "I need to know what you can tell me about the death of a man a few days ago here at the resort."

"Johnny Walker," I said, glancing over at Tomas, who stood to my left. I detected a slight nod of his head.

"No, the deceased's name was Davisson, Paul Davisson," she said with a frown.

"Yes, I remember the name from his room charges, but he drank JW Red." I shrugged. "I'm a bartender. I remember guests by what they drink."

"Right," she said, understanding the reason for my comment. "Was he a heavy drinker?"

"More than most, less than others. I'm sure you're aware we cut him off."

"Yes, Mr. Rodriguez filled us in about that," Ochoa said, indicating Tomas by his last name. "Probably a smart move. Prior to that, how many times was he in the bar?"

"Each night I worked last week. I don't know about the other nights."

"No, of course not. What do you remember about him?"

I thought about how to answer her questions. A man was dead, and I was being questioned by police, after all. I heard my father's voice echoing from my childhood, teaching me that when you tell the truth, it's easier to remember what you said. I would stick with the truth—except I wouldn't admit that I'd known Davisson. Unless I had to. He didn't recognize me when he ordered a drink from me at the bar so why assume I would recognize him? If Amir had not alerted me to Davisson's presence, would I have known it was him when I saw him at the bar? I would never know the answer. Davisson's name would have been familiar to me if I'd heard it or seen it in writing, but neither his first nor his last name was unusual. Few people knew of our past association. Maybe it wouldn't come up.

"Typical businessman," I answered. "Would drink in the bar, then head to his room, order more, charge to the account. We didn't chat much. You might talk to the servers. I would guess he had more to say to them."

Ochoa made notes and then looked me in the eye. I wanted to get the hell out of there. I didn't know if she had talked to Kyle or if they had me on the security video. I didn't know anything. All I could do, I decided, was create my own narrative and hope it gelled with the rest of their information. "He called the bar Friday evening. From his room."

"He called the bar," she repeated with surprise, the statement sounding like a question. "Why?" asked Ochoa. This was news to her, but then it was news to everyone because I'd made it up. "He knew you wouldn't serve him." She looked at Tomas and then at the nameless security guy.

"He asked about his bill, how many he'd ordered, that sort of thing." It was my turn to glance at Tomas. I rolled my eyes, like I had broken a rule. I looked back at Ochoa. "There was no one in guest services that would answer his questions. He didn't want to come to bar, said he was embarrassed." I looked at Tomas, and said, "You had gone home." I said this to Tomas, as if to ask, *what else did you expect me to do?* I turned back to Ochoa. "I told him I could print a bar total for the room charges and bring it up. He was thrilled, even sounded sober."

"You printed a summary of charges and took it up to his room."

"Yes."

"Did you leave anything else there?"

"I did," I said with a sigh. "I ran into a runner with an order for 418. They were busy so I offered to take it up for him. I was headed that way."

"How did he seem to you?"

"The runner? He was busy trying to keep up."

"Not the runner," Ochoa responded with impatience, as if I wasted her time. "The man in 418?"

"Oh, sorry," I apologized. "Of course. I didn't see him. He didn't answer the door. I left the tray and the report. Went back to the bar."

"Did you knock? Did you say anything to alert him to who was at the door?"

"I knocked," I said, thinking about it, as if I wanted to be sure. "I don't think I announced myself as room service or the staff from the bar. I didn't say anything. I was out of my element, I suppose."

"The runner says he got a five-dollar tip. How did that happen?" So, she did talk to Kyle. One question answered.

"I wasn't going to disappoint the kid or let him think I pocketed his tip. Runners rely on tips, like we all do. The tip came from me."

Ochoa nodded, deep in thought. "We didn't find anything like an expense report in the room."

"I left it on the room service tray," I said, as if that were my final word. "Couldn't say what happened to it."

"Okay Ms. Cordovan," said Ochoa. "Thanks. That will do. For now."

I nodded in Ochoa's direction, slowly stood, and told Tomas I was heading to the bar. I got the hell out of his office without looking at Mr. No-name.

***

By the time Mara left his office, Tomas was irritated. Griffin, who was part of the security team at the resort, had been present when resort staff were interviewed about Davisson by police. If an interview raised suspicion, it would continue at the department, but that situation had not come up. In addition to Griffin, Tomas asked to be there when Ochoa talked with Mara. He said she was dealing with health concerns and asked Ochoa to take it easy on her. He was allowed to be in the room if he stayed quiet and didn't interrupt. He agreed, but Tomas felt protective because of Mara's condition. Besides, they were all cooperating, and Tomas was convinced that no one had harmed Davisson but himself.

"There's nothing to find here—we told you that," said Griffin. "Mara's story backed up what the food runner told you. Neither of them had seen Davisson that night."

"That seems to be true, and your security video from the fourth-floor corridor does back up what Ms. Cordovan had to say," said Ochoa, nodding in agreement. "We only see her from behind and from above for eleven seconds, but long enough to see her approach, put the tray down, knock on the door, and turn to walk away."

"Yes, just as Mara said," Tomas confirmed, still irritated.

"There's no clear view of her face," Ochoa stated, "but you both identify the woman as Mara Cordovan, she says she was there, and the timing was right."

"Rebecca Hardin arrived at Davisson's room after he collected the room service tray from outside the door, as confirmed by the video," added Griffin, as if there was no further explanation. "She saw the tray inside the room. Ms. Hardin arrived after ten p.m. and stated Davisson was already drunk. She brought wine for herself, and he had killed off most of the whiskey by then."

"He bought the bottle around the corner," said Tomas, as if the story were simple. "He found a dealer that sold him drugs that he shouldn't have mixed with whiskey, came back upstairs, and partied alone until his friend Hardin arrived."

"I'm inclined to agree," said Ochoa. "We haven't accessed video from the store, but we know the bottle came from their inventory. Davisson didn't leave the room again and no one else entered except Hardin. I don't think she would have let him die, fallen asleep, then called for help when she woke up."

Ochoa gathered her things and thanked Tomas for the use of his office. She thanked Griffin for his cooperation. "I'm done here," she said, "but I still need a copy of the security video."

"Sent to your email, Detective," said Griffin. "From 1800 hours until Ms. Hardin called for help. Have a nice evening."

As she walked out of Tomas's office, leaving Griffin and Tomas to the rest of their evening, neither was sorry to see her go.

Chapter 26

Saturday had arrived. Sky Harbor, the international airport in Phoenix, is a large and busy airport but it never seems big nor bustling when I'm there. There are two working terminals, numbered three and four which is confusing unless you realize that numbers one and two no longer exist. Thankfully, the surviving terminals were never redesignated as one and two, which would have caused undue confusion and anger for the entire system—or so I guessed. Terminal One was demolished in nineteen-ninety-one to make room for the new parking facility. I can't say what became of Terminal Two. The two remaining terminals, still known as three and four, are named for Barry Goldwater and John McCain because, well, this is Arizona. Considering all this, Sky Harbor is simple and efficient to navigate. Simple and efficient if you are in the correct terminal. If you aren't in the correct terminal, as with any airport, neither simple nor efficient comes into play.

Joe and I left for the airport with of plenty of time to make our 9:30 a.m. flight to Vegas. Ed offered to drop us at the Departures area. Joe wanted to leave his car in short term parking where it would be waiting for us when we returned that afternoon. Ed insisted. He wanted to help and would be there to pick us up when we returned. Joe gave in.

Short flights are peculiar. As a traveler, you go through the same security measures and boarding process as with a longer flight but by the time you take off and your flight is under way, the cockpit crew announces they are beginning descent into your destination city. No time to settle in, read, watch an in-flight movie. While I thought about the up and down period, I did not dwell on it. A lengthy flight, like a lengthy road trip, was not possible for me at this point. We were taking this short, one hour and ten-minute flight thanks to Joe's consideration for my comfort and I was grateful for my brother's foresight. Traveling early in the day ensured that I would have the energy needed to deal with Fred. I had new motivations so maybe I could alter old patterns.

Our check-in was fast because we had no bags. We found our departure gate and had enough time before our boarding call to get coffee together. I had been thinking about how to have a conversation with Joe about my wishes for my personal possessions, but the coffee shop at Sky Harbor wasn't the place and there certainly wasn't enough time. Besides, the only plans I had formed concerned my house, the Prius, and of course, Avo. I had been thinking of leaving my house to Joe, but I wanted Lulu and Amir to continue living there, if they chose to, and I wanted Avo to continue to live there too. I had made these decisions but had no idea how they would be realized. One step at a time, I reminded myself.

Then there was the matter of my beautiful baby grand piano. I knew no one else who played piano. Maybe a school, a performance venue, or a recording studio would want it. Bequests are an ambiguous pursuit. As with all plans, we make them but, in this case, we must trust that our wishes will be honored. We won't be around to know or even care about our possessions. It feels like a waste of time and the effort can end up sordid by legal issues.

It might feel quite different to someone making these plans with years ahead of them and millions in assets to protect, but since that is not my situation, I wouldn't know. My focus is to keep my friends in the home we shared and ensure that Avo has love and care. My beautiful piano should enrich the lives of other musicians, either students or professionals. As someone preparing—most literally—to die, these are the things of importance to me. In that regard, I guess it is worth planning.

"Are you okay, Mara? You were a million miles away," asked Joe. I hadn't realized that I had been so deep in thought.

I pulled myself back from my mental retreat and acknowledged my brother's question. "I'm so sorry. I'm okay. I guess I was pre-occupied."

"No worries," said Joe. "As long as you are okay. They announced our flight, and you didn't react. Are you thinking about seeing Fred?"

I laughed as I shook my head. "Not at all," I answered. "I was thinking about more important things than our asshole uncle. We'll talk about it later, maybe on the flight or later this evening."

"All right," said Joe. He stood and offered me his arm with a grin. "Let's go."

I stood up, tossed the paper cup into the trash receptacle, and turned to face Joe. "Before we leave," I told him, "I want you to know how much I appreciate all you've done with this trip—giving up your Saturday, making the plans, going with me to Vegas—all of it."

Joe looked surprised by my words and then for a moment, he seemed embarrassed, but he made a joke of it. "Miss the chance to watch you rip Fred a new asshole? No way."

***

Two hours later we were in a rental car, speeding down the freeway on our way to Fred's house. Joe had called him while waiting for the rental car and Fred was expecting us. We would arrive at his home around noon which was the agreed upon time. We had provided Fred with few details about our visit. Fred had no idea when we had arrived in Vegas, and he didn't know how long we planned to stay. We had decided that it wasn't his business. If we needed an excuse to depart the pleasure of his company in a hurry, we could tell him we had a plane to catch, which was true. My intent wasn't to insult Fred, but I wasn't going to be falsely courteous either. His feelings had no bearing over the conversation I was planning.

Like so many neighborhoods, the street where Fred lived had seen better days. I had visited many times as a child and it looked different to me now—smaller, sadder, less-inviting. Pulling up to the plank-sided house, it was still painted the same pale yellow with the brown trim that I remembered. There had been a huge mesquite tree in the front yard, but it was gone. In its place was a circular rock garden centered by a trio of ceramic coyotes. I thought of my Aunt Rina. This had been her home and I had not returned since she died. I wondered if Fred was aware of that or had given any thought to how much time had passed.

I felt Joe's hand rest lightly on my back as we headed up the walk to Fred's door. I recalled the effort Aunt Rina put into her plants and surrounding shrubs but now it looked like no one lived here who gave a shit. Aside from the color of the house, nothing looked as I remembered. As we approached the front step at the entry, the door opened and there stood Fred.

Our uncle had aged and not gracefully, so much so that it took me a moment to recognize him. He was thinner, almost gaunt. He now relied on a cane for balance and was so stooped over at the waist that it was impossible to tell if he had lost height. Fred's hair had thinned to the point that he had but a small line of gray fuzz left over his ears. He wore glasses and due to the stooped posture, they could slide off his nose at any time. Fred attempted to look up in the direction of our faces as we stood before him resulting in a slight turn of his head to the left, and he repeatedly grasped his spectacles with thumb and forefinger of his right hand as if to assure himself they were still there. When he spoke, however, I knew it was Fred.

"Come in, come in," Fred said in his smug, irritating, voice that sounded neither friendly nor comforting. Fred had always sounded like that. I never liked Fred's voice with its fake cheerfulness. "You are right on time," he said, as close to a compliment as Fred would give. He carefully took small steps backward to allow us to enter his home. He had not yet looked either of us in the eye, but that was not odd. Eye contact required a degree of authenticity and Fred had none.

I don't know what I expected, entering Fred's home, but it didn't feel like a home. It was more like a temporary dwelling, a short-term furnished rental. My eyes searched but found not one item that recalled our Aunt Rina, her memory, or that this had been her home where a loved one still lived. Not one. No photographs, no mementos, no articles of decoration.

Joe tried to be civil. I heard him acknowledge Fred and offer his hand before Fred directed us to take a seat on his small, plaid couch. The television was large, too large for the room and it was on but thankfully, the sound was muted. The screen was split into two views featuring a horse race and a basketball game and I wondered on which event Fred, the gambler, had placed a bet. Possibly both.

"I can make coffee, if you'd like a cup," offered Fred. He waved an outstretched hand. "It's decaf, but it'll be fresh."

Joe and I looked at each other for a moment. Joe pointed in my direction, leaving the decaf decision up to me. "No, thanks," I answered. "Don't trouble yourself."

Fred nodded his assent and eased himself into the recliner on the opposite side of the coffee table, setting his cane aside but within reach. His head fell back with a motion that told us he was more comfortable off his feet, and it was now easier for him to keep his glasses on. "So how the hell are you two?"

We engaged in meaningless chit-chat. If Fred thought it was odd that we came all the way from Phoenix he didn't say so, even though we had not bothered to visit him at any point since Aunt Rina died. Joe returned the favor and asked Fred how he was doing, which initiated the recitation of a litany of ailments and the many woes of accessing services for people of his age. Then Fred started in on his financial troubles and that his meager, limited income barely covered the sparest of expenses. After a brief time, I couldn't listen anymore, and I had to interrupt.

"I am sorry, Fred," I said, giving him a moment to understand that I was commandeering the discussion. I glanced over at Joe. He responded with a slight, closed mouth smile and a tiny nod of his head encouraging me to get it over with. "Fred, I have news of my own. I decided to come tell you in person. Joe offered to come with me, so I didn't have to make the trip alone."

"News, huh? What's up? Did you win the lottery?" Fred laughed at his worthless effort at humor. From someone else it could have been possible to overlook the glaring offensiveness. After all, Fred didn't know that what he said could be taken as so awful. Fred, however had no class and with our history, his callousness was almost expected.

I looked him in the eye with disgust, deciding how to respond. I don't often feel at ease with speaking, especially under stress, but I felt my words come together in a rush. "Actually, my number has come up, Fred, but not in the way you mean." I felt Joe's hand on my shoulder, but it was meant as support. He didn't interrupt me. "I have been diagnosed with cancer," I told Fred. "The prognosis is bleak."

Fred didn't appear shocked or saddened but he did take a moment to decide on an appropriate response. "Sorry to hear this," said Fred. He rubbed his chin with the fingers of his right hand then the hand fell to the arm of the recliner. "Nothing they can do, huh?" He sounded bored by the subject.

"No," I said, bluntly. "There's nothing *they* can do."

Fred looked at the ceiling before he said, "That's how it was with Rina. They said she was sick and before you knew it, boom, she was gone." I was appalled at the lack of emotion as he talked about the death of his wife. I was surprised at how calm I was at hearing him mention it.

"Listen, Fred," I said, purposefully omitting the word *uncle*, "I wanted to convey to you how difficult my life was after our parents died. I should have told you years ago but that doesn't matter now. It is awfully hard losing your family when you are so young. Aunt Rina meant a lot to us, to Joe and me. She was the only family we had left, and she tried very hard to be supportive. It was another blow when we lost her."

He nodded slightly. His head resting back on the recliner and his eyes found the table between us. He said nothing so I continued. "It would have been quite different for us, for me, if you had been half as supportive, half as honest as Aunt Rina. Instead, you saw us as an opportunity. You took terrible advantage of our situation while we were too young. We should have been able to rely on your decency."

"What the hell are you going on about?" Fred tried his best to sound insulted.

"Our parents trusted you, well, I guess they trusted Rina. You were just an opportunist in a raw turn of fate. You robbed us of our inheritance, a little bit at a time until there was nothing left."

"Listen, I paid your bills. I made sure you stayed in school," said the asshole, as he pointed his arthritic finger at me.

"Oh, come on. Be honest for once. You didn't care that I stayed in school. You wanted me to work, to be responsible. That's all I heard from you."

Joe couldn't stay quiet. "Fred," he began, direct, but calm with a matter-of-fact tone. "You helped yourself to a lot of money because we had no way to stop you and then you covered your tracks. Don't lie," Joe told Fred, as he shook his head like he was admonishing an errant child. "Especially to Mara. Not now."

"That's all crap," Fred said, waving his hand in our direction. "I never took anything from you I didn't deserve. It took a lot of my time to manage your affairs—whether you believe it or not."

"It doesn't matter what you think we believe," I said, as I rose to my feet. "It never did. You are the worse kind of thief, Fred. You stole from your wife's relatives, from her grieving niece and nephew. That's what we believe because it is the truth. Plus, to top it off, you made Rina's life miserable. I won't forgive you for that either." I snatched my bag from where I had placed it near the couch. I wanted something in my hands to keep them from clenching.

"Excuse me." I turned and walked down the hallway to the bathroom, needing to be alone. I had managed myself as well as I could have expected, but I felt myself losing it. Losing it in front of Fred was not an option. He needed to see me strong, in control. I stepped into the bathroom and closed the door. I took time to calm myself and stretched my lower back from all the sitting on the flight, in the car, on Fred's ugly couch.

I took deep breaths as I looked at my reflection in the mirror. I had done it. After all these years, I had confronted Fred and it had taken a terminal illness for me to find the strength. He proved to be as unapologetic as ever, but I was going to consider my effort worthwhile, nonetheless. I said what I came to say, and I wasn't responsible for Fred's reaction or his lack of conscience. There was only so much I could expect or control.

On the bathroom vanity sat three medication containers. Two of the containers were amber in color with white screw-top lids. I picked up one of them and read the information printed by the pharmacist. The drug was a blood thinner prescribed for patients at risk of stroke. Fred had health issues it seemed, not that I cared. I picked up another bottle. The second one was more interesting. The label said it was Digoxin, a form of digitalis. Digoxin was serious business, that I knew. It was a regulator to control heart rate and rhythm, often in older patients with congestive heart failure. Fred needed the drug to stay alive. The bottle contained about a dozen Digoxin tablets. The third bottle was not a prescription but a common, over-the-counter analgesic.

Curiosity got the better of me and I examined the variety of medications. To my surprise, the Digoxin tablets and the analgesic appeared to be almost identical. Both were white and round and of medium size. The difference in the two were the tiny notations—the brand name on the analgesic and the number "50" imprinted on one side of each Digoxin tablet. The notations were easy to miss and unless you were trained to check such details—as a pharmacist, or a chemist are trained—you might not see them. I shook out a few of the blood thinners onto my palm and saw that they were small, flat white tablets. I put the small pills back in the container and returned it to the vanity.

Without a second thought, I took a mint tin from my bag and threw the few remaining mints into the trash. I poured the Digoxin into it, counting ten tablets as they fell into the tin. I opened the bottle of analgesic and counted out ten tablets, replaced the Digoxin with them, secured the white lid, and returned it to its place alongside the blood thinner. I hid the tin holding the Digoxin deep inside my bag and made sure to place the analgesic in its original position. I looked in the mirror and took one last, deep breath. I returned to the living room and told Joe I was ready to leave.

Chapter 27

We were soon on our way back to the airport. Joe was quiet, his attention on the midday Vegas traffic. I was exhausted and my back ached. The unappealing view of the traffic barriers that separated the lanes consumed my focus as we headed down the freeway, but my thoughts were on the medication I had stolen from Fred's bathroom. I wasn't sure why I had taken it other than having the medicine close by was important to Fred. The theft had occurred to me in the moment, there was nothing premeditated, and I had no answer as to why. Maybe I wanted to be mean and cause a problem for Fred. I had already killed a man, so I certainly was not above simple theft.

"Was I too hard on Fred?" I asked Joe, after a period of shared silence. "Maybe I should have backed off and been more diplomatic."

"Hell, no," said Joe. His eyes stayed on traffic. "I agreed with every word you said. I told Fred as much while you were out of the room."

"Did you?" I asked, with a surprised smile. "I wish I'd heard that. I would have enjoyed it." I reached into my bag to retrieve the bottle of Vicodin. I brought the Vicodin with me instead of the Fentanyl. It was easier on my stomach and not as likely to knock me out. At least I thought to place the stolen heart medication in the empty tin—no chance of confusing the Vicodin bottle with the one containing Fred's Digoxin. The last thing my body needed was to have my heart rate chemically altered.

"Fred tried to milk me for sympathy, as if I would have pity on him. I told him he should be glad that I was raised to control myself because what I really wanted to do was punch him in the face. That shut him up. Then I said he was lucky we couldn't sue him, and I told him I might try anyway. Maybe a civil suit, who knows?"

"Thanks, Joe."

"I told him he was a pathetic, old man and that he deserved to be sick and alone."

My eyes widened as Joe recalled for me his verbal assault on Fred. "Shit, Joe. I guess I wasn't hard on him at all."

"Yeah, well, I didn't mean to steal your thunder, Mara. The purpose of this trip was for you to give Fred a piece of your mind, but there were things I wanted him to hear. His attitude about the past got me riled and his response about your cancer diagnosis was not exactly kind."

"Maybe we should have confronted Fred a long time ago, Joe. It might have helped us both." Words and phrases like, *maybe, should have,* and *might have* sound especially sad to someone who is dying. The loss of possibility strikes hard, and the words are equally sad when it is your dying sister who says them to you.

Joe didn't answer but I could tell that he was thinking, formulating a response. "Hearing you tell Fred he was a loser made me proud of you, Mara, but I realized that I should have been around more, supported you when Mom and Dad were killed." I was touched by Joe's statement. My brother and I had not spoken much about those days. We survived that period as privately as possible, trying to make the best of things.

"You were grieving too, Joe. You were eighteen. You had college to think about and making plans for your future. I knew that to be true at the time," I said, "and it's not like we were close." I had to pause and think how to continue. It wasn't easy to talk about this and I wanted to express my feelings clearly "The situation already sucked but it would have been worse if I had been a burden on you on top of everything else."

My brother nodded and turned his head slightly to his left, toward the driver's side window of the rental. I suspected he had tears in his eyes, but if he had, he hid them from me. Joe's silence and his manner told me that he struggled to control his emotions. The sad truth was that as a sixteen-year-old with dead parents, I was going to be a burden to someone and it should not have been my brother, barely an adult himself at the time.

"Aunt Rina tried to help," I told Joe. "We talked often in the few years before she died. She didn't try to be a substitute parent, but I knew she cared. Rina talked to me about Mom and Dad, telling me what a wonderful job they did raising us and how well you and I turned out. She was proud of us."

Joe had recovered. He turned his head in my direction, and said, "Yes, she told me the same."

"I don't remember Rina ever mentioning Fred when we talked," I told Joe, thinking about the statement further. "I guess she knew he was an asshole," I concluded. She knew he wouldn't consider providing a home for his wife's orphaned niece. The unexpected comment made Joe laugh.

"Rina probably knew that to be true more than anyone," said Joe, as he exited the freeway. "Look, we'll be at the airport soon. What do you say we drop off the car, check in for our flight home and then find a bar?"

"That sounds good," I answered. "I think we both deserve a drink and that sounds better than taking a pill." The unopened bottle of Vicodin was still in my hand. I returned it to my bag.

***

We ordered four shots of tequila and two cold glasses of Pacifico and shared a plate of nachos. Joe was relaxed, I was feeling better, and we were enjoying each other's company. I was relieved to have the visit with Fred out of the way. I checked the time, seeing that we had another half hour until we boarded our flight back to Phoenix. I ordered another shot for Joe and a beer for me and told him his money was no good.

"Don't even think about it," I said, as he tried to argue.

"It was my idea, getting drinks. I should pay," he said to convince me.

"There was no arm twisting involved and besides, you have done enough. Although we might be leaving Vegas too soon, you know." I was feeling the tequila. "I didn't get to see you punch Fred."

"True," laughed Joe. "I was a model of self-restraint," he declared with mock pride, and we touched our glasses together.

"I have been thinking," I said, after a sip, "about what to do with ... things. I want Amir and Lulu to live in the house if they would like to stay there. If I leave the house to you, do you think that will work?"

"Mara," said Joe, the topic catching him off guard. I could tell he was uncomfortable with it. "You want to talk about this now?" Joe's expression had gone from relaxed to pensive. His palm held his chin, his brow furrowed. "No, ... wait, I'm sorry," he decided. "If you want to talk about it now, we will."

"Thanks," I said, emboldened by the drinks. "Hear me out about a few ideas and then we'll talk more later." Joe nodded, gesturing for me to continue. "Amir and Lulu's rent covers the mortgage payment and utilities. That leaves taxes, insurance, and maintenance. It would add expenses for you, but overall, it would be an investment. Then there's the equity. If you wanted, you could live there too. Just think about it." The practicality of the topic made it easy to keep the emotion out.

"If that's what you want to do, we will work it out. But you don't know if Amir and Lulu would even want to stay there," said Joe, not bothering to cap off the sentence with the words *after you're gone*, but I knew that's what he meant.

"True, but I think they will. If I'm mistaken, at least I've given them the option. I want Avo to stay there. Lulu and Amir will take care of him." I focused on the table as I mentioned Avo, and I couldn't look Joe in the eye. Sadness entered the conversation when I thought of my dog.

Joe reached for my hand. He didn't take it in his own but placed his hand over mine. "We all love Avo. He will be well cared for." He hesitated for a moment, making sure he had my attention. "Listen, I understand what you're doing. Do whatever you wish about the house, Avo, everything," Joe assured me. "We will each respect your wishes and work things out." I took a deep breath and when I exhaled, I met Joe's eyes and nodded.

"But, please," my brother pleaded, "don't try to keep things the same for us after you're gone, Mara. Nothing will be the same."

Chapter 28

The day, the emotion, and the drinks caught up with me and I nodded off before the return flight was in the air. Alcohol had that effect on me as of late. I preferred it to the pain meds. The taste was enjoyable, plus I didn't become nauseated, and the calories could not hurt. Dr. Edmunds would have her opinion about it but what difference would it make?

Joe and I were the last passengers to exit the plane. We made our way slowly through the terminal, taking our time for my benefit. Moving at a measured speed was the only choice I had anyway. Walking and being upright was good on my lower back and feeling the stretch in my muscles made me wish I had more energy. We stepped through the automatic door at the exit and the warm afternoon air hit my face. Lines of vehicles were making their way to the curb to retrieve arriving parties.

With perfect timing, Ed pulled up to the curb. He waved to us and got out of the Jeep. As he looked at me, concern filled his face, and he was quickly at my side. I leaned into Ed's frame and relished the physical support. His arms wrapped around me, and I returned the embrace taking in his scent.

Ed looked directly into my eyes. "Hey, are you okay?" he asked then looked at Joe.

"I'm okay, really," I answered, hoping to quell his worry. "Just tired."

"She napped on the plane," Joe told Ed. "We celebrated before we left Vegas. Mara handled the chat with Fred like a champion."

Ed was not eager to hear about the chat with Fred. He was concerned about my current state. "Let's get you in the car, Mara." Ed opened the front passenger side door and helped me in, then he turned to Joe. "Take the seat in the back behind the driver's seat, Joe.

Mara will be more comfortable in the front where she can recline." Joe agreed and went to the other side of the Jeep and climbed in.

"This is much better than on the plane," I told Ed as he helped re-position the seat. I was soon buckled in and ready to go. "Thank you," I said. I turned my head to look at Ed and smiled. He returned the smile and kissed me.

Ed took his place at the wheel and pulled out from the terminal. "Now tell me about Vegas and your visit with Fred."

Joe did most of the talking as we related the details. Ed nodded, glancing in my direction, as he absorbed the replay. He was more interested in how I was fairing than in what we had to say about Fred. I turned my head toward Ed and smiled at him again, savoring his attention. Ed was looking more attractive to me all the time and it wasn't the tequila.

"Have you eaten?" he asked me.

"We had celebratory nachos and drinks," I said. "The nachos were delicious, and the drinks took the place of pain meds." I rolled the back of my head against the car seat and glanced behind me in Joe's direction. "Joe and I had a chance to talk too. Thanks again for listening," I said to my brother as I turned back to face the front. "It was the best part of the day for me." Joe reached forward and gave my shoulder a squeeze.

I must have dozed briefly because I opened my eyes as we turned into my driveway. Ed parked next to Joe's car and before I managed any effort to move, he was at my side helping me out of the car and up to the door. Joe was already at the front door, giving Ed and I a moment of privacy. I hadn't planned on asking Ed to stay, but I didn't want him to leave. He had become such a comfort to me. "Could you stay for a little while? While I sleep?"

Surprise registered on Ed's face, then he smiled. "Sure. Will Lulu mind?" he asked. His question told me he was mindful that it was her home as well as mine.

"I'm sure she won't but we'll be polite and ask."

It was late afternoon. Lulu and Avo met us as we entered the house. "I wondered if you'd be home before I left for work," said Lulu, as I leaned over to pet Avo. His tail was waving back and forth, happy to see me. "How was the trip?"

"It was fine. I'm glad it's over." I straightened up, my bag still hanging from my shoulder. I reached for Lulu and gave her a hug. "Thanks for hanging out with Avo all day."

"No need to thank me. You know I love him," said Lulu.

"Sorry, everyone," I said, "but I need to lie down." I sounded exhausted even to myself.

"Avo and I just returned from a walk," said Lulu. "He'd probably like to join you."

Joe took a step in my direction. "If you don't need me for anything, I'm going to head out so you can sleep." He hugged me and quietly whispered in my ear, "We will talk soon."

"I'll be fine and thanks again, for everything," I told Joe as I returned the hug.

Joe turned to Ed. "Thanks for the ride," he said, and they bumped fists. Joe went out the front door adding that he would check in with me later that evening. I wondered if this was my new normal, having the people in my life check on me and not wanting me to be alone. I thought of Fred, ill and alone. In comparison, I was, by far, the fortunate one.

"I asked Ed to stay. Is that okay, Lulu?"

"Sure. I'm leaving for the casino soon," answered Lulu with a shrug. "It's a good idea as far as I'm concerned. Make yourself at home, Ed."

Ed helped me down the hall to my bedroom as Avo followed. I dropped my bag on the bureau and glanced around. I was glad the room was not a terrible mess since I was too exhausted to clean up if it had been. Stepping into the bathroom, I changed into a pair of shorts and a camisole and when I returned Ed was sitting on my bed. My bedroom isn't a small room, but it looked smaller with Ed in it and for some weird reason, that made me smile. It was all so natural, so unrehearsed. He had turned on the lamp on my bedside table, flipped on the ceiling fan to a low speed, and removed his sandals. Avo found his favorite place on the floor and stretched out.

"Thanks for staying. Sorry if I hijacked your afternoon, but I'm glad you're here," I said as I sat next to him.

Ed put his arm around my shoulder. "Is there anything I can get you?"

"A glass of water would be nice. You can grab something for yourself too. There's probably beer." I explained which cabinet held the glasses.

Ed rubbed my back for a moment. "Water will be fine. I'll be right back." He stood and left the room.

I looked at the bag I had placed on the bureau and remembered the Digoxin. I walked over, reached for my bag, and retrieved the mint tin holding Fred's heart medication. I placed the tin deep in a drawer in my bathroom vanity. I placed the bottle of Vicodin on the top of the vanity under the mirror.

The Fentanyl and the Zofran were both on the bedside table. I had picked up the Fentanyl bottle and was thinking about taking one of the pills. I heard Ed and Lulu speaking in hushed voices and a moment later, Ed walked into the room carrying two glasses filled with iced water. He placed one on the bedside table and closed the bedroom door.

"Do you like your water nearby or in the bathroom?" he asked.

"Here is fine. Thank you."

"You're welcome." Ed took a long drink from the glass in his hand then said, "I'll put mine in the bathroom out of your way."

I stretched out on my bed, pillows behind me, the bottle of Fentanyl still in my hand. I closed my eyes and took a deep breath. It felt good to stretch out. Ed walked to the other side of the bed and assumed a similar position next to me with pillows behind his shoulders. He raised his arms over his head, fingers linked behind his neck. He had one leg bent, knee toward the ceiling, his other leg stretched out.

"Lulu told me she would be leaving in an hour. I told her I'd be here with you for most of the evening."

"Sounds wonderful. Are you comfortable?" I asked. I patted his leg.

"Very," he assured me. "Are you?"

I nodded and smiled. "I'm glad you're here with me. I know I already said that. Sorry, I guess I'm tired."

Ed laughed. "You can tell me as many times as you want." He leaned over and kissed my cheek. "Do you need to take your meds?"

"I don't really need it," I explained. "My back isn't bothering me too badly. Besides, if I take one now, I'll need another dose in the middle of the night. If I wait and take them before I go to bed, I'll be back on schedule." I yawned.

"Makes sense. I could use a nap too," Ed said. We heard Avo snoring softly. "We should follow Avo's lead." I rolled over with my back to Ed, placed the bottle of pain meds on the table and turned off the lamp. Ed pulled the blanket over me, tucking me into the warmth as if I were a small child. He moved nearer and with his arms around me, I was enveloped by his tenderness. His head was tucked in behind mine and I heard him sigh. I could feel the closeness of his body next to me from my head to my toe.

"This is lovely," I said. Ed may have responded but I didn't hear it. I had drifted into a sweet sleep.

I napped for several hours. When I awoke later that evening, Ed had taken Avo out into the back yard where he was tossing a ball for the dog to chase. We fed Avo, had our dinner delivered, and talked about a variety of things—Joe and the day we had spent together, our visit with Fred, my decision to cut back on shifts at work. Ed listened, asked questions, and made comments but he offered no opinions or judgements, and I loved him for it.

Amir came home and we talked with him but not for long. His evening at work had been busy as weekends usually are. Amir was happy to finish my dinner. I had eaten as much as I could but there was food left over. I took a long, hot shower, finally took my meds, and went back to sleep with Ed beside me.

Chapter 29

Sunday began with coffee on the back patio. Avo enjoyed having Ed around and the extra attention was fun for the big, rambunctious dog. Ed suggested ideas for an early dinner together.

"You and Avo could come to my place again, that is, if you feel up to it," he offered. "If you want to stay home, if you want to rest, I get it. Selfishly, I want you to myself for the evening."

Smiling at his honesty, I leaned in with a kiss. "Privacy does have a certain appeal. I'm doing well this morning but then I slept well last night. Thanks to you."

"I slept well too," said Ed as he massaged the back of my neck, "and I tried not to disturb you. You hardly moved and were so quiet," laughed Ed. "The only thing I noticed was Avo snoring." By the time Ed left, we had decided to come up with a dinner plan later in the day and I promised to get a nap.

Mid-morning was filled with light housekeeping chores. Amir and Lulu were adamant that I was not to take on too many tasks in the communal areas of the house, so I concentrated on picking up my bedroom. I was setting clothes aside to launder when I heard my phone alert me to an incoming call. I expected it was either Ed or Joe, but it was Cameron Rowen's name that appeared on the screen.

"Hello, Cameron," I answered.

"Mara, I'm glad I caught you. Do you have a minute?"

"Of course," I said as I sat on the bed.

"I saw a news report that Paul Davisson was found dead." Cameron's voice was filled with alarm. "Here in Phoenix. Have you heard?"

"I did hear about his death," I answered, still surprised by the call. I held back, choosing to be cautious and not provide too much information. It was my conversation with Cameron, learning about Evan's illness and death, which put me on to Davisson in the first place. "I read sketchy details," I lied. "I was surprised to hear that he died here in Phoenix. I didn't know he lived here."

I tried to review our prior conversation, but I was caught off guard. Would Cameron make a connection between talking with me and Davisson's death? I told myself I was over-reacting. I had known all along that a connection was a possibility, that I might be linked to Davisson, but it was a risk I had factored in. The element of risk had not been enough to sway my actions.

"Apparently, he was here on business," said Cameron. "He was found in a hotel room. What a strange way to die, don't you think?"

"It is strange, Cameron. Very odd," I said. "To be honest, I don't feel much in the way of sympathy. I guess that sounds awful."

"No, it doesn't sound awful. It sounds honest. I won't grieve for that man," said Cameron, his voice colored by ire. "I'm still mourning my father, thanks to Davisson."

I couldn't respond. A man was dead, I had caused his death, and now Cameron and I were expressing our lack of sadness. It was as if Cameron were thanking me, and I kept quiet for fear that I would share that he was welcome.

"At any rate, I wanted to be sure you'd heard about his death," he added. "It couldn't have happened to a more deserving fellow if you ask me. I'd be interested to know if Richard Carling has heard about Davisson."

I changed the subject. I couldn't think about Davisson's death without blurting out more than was wise and I didn't want to think about Carling, the man who was as much to blame as Davisson for the tragedies in our lives. "I'm glad you called," I said. "How are you doing, Cameron? How is your mom?"

"We're okay. Taking each day as it comes. It does become easier, the grieving, as time passes."

I told Cameron I was glad to hear it. I asked that he give his mother my best.

***

It was hard for me to rest that afternoon. Lying on my bed, my thoughts kept replaying the call from Cameron and his reaction to what he had learned of Davisson's death. Cameron had mentioned Richard Carling, and although I drove thoughts of the lab inspector from my mind earlier, I couldn't get him out of my head now.

Reaching for my phone, I pulled up the ASC website and found the listing once again. Carling was thorough enough to note address and phone number for his business. The business address was in an industrial complex on River Road, an area of Tucson that bustled with a variety of businesses and heavy traffic. Henry had encouraged me to contact my former employer, to inform them of my fate. Henry felt that it would give me peace to speak my mind about what I was going through. In a very absolute way, I had contacted Presson-Hagee — by orchestrating the death of Paul Davisson. My actions were not at all what Henry had in mind, but it had given me a feeling of vindication.

Did I want to confront Carling? What would I say, if I had the chance? What did I want him to know? That I was dying, in part due to his greed? That Davisson had already paid the ultimate price for his own selfishness? This was something I would have to think about. Tucson was only a two-hour drive from where I lived in Phoenix. A conversation with Carling wasn't outside the realm of possibilities, however, I would have to initiate it. He wasn't likely to show up at the bar as Davisson had done and even if he did, what could I do? Spike another bottle of whiskey? Not likely either. I could drive to Tucson and confront Carling at his office but facing the man on his turf was a frightening idea. I would have to prepare myself by taking the utmost precaution. Maybe I would talk with Henry and hear his thoughts.

Chapter 30

The next few days were as pleasant as they could have been under the circumstances. I spent as much time as possible with Ed. I worked on Tuesday evening and then a short shift behind the bar on Thursday. I could not deny that I was more rested, and my back pain was less severe on my days off. During my shifts behind the bar, I found myself not wanting to be there anymore. I wanted to spend my time with Ed, with Avo, and at home with my roommates. Ironically, I had more of a life now than I had had for years and I was sad that it would soon end.

When I left the resort on Thursday evening, I left a note for Tomas to please cover my shift on Saturday. I also told Tomas that I had decided to give it two more weeks and then be done with the job. I would see Henry the following day and would talk with him about it. I knew what Henry would say: work if you want, quit if you want. It was up to me. There were things I could control and things I could not.

I arrived home a little after nine p.m. I had just let Avo in from the back patio and had sprawled on the couch when Joe called. I had talked with my brother briefly a couple of times since our trip to Vegas, but between our work schedules, this was the first I heard from him in days.

"Hey," I said. "What's up?"

"Mara, you're not going to believe it … Fred died!" Joe got the words out, but he was agitated, his words tumbling together

"What? We just saw him! How is that possible?" I sat upright, trying to catch my breath.

"I received a call from the police in Vegas. They called, maybe two hours ago. I've been on the phone ever since. This was the first chance I've had to call you."

"Was there an accident? What the hell happened, Joe?"

"According to his doctor he was not doing well, Mara. His health was failing." My mouth hung open with disbelief. I could not believe what I was hearing. Fred had been taking a low dose pain reliever instead of his prescribed medication because it was hidden in a tin in my bathroom vanity.

"He had seen his doctor recently. Fred's doctor was concerned about his memory, that he was confused. He wanted to put Fred in the hospital for observation and to regulate his meds under supervision."

"Why didn't he?" I managed to ask.

"Too late. Fred's neighbor found him this morning. She'd gone over to his house and saw him through the window. He was lying in the entry. The neighbor called 911 but there was nothing they could do. He was gone."

"I don't know what to say, Joe. I'm shocked."

"I know. Weird, right? Fred had me listed as next of kin with his medical provider. I talked with his doctor, Mara. Fred had been treated for a common condition for years. He's attributing Fred's death to that condition."

"Maybe we shouldn't have gone to Vegas. Maybe it was a mistake." The thought was out of my mouth before I could stop myself from saying it.

"It wasn't a mistake. Our visit had nothing to do with his passing. We told him how we felt. We both deserved the chance to do that, Mara. To be honest, I'm glad we went ahead with it before it was too late. Listen, the truth is that if Fred had been a kinder person, if we had had any desire to stay in touch with him, we might have known about his health concerns."

"You're right," I said. But I was aware of his concerns. I knew he was taking the medication and I had a good idea why, and yet I had removed the medication from his home.

"Don't blame yourself, Mara. I know the timing bothers you, but Fred needed to hear us out. You needed to say it, so did I. If he had been a decent person years ago, we would never have wanted to speak to him that way."

"I know. You're right," I said with a sigh. There was nothing else I could say to Joe at that moment.

"I'll return to Vegas to handle financial arrangements and close Fred's house. I will deal with what can't wait and handle the rest later. I don't want you to concern yourself with any of it, but you needed to know."

"Okay," I answered. "Sorry you have to deal with this, Joe."

"Mara, one last thing I've decided. I told the doctor I would arrange for cremation as soon as Fred's remains are released. There will be no service."

I couldn't talk anymore. At the mention of remains and cremation, I could barely breathe.

"I have to go, Joe" I murmured.

I sat in still silence, my hands over my mouth then I walked to the kitchen and got a beer from the refrigerator. I had already taken my pain meds and didn't like to mix with alcohol but right now, I didn't care.

Had I killed Fred? Maybe not in the truest sense, but I had certainly contributed to his death. My actions were less direct than with Davisson but still had impact on the outcome. If I hadn't intended harm or suffering, why did I take the meds from Fred's bathroom? The answer was simple: I hated Fred. He had been a poor excuse for an uncle, a guardian, and a human being. The man had made his own bed, as they say. His only living relatives wouldn't even have a service to mourn the loss. We felt no loss to mourn because Fred had treated us so poorly. Joe told me not to blame myself and he was right; it was bad timing. Besides, the timing had been bad only for Joe and me. I was convinced that Fred deserved what he got.

Chapter 31

On Friday afternoon, shortly before one o'clock, I arrived at Henry's for my weekly session.

"How was your week?" my therapist asked with interest, his manner at ease. Henry's expression held a slight smile, and he maintained eye contact as he took his seat across from me in his usual place.

"My week was okay, eventful in that I've made a few decisions. But eventful for another reason too. My uncle, mine, and Joe's, has died."

Henry may have been stunned but he tried to keep the surprise out of his reaction. Surprised or not, the pad of paper and the hand that held it hovered in the air above his lap for a moment. "Your uncle that we discussed last week. He'd been your guardian. You planned to see him last weekend." Henry spoke in statements; there were no questions, rhetorical or otherwise.

"Yes, and Joe and I did see him. That circumstance was an event on its own."

"What happened with your uncle? When did he die?"

"We saw him on Saturday. He looked much older but then I had not seen Fred in years. He didn't seem to be at death's door by any means—less so than I, I suppose."

I looked up at Henry who had been jotting notes as had become his practice while we talked. Henry wasn't impacted by the phrase about death's door, but in my ear, it stung. "That sounded ominous—*death's door*," I repeated.

"It is a common phrase. They sneak out before we know it." Henry paused for a few seconds. "Do you want to continue?" asked Henry. I nodded. "You talked with your uncle on Saturday with a definite agenda in mind and he died on Thursday. That's amazing. I'm sorry the man died, truly I am, but I can't be sorry that you had a chance to confront him. The timing is bizarre." There it was again, the timing issue. Timing was everything to me now that time was a limited commodity.

I nodded in response. "That's exactly what Joe said. That we were lucky to have had the chance, that we deserved it."

"Is there anything else you want to discuss about your uncle? I know you weren't close, that you had resented his treatment of you and your brother, but are you feeling any sense of loss?"

"Fred had no clue what we were talking about, wouldn't acknowledge our grievance but I had expected that from him." I paused to draw a deep breath and knew Henry heard my exhale. "I guess the timing was unfortunate." Timing again.

"What about loss?" asked Henry repeating his question that I had not answered.

"No," I said honestly, shaking my head. "I feel no loss. If he had died before last Saturday, I would feel loss about the missed opportunity to confront him because he would have robbed me of that too. I told him he had been an awful husband to my Aunt Rina too. I'd never stood up for her either. Now I have."

Henry looked at me, absorbing my words, thinking about their meaning or so I guessed. Finally, he nodded, said he was glad I had dealt with the situation and achieved closure regarding that part of my life.

"Let's move on, shall we? You mentioned making other decisions. Tell me about them."

Henry and I discussed my decision to quit working. My energy and strength were fading, I told him. I was enjoying my time in ways I had not for so long and I wanted more happiness. Ed was a part of that, I said. I described the intimacy we shared that wasn't based in the sensual but that we were compatible in that regard, as well. Then I explained the choices I had made about my home, my piano and

Avo. Before I could help myself, I was in tears over leaving my sweet dog.

Henry moved the tissue box to within reach. "I know it is hard. Remind yourself that the people you trust in your life love Avo and will take the best care of him."

I mopped my face with a tissue, nodding as I tried to relax. "I haven't figured out the piano. I don't know anyone who plays. I want to ask Ed's advice. He's very talented. He works as a graphic artist and he's musical. He might know a place, a school maybe."

"Ed is musical? Does he play an instrument?" asked Henry, sincerely intrigued that we had music in common.

"He sings. He trained in voice," I answered, remembering Ed's lovely speaking voice. I hadn't heard him sing.

Henry smiled. "How nice for you to have that connection, that mutual interest."

I nodded in agreement, but what I was thinking was whether I would venture to play for Ed and if I would hear him sing for me. Should we express the connection, the mutual interest in that intimate way or would doing so be too painful?

Funny that I had no desire to address the question with Henry. The only person I wanted to talk with about sharing our musical inclinations was Ed.

"Before you go," said Henry, his brow furrowed, "I heard about a guest found dead at the resort where you work. What a sad story."

I wasn't prepared for the question or for the sudden shift in the conversation. By the time I realized I was staring at Henry with a mortified look on my face, I had managed to nod my head—a repeat of my limited response about mine and Ed's shared love of music. The similar reactions to different subjects — one of pleasure and happiness and one of ugliness and secret revenge—was discordant and made my brain twitch. I forced an inhale because the surprise had made me hold my breath.

"Yes, sad," I answered, offering a verbal response.

"Did you know of this man?" asked Henry. "Had you interacted with him?" Henry's brow remained furrowed, and I was touched by his empathy, his compassion. His concern was for me and the possible impact this death might have on my situation. I nearly was embarrassed.

I looked at my hands and saw that they were clinched into fists. I opened my hands to stretch my fingers and rubbed my palms together. When I looked up, I saw that Henry was watching the motion of my hands and nervous energy compelled me to continue speaking.

"His name was Paul Davisson. He had been my supervisor years ago when I worked at P-H."

"You're kidding, right?" Henry was obviously stunned by the revelation.

"I'm not kidding. There had been some weird, ... um ... there were issues with him at the resort, but the death surprised everyone." This was true except for the surprise part—at least for me. "The hospitality industry often deals with strange situations," I added. "People do odd things away from home and family, whether they intend to or not. I don't mean to be insensitive, and this is a rare occurrence, but it has happened before."

Henry and I looked at each other. For a moment, I half expected him to blurt out the words, *you killed him didn't you, Mara?* Instead, he shook his head and said, "I guess that's true, but I find it so tragic. Unless you work in a hospital or in emergency services, we don't expect to have people die at our place of business or during our workday. And this was someone you knew many years ago."

When I had no response, Henry, concerned with the direction he had taken, apologized. "I'm sorry," he said. "That was an obvious statement and I suppose you'd rather not be reminded of it. The coincidence and the timing were unfortunate. That was really my point."

I uttered an expression of agreement, told Henry that I'd see him next Friday, and got the hell out of his office. I did not want to discuss Paul Davisson's death another minute. At a point in my limited future, the situation may require further explanation, but for now, the less I talked of it, the better. Perhaps the need to explain would outlive me.

The drive home gave me time to process my session with Henry. There had been a range of emotions as we talked about Fred's passing, and the sad—Henry's word, not mine—death of Paul Davisson. We talked of the support of my friends and Joe and the closeness that had developed with Ed. Then I thought of the sadness that overcame me talking with Henry about leaving Avo. In contrast, I had not the smallest sense of loss, remorse, or regret about Fred's death. As with Davisson, all I felt was relief.

Arriving at home, I was tired. My back ached from sitting. I needed to eat something and take my meds. After I let Avo outside, I found a snack in the kitchen and took it to my bedroom. I ate the few bites and took pain pills then reclined on the bed with Avo. Stretching out relieved some of the pain in my back and the pills would take care of the rest as I drifted off.

I ran my hand over Avo's back, stroking the soft fur and my thoughts fell to Richard Carling, the lab inspector now living in Tucson. I had intended to talk with Henry about him, his deceit, and his role in my illness. It was Henry who had suggested clearing the decks of unfinished business so I was safe to assume he would encourage a conversation with Carling. Our hour-long session had been taken up by more important topics and Carling had slipped my mind. I was going to have to start writing things down—things to discuss, decisions to make, plans to complete. If I continued to let topics slip, the day would come when I would not have the chance to re-visit them. I'd give more thought to Carling and perhaps discuss it with Henry at our next session.

Chapter 32

I woke from my nap hours later to a forwarded email from Cameron. In the subject line, he had written the words, *these people have no shame.* The email had been sent to his father's account. The attachment was a notice from a professional journal about the sudden death of Paul Davisson. The notice was an obituary of sorts that began by including the sanitized particulars of how he died, his professional accomplishments, and how admired he was within the industry. As I read the notice, its intent was to make the reader know that the departed's death was a grievous loss. In this case, however, the extent to which this intention was taken was almost comical until I read the following:

"Mr. Davisson was a pillar of integrity in an industry sometimes plagued by less-than-scrupulous practices and the temptation in the past few years to risk the use of unqualified staff. Davisson resisted the call to ignore basic requirements of education and training and he refused to gamble with the health and safety of his employees. His ability to always place safety and precision above profit is why he will be sorely missed."

The obituary had been written by none other than Richard Carling.

I was with Cameron. They had no shame. With what Carling knew of Davisson there was no way he could claim the man to have been honorable. When you add in that the two of them had profited from their mutual lack of honor, it was an affront to have lauded Davisson as a paragon of integrity. The pair of them had embodied unscrupulous practices and gambled with the lives of their employees.

Re-reading the obit, I grew more outraged by Carling's nerve. I was cheated out of my health and my career in the field to which I had committed myself. Evan, Cameron's dad was cheated in the same way and when he called them on their bullshit practices, they had threatened to ruin him. Evan had already paid with his life, and I was headed down the same agonizing path.

Carling and Davisson used the system to make themselves wealthy men by accepting bribes, falsifying records, and throwing suspicion away from each other. With Davisson gone, Carling was hedging his bets. He was calling on the dead man's counterfeit reputation to guarantee his continued profit based on lies and deceit. He wasn't going to let Davisson's death put an end to a good thing and it pissed me off.

I stretched out on the bed, tried to think through the anger I felt for Richard Carling. He was as responsible for my illness, for Evan's illness and death, as Paul Davisson. He didn't deserve to live any more than Davisson did. For me to deal with Carling—whether I caused him embarrassment, ruin, or even death—was a different concept and needed a more complicated plan. Davisson had come to me, in a way, into my midst. When he stood at my bar, fate had enabled me with a mission, a plan, and means for revenge. Carling wasn't going to simply show up within my field of vision and purpose as Davisson had done. I had no way to place him in my crosshairs. I would have to go to him and face him.

I'd been encouraged to confront Carling. Whether I left the confrontation at that level or took it further was up to me. Could I kill him? Could I kill Carling as I had chosen to do to Paul Davisson? It was easy to spike that whiskey. I had had a chance to watch Davisson, knew his habits, his choice of drink. I had an in with Vinnie to obtain the drugs that I combined with the alcohol, and I had days to prepare. Yes, I told myself, Carling was as deserving of my vengeance but the plan, the formula, the execution, literal as that sounded, was a different consideration altogether.

Davisson never knew I caused his death. He didn't recognize me, never spoke to me as someone who he had known years ago. That fact was part of the reason his death had been relatively easy to manage. He never suspected me or that I was aware of his treachery. While this was true, I felt cheated. I hadn't had a chance to look him in the eye and see the realization on his face. I took a deep breath and knew I wanted things to be different with Carling. He would not only see me coming but would be compelled to acknowledge me and my impending death from cancer—a death that could have been avoided. Given the chance, I would give Carling a choice. He would have that courtesy, one that I had not allowed Davisson, a choice that neither Evan nor I had been given.

I sent a quick one-word reply to Cameron: *unbelievable* was the word I chose. I searched the registry of chemists and found Carling's contact information. I hit the phone link on the website and called his office in Tucson.

The call was answered after two rings.

"Laboratory Solutions," said a male voice at the other end of the line.

"Hello. My name is Mara and I'm with Valley Chemical in Phoenix. I was hoping to reach Richard Carling. Is he available?"

"I'm sorry. He's out of the office until Tuesday. This is Marcus. How can I help you?"

I explained that I had been acquainted with Carling years prior, thus the reason for seeking his services. Then I concocted a story that I managed a lab in need of an inspection. Time was short as we had contracts to honor and feared a shutdown. Before I knew it, I had fabricated my way into a meeting with Carling. After expressing difficulty with scheduling an earlier meeting, Marcus said that Mr. Carling was available to meet with me the following Tuesday at the end of the day.

Carling was used to doing things his way. He conducted business by bullying and swindling his way around other's defenses. That impression had been supported by how he had treated Evan. If I were to confront the man, I needed to ensure that I would have the upper hand. What better way to have the upper hand than to confront Carling with what I knew?

I started by organizing my thoughts on paper. Within minutes, I had a timeline established and an outline of the main points beginning with my tenure at Presson-Hagee and the closing of the lab to the news I'd received from Cameron about his dad's death from cancer. Then there was the sad fact that I was dying, and that Carling and Davisson were to blame. I had to decide whether to include my diagnosis at the beginning of the narrative or end with it. Slowly, I was formulating a plan of action.

Tuesday's meeting with Carling was forming in my imagination and I decided a meeting with Carling in his office at the end of the workday would do nicely.

***

There were other important business matters I needed to consider. I would feel better about meeting with Carling knowing I had addressed them. I had prepared a list of attorneys who specialized in estate law. I perused the short list days earlier when I knew that writing a Last Will and Testament was something I needed to do. It was after business hours, but on Monday I would schedule an appointment. Then I emailed the Director of Human Resources at Anasazi Resort. This had been Henry's idea. Make sure, he said, that you know where you stand on benefits.

I heard Lulu down the hallway and called out to her. She approached my bedroom door and stopped in the doorway.

"Hey," she said. It was obvious she had been sleeping. "How are you doing?"

"I wasn't sure you were home." I moved over, pulling Avo along with me, and motioned for Lulu to join us. She slumped into the room and sat at the foot of the bed, then sprawled across it. "Are you working tonight?" I asked.

"I'm not," she answered with a yawn. "But I have a long shift tomorrow. I'm so glad to be home. It has been a long, few days. I need a break."

"What's your schedule next week?"

"I work tomorrow and Sunday. Then I'm off until Wednesday evening," she answered, her curiosity piqued. "Did you have something in mind?"

"How about taking a day trip to Tucson with me on Tuesday? I have a meeting there in the afternoon. If I'm too tired, you can drive home. I'll buy dinner."

"I can do that," said Lulu, as she petted Avo. "No problem. I'll drive both ways then you can nap on the way."

"I really appreciate this, Lu. We don't need to leave early. My appointment is late afternoon."

"What's up, Mara? What's this about?" Lulu's face turned red. "I'm sorry. I didn't mean to pry."

"It's fine, Lu. I don't mind telling you." I sighed, thinking how to explain my intentions without alarming Lulu. "Henry has encouraged me to put old business to rest, you know, clear the decks. There's a former business acquaintance in Tucson that I want to speak with. There are things I want to get off my chest. Nothing too important. Anyway, I can meet with him Tuesday. I'll feel better when it is over."

After she considered what I was asking of her, Lulu had a question for me. "Will you want me to drop you off at the appointment and pick you up? Or do you want me to go with you?"

Lulu could not be present at the meeting with Carling. I would protect her from knowing anything. "Honestly, it's something I need to do on my own. I shouldn't be more than an hour."

"Whatever you need to do. I'm glad you asked me. I don't mean to tell you what to do, Mara, but you should not take road trips alone, even a short, day trip to Tucson."

I nodded. Lulu was right. I had arrived at a point in my condition where I needed to listen to people who cared about me. I appreciated the doctors and therapists who were caring for me and I trusted them, but they are paid for their professional opinions. My friends were involved out of love.

Chapter 33

Joe had taken Friday off and was in Las Vegas organizing Fred's affairs. There would be more to manage later but for now Joe didn't want to deal with any more than was necessary. He left a message that he was staying in Vegas for the night. He planned to return to Phoenix on Saturday afternoon.

Amir and Lulu had known Joe for years and they got on well together, but he didn't spend much time with us. Joe had been around more lately because of my diagnosis. My friends knew how supportive he had been, and the circumstances had brought us closer out of necessity. He was proving to be there when I needed him, as the cliché goes. Was it my fault he'd been excluded, kept on the outside of the closeness I shared with my friends? Had I kept Joe at arm's length from my friends because of my own hang ups? Again, I started to blame myself. I let the question go because I couldn't change the past. All I could do was be glad of the present.

On Friday evening, the four of us enjoyed dinner together. Ed was accustomed to enjoying weekend evenings as he saw fit, but for Amir, Lulu, and I, it was a rare event. It was cool enough by late evening to dine outside. Avo entertained us with his canine antics of fetch, refuse to fetch, and then pestering us to throw the ball so he could fetch again.

Ed's affection toward me that evening was so natural in front of my friends. I basked in the warmth of his gestures as he reached for my hand, smiled at me, placed an arm around my shoulder. There was a lull in the laughter and we each surveyed the table, full of dishes and glassware. When Ed rose from his chair and started to collect items, Lulu stopped him.

"No, no. I will do that, Ed. You've helped enough," she said as she took the plates from him.

"Thanks, Lu," I told her. "I'm going inside. Do you mind if Avo stays out here with you? He's having fun."

"Of course not. Amir can play while I clean up." She looked to Amir who was on the ground wrestling with Avo. "Okay with you, Amir?" Amir nodded, busy laughing at Avo trying to get his ball from Amir's grip.

Ed turned to me with a smile and said, "There is something I'd like you to do, Mara."

"What's that?" I asked him, returning the smile.

"Would you play for us?" asked Ed.

I considered the out-of-the-blue request, deciding what the hell, why not? "I will if you sing," I answered. "Let's find a tune we both know."

"That sounds marvelous!" exclaimed Amir, having overheard us.

Lulu clapped her hands with enthusiasm. "Excellent! Please leave the door open so we can hear."

Ed helped me up and into the house and I took my place at the piano while Ed stood nearby. I thought of a song and if Ed knew this one, it would confirm for me how special a person he was. Finding the keys, I went through a couple of warm-up trills then began to play *Stardust*, that mellow, haunting melody written by Hoagy Carmichael in 1927. Nat King Cole's version made the song famous in the 1950's.

Within seconds, Ed sat next to me. He hummed the complicated melody and cleared his throat. We exchanged a glance, nodding our approval. I began again and Ed started to sing:

And now the purple dusk of Twilight times/steals across the meadows of my heart

The old song had been my grandmother's favorite. She often played the tune at this same piano. Ed's voice was perfect for the melody. Grandma would have loved hearing him sing and as I listened to Ed, I imagined her beaming with approval. Even though it was about a memory of a love that was no more, I didn't regret the choice. I was touched Ed knew the song, but I was not surprised. He had a beautiful voice, and I was fortunate to accompany him while he sang it.

When we finished the performance, Ed kissed me, and we shared a laugh as applause floated in from the backyard. Amir and Lulu begged for another number.

"How about something more recent," I said. I played the first few notes of the Beatles, *You Never Give Me Your Money*. Ed recognized it instantly and began to sing. One of my favorites on piano by the Fab Four, I enjoyed it even more with Ed on vocals. The song was written in a higher register than the Carmichael, so it really displayed Ed's talent and he sounded superb:

You never give me your money/You only give me your funny paper.

When our eyes met as Ed sang the line, "*Oh, that magic feeling*," I became so distracted that I nearly blew the melody. As we finished the song, Ed nuzzled my ear and whispered, "I'm glad you didn't choose *Golden Slumbers*. The song reminds me of my mom. I don't know if I could have sung it without getting emotional." *Golden Slumbers* is a beautiful piece, but McCartney filled it with longing for days past. I couldn't have made it through the song either.

"One sweet dream came true today," I whispered back, repeating a line of the lyrics. Ed responded with an embrace.

"Let's do one more, okay?" I begged.

"One more," Ed agreed, with his index finger extended.

"Let's try a show tune." My hands returned to the piano keys and played the first few notes of *Send in The Clowns*, from Sondheim's *A Little Night Music*. Ed picked up on the beautiful song of regret. He knew every word.

Isn't it rich? /Are we a pair? /Me here at last on the ground/You in mid-air.

Ed sang the song beautifully, each note with perfection. Lulu and Amir applauded with gusto.

"I am impressed. How do you know it so well?" I asked, knowing there had to be a story.

"Would you believe I was in a production of the musical in college?"

"Of course, I believe it," I laughed and kissed his cheek. "Tell me about it."

"I played Fredrik, the male lead. *Send in the Clowns* is sung by the female lead, Desiree, but the two characters sing it together in the reprise."

When we finished, I was exhausted. As I stood up, the dull ache in my back turned into severe pain and I felt as if the floor came up to meet me. Ed caught me and I sat back down.

"I'm okay, really," I apologized, knowing I had tears in my eyes, and took a moment to pull myself together. "I enjoyed tonight. I want you to know that." I looked at Ed as he rubbed my back. "I guess I overdid it, but I'm joyful too." I wiped my eyes with a napkin that appeared out of nowhere and I was reminded of Henry moving the tissue box closer. It meant so much to enjoy myself—to feel alive and happy. Dinner, laughing together, having fun with Avo—finally hearing Ed sing for me.

I felt weak. I noticed a change in the back pain over the past few days. It had intensified and was no longer confined to my lower back but was spreading to my legs and hips. The Fentanyl provided relief if I stayed on schedule with the doses.

Ed helped me up and we walked down the hallway to my bedroom. Although the evening passed quickly, I had sat much too long. I knew better, of course, but was enjoying myself. Lying down took the edge off the pain although not as much as I had hoped. I took my meds and Ed helped me find a comfortable position. I inhaled and exhaled deep breaths and felt Ed's hands stroke my hair away from my face. Soon I was asleep.

***

The weekend drifted by. I made pots of coffee during the day and switched to beer in the afternoon. I forced myself to eat even though I wasn't interested in food. I managed a few bites and napped intermittently with Avo or Ed at my side.

Joe did not return from Las Vegas until Sunday. He came by the house and shared a few details but wasn't interested in talking about Fred any more than I wanted to waste precious time hearing about him. Waking from a nap on Sunday afternoon, I heard hushed tones in the living room. Amir and Joe were speaking in quiet voices. I couldn't make out what was said, but it was clear they were talking about me. I wasn't offended. I was fine with it.

Ed spent the weekend with me. He didn't hover but I knew he was concerned. We spent much of our time in the backyard with Avo. Ed and I found no shortage of things to discuss, and cancer and death were not topics we shared. I craved his being there and I told him as much. I wanted him to know how endearing it was to drift off to sleep with him next to me and wake up with him by my side.

I rested during the weekend and was feeling the better for it by Sunday evening. I insisted that Ed spend Sunday night in his own place, knowing he worked on Monday morning. He agreed, but only if I was very sure. He knew I worked on Monday and that I had an appointment in Tucson on Tuesday. Ed didn't ask who I was meeting or what it was about, but he was relieved that Lulu planned to accompany me.

Chapter 34

Monday morning, I spoke with the assistant of an estate attorney. She was a young woman who repeated her name for me several times, but I still forgot it. The woman asked me questions and set an appointment for me the following week. The young assistant would send a preparation questionnaire about my assets and wishes. She made it clear that the questionnaire must be completed and brought to my meeting. I explained that I hoped to complete the process as soon as possible, but I did not disclose the reason for my haste.

It took me a couple of hours that afternoon to finish the notes I had amassed about Presson-Hagee, the lab closure, and the information from Cameron about Davisson and Carling. I included the details I knew of Evan's illness and death and of my own situation. I had not prepared a chronological report of this sort in years. The finished document was five pages in length. I printed two copies and placed each copy in a separate manila envelope.

I was scheduled to work Monday and Wednesday because of the trip to Tucson. I tried to give Tomas two full weeks, but I didn't have the energy—and I wanted to be done with it. Before my shift on Monday evening, I met with Renee in Human Resources. She had spoken with Tomas and knew that I was ending my employment but did not know the reason. Renee was a nice person and knew her job well. On the rare occasion I had met with her throughout my employment with Anasazi, I was impressed with her attitude in fulfilling her job responsibilities. Renee knew I was close to Amir and Lulu and for all these reasons, I was comfortable telling her that I was dying of cancer.

"I am so sorry to hear this, Mara," I was touched by her sincerity.

"Thank you," I answered.

"I don't want to presume, but you seem to be dealing with things. I admire your strength."

"Dealing with it becomes easier." I sighed and tried to find something to do with my hands. "I've been working with a therapist. He told me that my initial reaction would not last and that I would move on to other responses. At first, I couldn't conceive of what he was telling me, but he was right. I get it now. Like everything else, it took time to get used to it, to talking about it and living with it."

Renee nodded. "I'm sure that's true. I won't say I understand what you are going through. No one does unless they have been in your shoes."

There were more details to go over than I could have imagined, but Renee had thought of everything. We agreed that my last shift would be on Wednesday. The resort would continue to cover benefits through the end of the month, and I would have the option to cover the premiums myself after that time with COBRA. Renee and I didn't talk about prognosis, but I doubted it would be necessary for me to cover premiums for very much longer, if at all.

The resort had a life insurance option that I had forgotten. Years ago, when I first worked for the company in college, I had set up the policy and named Joe as the beneficiary. This was a pleasant surprise, as was a small profit-sharing benefit offered to employees after five consecutive years with the company. As I gathered details, I thought of how they would all find their place on the questionnaire for the estate attorney. I took a deep breath and told myself I was certainly getting my ducks into a tight row. I felt proud of myself and to be honest, I felt quite relieved.

I worked an uneventful shift behind the bar and was off work once everyone had a break. Mondays were usually low-key, the dinner crowd lighter, mostly guests staying in the hotel. Tomas stayed longer than usual into the evening. He might have been worried about me, but he didn't get in my way as I prepared orders. It crossed my mind several times that evening as I served guests at the bar that it had not been so awfully long since Paul Davisson stood there and ordered a JW Red. How differently things might have turned out if Davisson had recognized me or if I had not been working that night. If I was giving myself a chance to regret my actions, it was for naught. I did not regret his death or my part in it.

Chapter 35

At one-thirty on Tuesday afternoon, Lulu and I climbed into my Prius and headed south on the 10. It was a beautiful afternoon—warm, bright, and clear with a slight breeze—and we should reach Tucson by three thirty depending on the flow of afternoon traffic. I slept well the night before and I felt reasonably okay which meant that I was alert and the pain in my back and legs was minimal—at least for now. Lulu wanted to drive which was fine with me.

I wasn't concerned about talking with Carling. I felt the same before I talked with Fred—there were things I wanted to say, things I deserved to say, and I was fortunate to have the chance to say them. While this was true, I would be glad to have the meeting behind me. When I confronted Fred, it had been about my past and my unexpectedly shortened future. With Carling, his own future would come into play. I brought a copy of the report I had prepared, leaving the other at home. I was ready.

My thoughts drifted between topics on the drive south. It was easy to talk casually with Lulu because I felt ready and relaxed for my meeting. The topic of our conversation soon came to rest on Ed. "He's a great guy, Mara, but you know that," said Lulu. "He obviously makes you happy. I'm glad for you."

"We have gelled together well," I answered with a smile. I looked out the window at the desert landscape of the Santa Cruz flats with Picacho Peak in the distance and realized we were halfway to Tucson. "He's very kind and he makes me laugh. I feel lucky every day to have met him."

"That voice!" said Lulu. "It's like listening to McCartney or Elton John. He's been trained I know, but he had the basic talent already. Such a beautiful tone."

"I love Ed's voice," I said, agreeing with Lulu. "When he first told me he sang I wasn't surprised because his speaking voice is so nice." I sighed, turning my head to look at Lulu in the driver's seat. "I could listen to that voice all day."

Lulu grinned then she added, "And all night too, apparently."

"You're right about that," I said with a laugh. The seriousness returned. "I really am lucky. Ed knows what's happening and still chooses to be with me. I gave him a chance to back off, no regrets, but he wanted to stay. You and Amir have been so nice about Ed spending time at the house with me. It does me good, having him there."

"He is more than welcome. I like Ed, I know Amir feels the same, and you know what? Avo likes him too."

I laughed. "Speaking of Avo ...," I said and went ahead to ask Lulu about the future of my beloved pet. "Avo loves you all. I'm not sure who to ask to take responsibility for him."

Lulu didn't speak. She listened, nodded. When I had started a similar conversation with Joe at the airport bar, he became uncomfortable and asked if I really wanted to talk about these plans. I watched to see if Lulu became emotional, but she appeared to be thinking as she listened. I was grateful for her strength, knowing this must be hard for my friend to hear. "I know it is hard to talk about," I said. "But I honestly want to know what you think."

Lulu approached the topic logically and viewed it from all sides. She expressed a variety of concerns, from whom Avo felt most secure with to which home had the most room for him.

"Avo should remain at your home if that is at all possible. It's his home too." Lulu didn't say it but we both knew that Avo would have a lot to get used to—especially my absence. "Will Joe want to live there? At the house, I mean?"

"I don't know. We haven't talked about that, but I want you to stay there. You and Amir. I don't want things to change for either of you—and not because of Avo."

Although she was driving, Lulu looked in my direction as best she could. "Mara, that's very generous of you, of Joe too. I'd be thrilled to stay in the house, at least for a few months, longer if I can. This might sound odd coming from me because you know I love that dog, but Avo needs to be a package deal with the house. When you put the house in Joe's name, he should be Avo's registered owner too. It's what's best for Avo."

"I hadn't thought of that. You're probably right." I paused for a moment and let it sink in.

"Besides, we will all love and care for him no matter what."

I started to cry. She came to my rescue by saying, "Auntie Lulu will have visitation rights!" I laughed. The sadness fell away.

We made our way southeast on the highway and I saw the signs for the city limits of Marana, just north of Tucson. Further down the road, I instructed Lulu to take the Miracle Mile exit and then merge onto River Road. I checked the time. Our arrival at Carling's place of business would time out perfectly.

I recited the address. "It should be just down on the left." Lulu waited for traffic and turned into a business complex. We found the office and I was secretly thankful it was on the ground floor. Climbing steps had become difficult.

I pointed to the entrance in the event Lulu would need to come for me. In my weakened state, it was a possibility. "It's the doorway where the sign says Laboratory Solutions." Gathering my bag from the floor of the car, I added, "I'm meeting with a man named Richard Carling. It's his company. He did business with P-H when I worked there." Lulu noted the entrance to Carling's office and nodded.

"Google Maps says there's a coffee shop down the block and a café two streets over," I told her as I opened the passenger door and stepped out. Exiting vehicles had become slow and cautious. I turned and closed the car door and said to Lulu through the opened passenger door window, "I'll see you in about an hour, okay?"

"I will be here waiting for you in forty-five minutes," she answered, leaning toward me from the driver's seat. "Call me if there is any issue and I'll be back in a flash."

I attempted a smile. "I will be fine. In fact, I'll be better after this meeting." Lulu drove off as I walked toward the building.

The inside corridor was sterile, unadorned, the floor covered with polished concrete. According to the signage, Laboratory Solutions was on the left at the end of the hallway and restrooms were on the right. In the ladies' room, I studied my face in the mirror over the basin. There was a calmness, an ease about me. I should have been nervous about meeting with Carling, but I wasn't. I anticipated the look on his face when he heard what I had come to say. My phone said it was exactly four p.m.

Leaving the restroom, I walked to the doorway of Laboratory Solutions. The sign listed Richard Carling as proprietor. Inside the entrance, a reception desk was positioned to the left, but it was unmanned. To the right were uncomfortable-looking, rigid plastic chairs and a large, potted palm. As I turned back to the reception desk, a young man appeared from the hallway behind him. He was dark-skinned with curly black hair that shone with a carefully applied grooming product. His face was clean-shaven but the line where whiskers grew was plainly visible. Tall and thin, probably in his early thirties, he had an athletic build that suggested a passion for either running or basketball.

"Hello," he said, his hand extended. "You must be Mara. I'm Marcus. We spoke on the phone."

"Yes," I said tentatively. "I'm Mara Cordovan. Nice to meet you. I appreciate you putting me on Mr. Carling's calendar so quickly."

"It was no problem. Richard recognized your name on his appointments. He mentioned that he hadn't seen you in quite a while." Carling remembered me. I wasn't sure what that implied, but I didn't care.

"It has been years. I was with a different lab at the time. I'm flattered he remembered my name." I smiled, having decided to play the role for all it was worth.

Marcus returned the smile and said, "Richard is finishing a call. He will be with you shortly," he gestured toward the ugly, plastic chairs. "Is there something I can get you? Water or coffee?"

"Coffee perhaps, if Mr. Carling will join me. Thank you." Not wanting to sit, I took two steps toward the chairs but remained standing. Luckily, there were items on the wall that I could pretend to study with interest. Marcus nodded, asked that I excuse him, then returned down the hallway from which he had come.

Chapter 36

Two minutes later, a door opened, then footsteps approached in my direction. Richard Carling appeared from around the corner. Except for the eyes, I would not have recognized him. Carling looked nothing like the more recent photo on the ASC website. He was much older and thinner, his color ashen, his cheeks hallow. Carling was in poor health.

He wore an expensive suit that looked almost new, but the way it hung on his frame told me that the man had lost weight recently. He managed to work up a closed mouth smile on his thin face. "Mara Cordovan," said Carling, as he offered me his hand. His voice was restrained as if speech required effort.

I returned the greeting in the same vein. "Richard Carling," I said, as I shook his hand. "It has been a long time."

"Yes," he said as he released my hand. I tried to get a read on him, but it was hard to do. "Let's go to my office."

He led me past the empty reception desk, down the hallway into which Marcus had disappeared, and to another short hallway to the left. The floor was covered with the same polished concrete used in the outer corridor. Bland, boring but easy to maintain. We entered Carling's office, and he closed the door. The room was large and furnished as one would expect: a huge desk with a leather office chair behind it. There were two guest chairs facing the desk on the opposite side. To the side of the desk, was a sitting area with a small couch and two thinly upholstered chairs with a coffee table. The outer office and Carling's private space had the same sterile, unappealing feel of the communal area of the building. The place was not old or unkempt. It was simply bereft of ambiance.

Carling motioned to the guest chairs at the front of his desk and then sat down at his chair on the other side. Apparently, my presence did not call for the informality or comfort of the sitting area. I wasn't going to inquire about the offer of coffee.

"How are you, Mara?" asked Carling, as he looked at me directly for the first time. "And how might I be of service?" He stifled a brief cough, more a clearing of the throat and I realized it was the third time he had done this.

"Well, Mr. Carling ...," I began, but he interrupted.

"Please, call me Richard. I know we weren't on a first name basis years ago, but it's appropriate now."

"Thank you, Richard. We weren't really on any basis years ago. I was just a lab chemist when you knew me at Presson-Hagee. You interacted with management."

Carling nodded his assent. "You mentioned to Marcus that you are with a lab in Phoenix now, is that correct?"

"It is," I lied, "But, honestly, that not why I'm here. I wanted to talk with you about Paul Davisson."

Carling was surprised. I'd caught him off guard. "Davisson?" he asked, and for the first time coughed outright, not merely a clearing of his windpipe. He held a handkerchief over his mouth and tried to hide the convulsing cough. I waited for him to recover. "Are you aware Paul Davisson is dead?" he asked with sadness.

"Yes, yes, I am," I replied. "I am aware that he died recently. I read the obituary you wrote. Very thoughtful," I added, hoping to conceal my contempt.

Carling nodded, but his eyes did not meet mine. "Paul will be missed in the local industry. I heard that his death was an accident." Carling made eye contact with me for the slightest moment, then he looked at his desktop and said, "An unfortunate accident."

I didn't offer any opinion but chose to plunge ahead. I was not going to waste his time or mine. "You might not be aware that I left Presson-Hagee when the lab closed. Do you remember when the decision was made to close the lab?"

"Yes, I do," Carling answered thoughtfully. "It was a difficult decision for the company, for Davisson, and for the management team at the time. They were proud of the team they put together, of which you were a part. The work that was done there had been on the forefront." Carling's comments might have been sincere but to my ear, smacked of flattery and condescension. When I didn't react, he continued by asking, "Why would you be interested in that situation after all this time?"

I ignored the question. "If I recall, you were with the company authorized to inspect the lab."

For the first time since entering his office, Carling looked at me with something akin to suspicion. He placed his elbows on the desk, his hands clasped together. I watched his eyes narrow over interlocked fingers.

I waited for a response, but none came, so I forged ahead. "Isn't that correct?"

"Ye ... es...," he finally managed to stammer slowly. "Excuse me, but it has been a long time. The condition of the lab had nothing to do with its closure. The lab itself was sound. There were no issues that I recall. I do remember that the decision was purely due to finances." He hesitated for a moment. His expression revealed that a thought crossed his consciousness. "I was told the reason for the decision was made clear to the staff. Were you told otherwise?" Carling moved his head, furrowed his brow in such a way as to appear to be genuinely concerned that I may have been deceived.

Again, I ignored his question. It didn't matter what Carling knew or didn't know, understood, or did not, or how the truth was manipulated. My agenda was paramount to his.

"Do you remember a man with P-H by the name of Evan Rowan?" I asked the question casually and watched Carling's face drain of color when I mentioned my co-worker's name. "Evan left the company a while before the closure." I waited but Carling did not—or could not—respond.

"Ah," I said. "I can see that you remember him. I thought you might." Carling looked like a cornered beast who was losing his fight, but I wasn't letting up. "I'm sure you know that, like Paul Davisson, Evan is dead. I've been in contact with Evan's family. I was told you spoke with him just weeks before he died."

"That is true. I am sorry for Mr. Rowan, sorry for his family. What does this have to do with me?"

"We will get to that. Be patient," I snapped. "Are you still insisting that the lab at P-H had no issues, that all was safe, and the working conditions passed the requirements?"

"Of course, I do, yes. Who said otherwise? Rowan? He was a well-respected chemist, but he was not an inspector."

"Evan knew a lot, but he isn't saying anything anymore. He's dead."

"Yes, I realize that...." Carling began but I cut him off.

"He had cancer and it killed him. But then you already know he had cancer because Evan told you."

"Sad, very sad, but an unfortunate coincidence," he said, shaking his head.

"Are you willing to stake *your* life on that?" I'd hit a nerve, but then that had been my intent. "I'm betting you've been asking yourself these same questions." My gut told me I was going in for the kill shot, but I refused to veer from it. "When were you diagnosed?"

"What? What are you talking about?" he asked with disbelief.

"You have cancer, I'd stake *my* life on it. I can see how sick you are, Richard," I spoke his name with contempt, my eyes boring into the man on the other side of the desk, "Because I have cancer. I'm dying. You, me, Evan—we're members of the same club."

Carling began to cough. The handkerchief went to his mouth. It took time, but he recovered from the exhausting bout. "I am sorry to hear you are ill, "he said. "Whether you believe me or not, I wouldn't wish this pain on anyone, and yes, you are right—I have lung cancer. I've known for a few months."

"Your apology is much too late. We know the cause of our illnesses. There is no coincidence. The lab was closed for financial reasons, but also to hide the fact that everyone there was in danger of exposure to chemicals. You and Davisson knew you'd been found out."

As the man tried to regain his breath, I reached into the bag at my feet, retrieving the manila envelope. I tossed it on his desk within his reach. "The document inside this envelope is a summary. It contains every piece of information I am aware of about the situation at Presson-Hagee. Many of the details I learned from Evan's son, the rest I put together. I have detailed each aspect of your deception and I hold you and Paul Davisson responsible."

Carling removed the papers from the envelope. He reached for the reading glasses that sat on his desk. He put them on then began to scan the information I had put together. As he read, his physical presence seemed to diminish before my eyes. Carling turned to the second page of notes, then the third. Occasionally he looked up from the page, our eyes would meet, then his attention would return to the papers he held in his hands. Carling's eyes reflected shock and disbelief while I kept mine clear of emotion.

"What good does this do now? Why would you care at this point?" Carling sat back in his chair, resigned, no fight left in the tired, sick man. He tried to breathe deeply but his failing respiratory system only allowed him to take short gasps.

"Are you hearing yourself? Why would I care? A huge injustice was committed. Evan and I were robbed of our health, of years of our lives! I ask myself daily how many other victims there might have been of your greed. Don't they deserve to know of your deceit?"

"I'm a victim too," he argued with as much effort as he could summon. "Yes, of my own making, but I've still paid a price," said

Carling. "What difference does it make now? There are no records. You can't prove anything."

"You didn't finish reading, Richard. There are records." I pointed to the paper in his hand, urged him to continue reading the document. "You know how meticulous chemists are in their documentation. Evan had the solvents analyzed. There was no mistake. He kept the lab reports, the correct ones, the ones you should have taken responsibility for producing. By the way, this copy is for you. I have others."

The papers dropped from his hands and landed on the desk as Carling leaned forward. He removed his glasses and tossed them on the desk. Carling placed his elbows on the desk, his forehead on his fingertips. "I've regretted my part in this for so long. I doubt you'll believe me, but it is true."

"Then why didn't you own up to it? Alert the authorities to the risks we had been exposed to? Instead, you threatened Evan. You threatened to claim that he was complicit in your crimes. That was the threat you held over the head of a dying man."

"No, no, I never threatened Evan," he exclaimed, shaking his head. "I just wanted him to see reason. There was nothing to be gained. So much to be lost."

"Spoken like a man with everything to lose except his self-respect. That you sold years ago, however. You and Davisson."

"Davisson never forgave himself for his part in this. It haunted him. That's why he struggled with alcohol, with drugs. It is why his private life was a mess. I believe he hated himself."

"If any of this is true, there were steps that could have relieved your guilt. Neither of you chose them. You get no sympathy from me."

"What are you planning to do?" Carling asked with fear in his scratchy voice.

"What do you think? I'm going to expose you, finally. I'm releasing the information to the media. I want the public to know the story. I want people to know what happened—that people trusted you and you put money ahead of their well-being."

"Please, please...don't do that," the man pleaded, his palms raised toward me as if fending off an attack. "My family is already suffering because of my illness. This would cause them pain and sadness they don't deserve."

"What of the pain and sadness suffered by Evan Rowan's family? What of my family?" I raged. "Your family could have been spared the news of this—all our families could have been spared. We could have been spared from dying the painful deaths we're consigned to." I was repulsed by our discussion. I tasted bile. "Evan didn't deserve this," I said shaking my head from side to side. "I don't deserve it." I fought tears, determined to keep control.

It was nearly five p.m. Lulu was waiting for me. "I need to go. I've said what I came to say. Don't try to intervene or I'll expose that as well. Thanks to you and Davisson, I have nothing to lose. If you try to stop me, a copy of the document will be delivered to news outlets across the state and to law enforcement." I was lying but Carling didn't know it.

"Media?" he asked with desperation. "Law enforcement? No, no! Please reconsider!" he begged.

I pulled one other item out of my bag. It was a small package holding a carefully considered assortment of pills in a clear, plastic packet. I placed the packet on Carling's desk. "Maybe you'd like to consider taking the easy way out. If that appeals to you, then consider this a favor. The white oval pills are Zofran, an anti-emetic. These two," I said, pointing at capsules, "are Fentanyl. They will help you relax. You might be familiar with that option for pain relief already, as I am. These four round tablets are Digoxin. In this concentration, they will stop your heart and thanks to the Fentanyl, you won't feel a thing. The choice is yours. The Zofran should keep you from throwing them up."

The Zofran and the Fentanyl were mine. The Digoxin tablets, of course, were stolen from Fred. I found a use for them after all.

I stood up and felt instantly lightheaded. The meeting had wiped me out. I wanted out of that office and quickly. I put the strap of my bag over my shoulder and looked at Carling. There were tears of defeat in his eyes. His shoulders had fallen slack, his face in his hands. "Goodbye, Richard. I wish you a slow, painful death unless you can summon the strength to end it here and now."

With surprising speed, Carling grabbed the envelope and stuffed the papers back inside. He grabbed the packet of pills and crammed it into the envelope with the papers. "Take this with you," he said, trying his best to sound strong while holding the envelope in my direction. "I don't need a reminder of those details and I certainly don't need your help with my end-of-life decisions."

"Your choice," I said. I reached for the envelope and returned it to my shoulder bag. "But returning the papers to me doesn't change a thing for either of us. I won't be dissuaded."

"Do what you have to do," he told me, his hands splayed in front of his face. "I can only do the same." Carling remained at his desk as I left, closing the door to Carling's office without a backward glance.

Marcus was seated at the reception desk, his fingers tapped away on a PC. He didn't raise his head, but eyes flicked in my direction for a quick moment. "Thank you, Ms. Cordovan," he said, without missing a stroke. "Have a nice day." I managed a nod as I made my way through the office space to the exit, hoping I didn't collapse on the floor. As I opened the door to leave Carling's place of business, Lulu greeted me in the outer corridor.

"Hey," she said. She took another, closer look at me and asked, "Are you okay?"

"I'm fine. Just very tired. Let's get out of here." I felt myself slump toward the wall in the corridor. Lulu took me by the arm.

"Lean on me," she said, supporting me. "I'll help you to the car."

As we turned to leave the building, we heard a loud, concussive noise that forced us both to jump. Instinctively, we cowered as we turned to look down the hallway in the direction from which the sound had come. It was a gunshot. It came from Carling's office.

Chapter 37

Lulu and I stared at each other in horror. "What the hell?!" she yelled. "Was that a gunshot?" She turned to me and said, "Let's get out of here. Now!" Lulu led me quickly from the building and to my car, which she had parked spaces away from the office entrance. Even if I had been capable of protest, which I was not, I was too shocked, too weak to argue. Lulu helped me into the passenger side then ran around to the driver's door, climbed in, and locked the doors.

"Who's in there, Mara?" she asked in a panic as she started the car. "What the hell happened?"

"Only Richard Carling and an employee, a guy named Marcus." I answered slowly, as if my words tumbled out in slow motion. "We talked. That was all." I stared in the direction of the entrance to Carling's building. There were other vehicles parked in the lot, but except for Lulu, I had not seen another person in the building or in the parking lot. I wanted to throw up.

As I tried to control my gut, I saw Marcus run from the building. He was waving his arms to get our attention, obviously alarmed. I tried to make sense of it, but I knew what had happened. I looked around, waiting for people to come running to find out what was going on, but there was no one.

"Is that Marcus?" asked Lulu.

"Yes," I answered, although I couldn't hear myself speak.

"There was no one else there?"

"No," I answered with more certainty than I felt. "Not that I saw."

"Stay here," Lulu told me. She opened the car door and stepped out. I wanted to stop her, but I couldn't move, couldn't speak.

"What happened?" she called to Marcus. "Are you okay?"

"It's not me, it's my boss!" Marcus shouted, pointing to the office from which he'd come. "He shot himself!"

"What?!" screamed Lulu. The events started to make sense to Lulu as she quickly looked in my direction then turned back to Marcus. "Have you called 911?" she asked with urgency.

Marcus was shaking his head. "I heard the shot and opened his office door. He's at his desk, blood everywhere! I ran for help!"

Lulu was out of the car by now. "You better sit down," she told Marcus, motioning to the shade at the curb of the parking lot. "I'll make the call." Lulu reached for her phone, which was the last thing I was aware of until I heard the sirens.

***

Police officers responded to the scene within minutes. They secured the office building and spoke with Marcus, with Lulu, and with me. Lulu was by far, the most helpful. Marcus and I were both in shock, our recall was spotty, but we answered their questions as accurately as possible. Lulu made it clear that I was unwell and that she was concerned about me. After that, one of the emergency responders hovered nearby. There wasn't a lot for them to do inside.

Marcus had been in the office the entire time I'd been in the building. He said goodbye and saw me leave the office before we heard the gunshot. I doubted there was time for Marcus to shoot the man before Lulu and I heard the shot. There might be prints other than Carling's on that gun, but they weren't mine.

The officer in charge, a detective named Stevenson, completed initial interviews with Lulu and Marcus before he talked with me. I was glad of this. I desperately needed the time to rest and recover from the shock of what had happened. In truth, I wanted time alone to get my story straight.

I could not fathom my stroke of luck that Carling had returned the papers and pills to me before I left his office. The same good fortune intervened when Davisson's friend did not drink from the adulterated whiskey. What of Fred? I hadn't killed him, but I managed to withhold life-saving medication. You would think a nefarious angel had aided my vengeance, but you can't accept that angels, nefarious or otherwise, are helping if you do not believe they exist. Then why would I believe in luck? It was a question for which I had no answer.

Stevenson was young. I doubted he was my age. He proved, however, to be thorough and tenacious, and asked his questions without leading us to answers he wanted to hear. He was patient and waited for my responses. That may have been for my benefit or because he couldn't tell how reliable I was due to my condition, medication, or whatever. I was still sitting in my car with the seat slightly reclined, as comfortable as possible under the circumstances. Stevenson stood next to the car as we talked.

"How were you acquainted with Mr. Carling?" Stevenson asked me. "How long had you known him?"

"I knew Richard years ago," I answered. "Our interactions occurred over a few years. They were work-related, not personal. I had not spoken to him in a long time." I told myself that using the man's first name made me sound less inclined to wish him ill.

"And you had an appointment with him this afternoon?"

"I did. Four o'clock." I knew Stevenson was confirming what he had already heard from Marcus and Lulu.

"What was the nature of your business with Carling?"

"A former colleague recently died. Someone he knew well. The man who died had been my employer." On the face of it, that was true.

"You wanted to talk about this man who died?"

"Yes. His death was sudden—an accident," I shared, knowing it was partly true. Davisson's death had been sudden.

"What was the name of this colleague?"

"His name was Paul Davisson," I stated, with a hard exhale, as if it didn't matter anymore. I watched the detective jot down the name, noted the correct spelling for him.

"I informed Richard about my illness. I wanted him to know of it," I said, with a shrug. "To be honest, I don't have long."

"I am sorry, Ms. Cordovan. If a conversation is too much for you right now, we can talk tomorrow."

'I'd rather go ahead with it now. I'm here." I waited for a beat before I continued. "I've contacted many people I haven't seen in quite a while. It is what you do at this point, Detective, for a variety of reasons." I paused to let that sink in.

"I appreciate that you are willing to continue, Ms. Cordovan. It's very helpful to us. How did Carling respond to your news?"

I sighed. "He was sorry to hear it and I appreciated his kindness." This was a fabrication, but it was the believable sentiment, I supposed. "Then Carling told me he was suffering from cancer, too. Neither of us had any idea the other was ill," I said, shaking my head. "Another colleague of ours died of cancer months ago."

"And that colleague's name?"

"His name was Evan Rowan. He was my mentor, you could say."

"Three colleagues with cancer? And another died due to an accident?" asked Stevenson. "That's unfortunate. Were the diagnoses coincidence or were the circumstances related?"

"Hard to tell," I said. This was a lie, but it would be hard to prove it. "We each worked with industrial chemical labs. But that was a long time ago, at least in my case."

"Carling and the other man who died, they still worked in the industry?" I nodded as Stevenson thumbed back a page in his notes. "Carling's company was called Laboratory Solutions. What did he do here?"

"His company was contracted to inspect commercial labs." He jotted down the information.

"So, Ms. Cordovan, how did Mr. Carling seem to you?"

I thought about it. "Difficult to say. I didn't know him well and hadn't seen him in so long. Based on what I knew of him years ago, he had changed significantly. Older, of course, and he was obviously ill." Stevenson didn't respond—he was taking notes. When he stopped writing, he looked at me, but still said nothing.

"You want to know if he seemed like he was about to take his own life?" I asked with sarcasm. I remembered the assortment of pills, the pills now concealed in my bag on the floor of the car. I recalled how Carling had tossed them into the envelope. I stared out the windshield and shook my head. "No, he did not," I said. "I can't believe he chose that moment to do it. Why would he do that?" I asked rhetorically. I faked the quandary because I knew the answer.

"Tell me what happened, from the time you arrived until you heard the shot."

"I arrived at four," I answered, taking a deep breath, thinking about what to say. "Marcus, Richard's assistant, greeted me and introduced himself. He said Carling was on a call but would be with me soon. I waited for a brief time. Carling greeted me in the waiting area, and we talked in his office. I became very tired. Carling and I said goodbye and I left a little before five. Marcus told me goodbye and thanked me as I left."

As Stevenson noted my responses, it occurred to me that I had not disclosed my ruse of needing a lab inspection to schedule my appointment with Carling. Marcus had not been aware of my intent to speak to his boss about Paul Davisson or Evan Rowan. I wondered what Marcus had told Stevenson about the reason for my visit. Had Marcus been asked why I was there? Did I care? Either way, I couldn't worry about that now. The question wasn't important enough to me to waste precious energy on it.

"I was exhausted," I continued. "I felt weak. I was relieved to see Lulu waiting for me in the outer hallway. I was barely able to make it out of the building. Lulu had to help me. We had just turned to leave when we heard the shot. We were both scared, alarmed. Lulu got us out of there. We had just climbed into my car when we saw Marcus run out of the building. Lulu must have realized he needed help. At least she was thinking clearly. Honestly, I was not in good shape. I'm a little better now."

"Okay, Ms. Cordovan. I appreciate your cooperation. You and Ms. Vasquez can go, however, there might be additional questions. I will need your contact details." Stevenson handed me his card. "Are you sure you can make it home? I can provide an escort, if needed." Stevenson sounded genuinely concerned about me. "I know you have a two-hour drive."

"I'll be fine. I just want to go home."

Chapter 38

I slept on and off for hours. While awake, I thought of the sound of that gunshot and when I slept, I heard the jarring sound within my dreams. I hadn't spent time around guns, didn't shoot them, and never liked them. Open carry was legal in Arizona, but I didn't know many people who owned a handgun.

Wednesday evening would be my last shift behind the bar. I had a multitude of mixed feelings about it. Bartending is a skilled position in the hospitality industry. It can take years of practice to become proficient and the only real training is on the job. I've worked with graduates of bartending schools and the poor souls flounder for the first few months, confusing Cognac with brandy and topping draft beers with two inches of foam. There were many aspects of the job that I enjoyed, and I was fortunate to have worked with a good crew. I never had the urge to bail because the conditions were hellish or the clientele impossible.

My thoughts were on my therapy appointments with Henry. The sessions had been helpful to me, I couldn't deny it, but did I need to keep going? I was *dealing with things*, whatever that meant. As for the stages of my grief, I had overcome the initial stage of shock and denial, then the emotional pain and guilt. I had experienced anger, but not bargaining. My anger had not been directed at the diagnosis but at the cause, the source—the exposure to carcinogens. Depression was supposed to come next, but it had been a part of my life since my parents were killed. How would I know how it had factored in now?

I had reached that stage in the grieving process referred to as an upturn. I had worked through unfinished business and made decisions about spending my time and how I wished to leave this world. My actions were extreme, but they were fair and just, at least in my estimation. With Henry's encouragement and the support of my friends, I was approaching the acceptance and hope that would allow my life to end in peace.

There was one last task I wanted to complete, and it involved some research. I pulled up the ASC website once again and as morbid as it was, my attention was directed to member obituaries. I learned that in the last ten years, seventy-two members had died and allowed obits to be posted in place of their bio. A quick filter of the information revealed that fourteen of seventy-two had been employed at Presson-Hagee. Twenty percent of chemists listed in the ASC who'd died in the past ten years were affiliated with P-H. Eight of those fourteen were under fifty years of age at the time of their death. I would be the ninth.

I printed the information and placed it in the manila envelope with the second copy of the report I had created prior to my appointment with Carling. I still had that first copy, the one that I had shown to Carling, but the pills I had offered to him had been flushed that evening.

***

Arriving for work half an hour early, I hoped to end my shift early as well. Tomas was there, as were several members of the bar crew that I seldom worked with, which was unusual. The place wasn't busy, but it would be rocking in an hour or two.

A huge bouquet of flowers sat at the end of the bar. Tomas asked that I check the name on the card because he wondered if they had been left by mistake. I reached for the envelope and saw my name. The flowers were compliments of the management of the resort. I laughed and told Tomas they were beautiful and that I doubted the big arrangement would fit in my car. I was touched by the thought. I had not known of another bartender to be honored with flowers on their last day. It occurred to me how nice that the enormous, fragrant creation had not been sent to my funeral because having them here tonight, I could enjoy them too. Weird thought, but it popped into my head, nonetheless.

I soon realized that many of the staff were there for my send-off. My co-workers, including Debbie, the beautiful danseuse, had planned a party for me. They applauded after I read the card and acknowledged the bouquet. One by one they spoke to me for a moment. Many of my co-workers placed a note or a card in my hand. A few of them stayed and ordered a drink, while others took their leave, many of them scheduled to work that evening. Other than Tomas, none of them were aware, as far as I knew, that it was more than my employment that was ending.

Word got round about the get together, thanks to Amir. By five o-clock, Ed was there, along with Joe. They ordered Manhattans and wanted me to make them. I remembered that this was where Ed and I had met, and I reminded him of it. Ed said it was a happy thought and he kissed me. Amir was off work by six and joined the party too. Lulu took a break at seven. She joined us during her dinner break even though she couldn't celebrate with a drink because she had to return to her table in the casino.

I worked behind the bar, like any other evening, except that I was accompanied by another bartender who completed the orders. Craig, my co-worker behind the bar with me, wouldn't let me do much of anything except pour wine or draw beer and he and Dean, the bar back did everything else. Every tip collected that evening landed in an oversized brandy snifter. At seven thirty, Tomas said I was done for the evening. He escorted me to the table occupied by my friends. The snifter was moved to my table. Debbie and the other servers continued to put their tips in it, one by one. The cash in the snifter was my gift from the crew.

The place was packed, loud and busy. Amir ordered food for our table, and I ate enough to keep the others from noticing. Fresh beers showed up non-stop in front of me. I drank a few but passed most over to one of the guys. I joked that if I'd known how much fun it was to quit the job, I'd have done it long ago. This was my evening of celebration. My co-workers were cheering for me, assuming I was moving on to a new adventure. I didn't dwell on the true reason for my departure. I savored sitting there with Ed's arm around my shoulder, listening to him talk and laugh with my brother and Amir, both of whom kept eyeing Debbie. I had a great evening and other than Avo, everyone I loved was there with me.

The last time I left employment had been when the lab at P-H closed. I hadn't made that decision for myself. I hadn't known what my future would hold, and I didn't know I would not work as a chemist again. Those were dark times, but I managed to keep my house, save my money. My sweet Avo comforted me. I suffered bouts of depression over the next few years not realizing that this might have been due to the unknown precursor to the cancer festering in my bones.

Tonight, the situation was different and as hard as it was for me to believe, the feeling was upbeat. I was leaving my job because I was no longer able to work, but it had been my decision. My friends were there with me. I enjoyed my evening enough to forget about the pile of bodies.

The bar was hopping with hotel guests by nine and I was ready to call it a night. Staff were busy serving which made it easy for us to depart gracefully. Joe and Ed had arrived together from the office, so at the end of the evening Ed drove me home in my car. He carefully placed the bouquet behind the front passenger seat. The arrangement extended nearly from floor to ceiling in the compact car. The scent was heavenly.

"What a great crew," Ed sad, as we left the bar. "I don't know many people in the service industry, but I guess co-workers are co-workers—they can be wonderful or awful. I'm glad you had a tight group to work with, Mara."

"You're right for the most part. The only ones I've been close friends with are Amir and Lulu, but I can't complain. Tomas has been a good boss. I've worked with managers in the past who were real pains in the ass. I would like to think that the service industry is becoming as enlightened to harassment and gender equality as any line of work, but it's hard to say."

Ed reached over and took my hand. "Nice man, Tomas. He told me he will really miss having you behind the bar and made me promise to bring you in for dinner soon."

"Ha," I laughed. "That was nice of him, but I'm not craving resort cuisine. It is edible, but nothing like our Indian place." The statement was out of my mouth before I realized it. I had referred to Jhankar Mahal as *our place*, and made it sound like we were a couple.

Before I could backtrack, Ed kissed my hand. "Nowhere is like our Indian place," he said. "We should go this weekend. If that sounds okay to you, that is."

I smiled at the thought of dinner with Ed, when I remembered that it was Wednesday evening and Ed had to work in the morning. "Shit," I said.

"What? You liked Jhankar Mahal. You just said so."

"No, no. I do. Dinner would be lovely. 'Shit' was about tomorrow morning. I don't work anymore, but you do. Your car is at the office, isn't it?"

"My car is at my apartment. Joe and I dropped it off there. Before we left the party, I told him I would take an Uber from your house. Neither of us wanted you to drive."

"But now you are inconvenienced. I'm sorry. I didn't think it through."

"It is not an inconvenience for me, Mara. I did think it through. Relax. Let me do things for you."

I took a deep breath and looked over at Ed, driving my car with no wheels of his own. "I don't need my car until Friday for my appointment with Henry. You can take it, or if I'm up early enough in the morning, I can drive you home before work. It's early. Maybe I'll sleep well."

"Is that an invitation to stay at your house?" asked Ed, with a grin.

"Well ... then I know I'll sleep well," I answered, and returned the smile.

"I'd love to spend the night with you, Mara. Perfect end to a fun evening—an evening in your honor."

Chapter 39

I had hoped for a romantic episode of passion with Ed, but I didn't have the strength. As with all things that were important to me at this stage, I had to prioritize and factor in the stamina and the energy. I told Ed that I had made a promise to myself to be more energetic by the weekend.

Ed's Uber arrived early Thursday morning. He kissed me goodbye while I was only half awake. He refused to have me drive him home saying that I needed my rest. I think I wished him a nice day at work, and he may have asked that I text him when I was up for the day, but I was not awake enough to be sure.

My eyes opened and I looked at the clock by the bed. It was eight thirty in the morning. I did the math and figured I had slept the better part of ten hours—more than I usually slept in three days. I hadn't had a lot to drink the night before, but coupled with the pain medication and Ed's company, I had managed a noteworthy amount of rest and I was happy about that.

I rolled over onto my back and bumped into Avo at my right side. The big dog rousted but didn't move from the bed. I stretched before I got up, then slowly rose to sit on the side of the bed. I had learned to take inventory each morning by checking in with myself. Was I in pain? Were my feet and legs strong enough to support me? I did a series of mobility tests to be sure. Was I dizzy? Was I nauseous? How was my gut? I was taking so much Fentanyl and Zofran that I suffered alternating bouts of constipation and diarrhea. Or were these problems related to the cancer? Hell, I didn't know. I had little appetite for food but tried to eat small portions at least twice each day. I consumed coffee and beer. With the support of my bedside table, I stood. So far, so good.

With Avo at my heels, I walked to the kitchen. There was a note from Amir. Before leaving for work, he had run Avo in the backyard and fed him. He enjoyed being part of my celebration at the bar the night before and hoped I'd slept well. After I made coffee, I texted Amir to thank him. Lulu's car was in the driveway, so I assumed she was sleeping.

I poured a cup of coffee and relished the first sip of the morning while I looked out the window at the back patio. I poured a second cup and pulled out the estate planning questionnaire I had received from the attorney. I leaned over the kitchen island as if it were a tall desk and perused the document. The questionnaire seemed straightforward, and I was as impressed with the level of detail as I had been with Renee in HR. I told myself that if any profession demanded an eye for detail, it was law. That is, any profession short of brain surgery, rocket science or, of course, chemistry.

I grabbed a pen and began filling in the blanks on the questionnaire regarding my assets, my banking information, my thankfully few liabilities. I named beneficiaries—Joe, Amir, and Lulu. I paused for a moment thinking of Ed. He had become a special part of my life in a brief time. I would remember him in a way that was fitting of the affection and regard I had developed for him, but for the moment, I did not know the shape I wanted that remembrance to take.

***

Friday at one p.m. I found myself at Henry's office. After he greeted me in the waiting area and I followed him to the private office, I took my usual seat across from Henry's chair.

"Mara, you look rested," said Henry with a slight smile. "Tell me how you're doing."

"I've been sleeping well, maybe because I'm not sleeping alone—and I don't mean with Avo," I joked.

"You're spending time with Ed? How nice for you." I was impressed that Henry remembered Ed's name—or had recently reviewed his notes.

"Yes, it is nice, and I've quit my job, Henry."

"That's a big step."

"It was time." I shared about my waning energy and lack of strength. "I've been consciously trying to enjoy my days. Except for Tuesday." I stopped and took a deep breath, exhaling slowly.

I told Henry about Richard Carling's suicide and that the man was a chem lab inspector that I had known during my days at Presson-Hagee. I shared about speaking with the police but withheld the parts about the document I had used to threaten him and the offer of narcotics.

Henry stared with eyes wide, absorbing my words. "That is bizarre, Mara." He placed the tablet and pen on the small table next to his chair. Henry shook his head and leaned forward, his chin in his hands, his elbows on his knees. "The man suffered from lung cancer?" he asked. "He shared this with you?" Henry was incredulous.

I nodded. "I don't mean to sound cruel, but if he had waited five more minutes, Lulu and I would have been down the road and aware of nothing more than sirens in the distance. Instead, we found ourselves talking to responders." I knew why he killed himself and my disappointment had more to do with why he hadn't swallowed the pills I provided him. That was the ending I wanted, instead of hearing that damned gunshot.

"I could start a society," I said, with sarcasm. "It would be very exclusive except all the members would be dead. The upside is that the entrance dues are prepaid."

Henry said nothing. He merely blinked.

"Evan, Uncle Fred, Paul Davisson, and now Richard Carling. I'll soon join them." Henry looked at me. The shock had subsided. He appeared to be deep in thought. A well-trained therapist, his expression did not bear surprise, irritation, or judgement.

He nodded, moving his gaze to the pad of paper he held. "You have been surrounded by the deaths of others, Mara, nearly since you received the news of your own diagnosis."

I could only nod. I looked at my hands.

"These circumstances are unique," said Henry. "Let me ask a question about Richard Carling. Why do you think this man Carling chose to kill himself that day?"

I sighed. "Richard expressed remorse for his part in the lab exposure. It is possible that seeing me, learning that I was dying, was more than his conscience could handle," I explained, giving Carling the benefit of feeling guilt. "We discussed Evan. Richard had known him but didn't know he had lost his battle with the disease until I told him." This was untrue but I said it anyway.

"Tragic," said Henry. "Did Carling know Paul Davisson?"

"Yes, they knew each other. Carling and I discussed Davisson's death. He mentioned that Paul had been involved with the shortcuts at Presson-Hagee, that he blamed himself for his part in it. Carling thought that was the reason for Davisson's excesses."

"Carling thought that Davisson had regrets and abused drugs and alcohol to forget?" Henry asked.

"He seemed to believe that."

'Do you believe it, Mara?"

"I don't know. I only know that Davisson made his choices."

"At Carling's office, you and your friend Lulu spoke with the police. What have the police determined?"

"We haven't been contacted since giving statements. They might not have reached an official conclusion, but there is no doubt of how he died. He was alone in his office."

"You said that Carling expressed remorse. Does that change the way you feel about him? Do you regret speaking with him?"

I had to think about my answer, but I didn't need long. "No. Taking his life made him no less negligent. He made a choice. He harmed himself and brought grief to his family. I'm dying because of choices he made in the past." I shook my head. "I feel no different about it. I had a right to confront him."

"You said the same about your uncle, that you had a right to speak your mind."

"Yes," I said, taking a deep breath that I hoped Henry took for regret, remorse, or sadness.

"You couldn't predict that either of these men would die. They were both in failing health. Do not take away from what you needed to do for yourself. Again, the timing was bad, but the timing was not your fault." Timing. I could not get away from it.

"True. Thank you for saying so, Henry."

"It is possible that if the police are thorough, you won't need to speak with them again. They could find it rather simple to rule the death a suicide. Talking with this detective wasn't exactly easy—you were exhausted and weak. I hope they took your condition into account."

"I was glad to get it over with and Detective Stevenson was as decent as he could be under the circumstances. He was concerned about the drive ahead of me, but I was okay."

"Detective Stevenson."

"Right." I paused. There was but one last issue I wanted to discuss with Henry. I forged ahead. "Henry, I'm doing as well as can be expected. I've made use of the time in therapy. I've taken care of my affairs and resolved unfinished business as you have encouraged me to do."

"You have made progress in those areas, Mara," agreed Henry.

I looked at my hands in my lap then back at Henry. "I don't feel the need, as greatly as I did, to talk with you. I think we're finished."

Henry was surprised by my decision. Color rose in his face. His expression bordered on embarrassment. "If that's how you feel, we can leave it here."

"I think I'm at a good point," I said slowly with a nod, my eyes meeting Henry's. It was difficult to read the expression on Henrys face, but he voiced his thoughts soon enough. He wasn't going to make this easy for me.

"Mara, I have concerns about this rather abrupt decision. With the strange circumstances that have surrounded you lately, it would be good for you to talk about them. It may not feel that way now, but you may change your mind. Would you consider a couple more sessions? Just to be sure?"

"Here's the deal, Henry," I began, pausing to take a deep breath. "I don't want to talk about any of it. Not anymore. When this arrangement started, you said it was up to me whether I met with you once or a hundred times."

"Yes, of course it's up to you, but..."

"The truth is," I interrupted, "I came here to talk about my diagnosis, my impending death. I don't want to pay you to talk about people who meant nothing to me. If that sounds shitty, I really don't care. What I need now is time at home with my friends and family. That's how I want to spend my time." I sounded more irritated than I was, but I wasn't sorry for it.

We stared at each other for a brief second, our cases made. Henry attempted to make one last point.

"Considering what happened—a former colleague killed himself just feet away from you after the two of you talked—are you certain you don't want further help to process this?"

I looked Henry in the eye with resolve. "I have nothing to process."

Henry appeared stunned by my response, but the shock lasted only a fleeting moment before he recovered. "Okay then. One last thing though: will you call if you need to talk? Or just *want* to talk, or if something comes up?"

"Of course," I answered, having calmed down. "You've been very helpful, Henry."

As Henry and I shook hands, he covered our clasped right hands with his left and looked at me. With eyes full of compassion and care, he said, "You have the support of friends, and you have your brother. I wish you the best, Mara."

On that note, I left Henry's office and looked forward to a weekend filled with love and relaxation with Avo and my friends, with Joe, and with Ed.

Chapter 40

Henry Maloney sat in his office, looking out the window. He was thinking about the session with Mara Cordovan. He had thought of little else in the past few hours. Henry believed in coincidences, but as with most reasonable people, he trusted them only to a certain point. He contemplated a phone call. Henry would listen to his gut, but he wanted guidance and decided to make another call first.

He reached for the office phone and dialed the number of a friend who had been Henry's mentor when he began his practice. His friend was now retired, but his specialty had been caring for the psychological needs of the incarcerated and Henry appreciated his friend's no-nonsense view of their profession.

"Henry," his friend answered. "Good to hear from you and on Friday too. Where are they pouring cold beer?"

"Hello, Bill. I need to run something by you. Something that might sound odd. Can you meet me at the Blue Coyote? In about an hour?"

"Sure, Henry. I can't wait to hear this one."

***

Henry walked into the Blue Coyote Brewery at 5:30 pm sharp. Bill was already at the bar with a tall, cold one. Henry walked over and smacked Bill on the back.

"Nice of you to wait for me, ya' big lush," said Henry, trying to sound put out.

"Hey, Hank. It's Hammerin' Hank," said Bill, half turning to look at Henry with a smile that reached from ear to ear.

"Shit," said Henry. "I can't believe you still call me that. I haven't played ball since my undergrad days, and you damn well know it."

Bill continued to enjoy the joke at Henry's expense but moved on to more important matters. "What are you drinking, man?"

"Whatever you're having. Mind if we get a table outside?" Henry gestured toward the patio with his thumb.

"Sure, Hank," Bill agreed, as he glanced toward the door leading to outside seating. "Grab a table. I'll be right out with the brew."

"Thanks," said Henry, "and an order of chili fries. I'm starved."

Henry and Bill spent time catching up with each other's lives. The two men were each on their second beer and they had eaten half the chili fries before Bill asked what was on Henry's mind.

"What did you want to run by me?" Bill asked, as he watched Henry wipe chili from his whiskers. "You said it might sound odd, but I've got news for you—I haven't been amazed by much in a whole hell of a long time."

Henry sat back, took a long drink of pale ale, deciding how to begin. He stuffed a fry covered with chili into his mouth. He tried to avoid his mustache, but it proved impossible. He reached for a napkin and swallowed.

"I have a patient with an untreatable condition. This patient was referred for end of life support—making choices, unfinished business, finding peace. The prognosis isn't good, and the condition was likely caused by workplace exposure to chemicals years ago. She signed a detailed NDA. For reasons of her own, she has chosen not to pursue employer responsibility as a "reasonable exception" to the NDA."

"That's very unfortunate," responded Bill, listening attentively.

"It gets much more unfortunate. Soon after receiving their diagnosis, she learns that a former colleague died months ago. Cancer," Henry shared, shaking his head.

"Same NDA?"

"I assume so, yes." Henry took a drink of beer, swallowed, then continued. "Further, this patient is now employed in the hospitality industry, and a guest died of a drug overdose at their place of business."

"Okay," answered Bill. "Something similar occurred recently at one of the casinos. I read about that."

"Exactly the incident to which I refer," said Henry. "Now imagine that this patient had an elderly relative in poor health. There was some history between them, and it wasn't pleasant. The relative dies. Their passing was not unexpected due to the shape they were in."

"It does happen," concluded Bill with resignation.

"It does. Yes, it does. Then my patient wanted to confront a business professional who might have been responsible for the negligence that could have caused their illness. This business professional was, at the very least, aware of the exposure."

Bill pulled the corners of his mouth down as he often did when he was deep in thought. "Confronting this person could be cathartic, to accept the hand they've been dealt."

"Right, I agree. I might encourage such an interaction. A conversation takes place. The unfortunate patient learns that the business associate is dying of lung cancer. What are the odds, right? Then immediately after, within minutes, the former associate blows their head off—in their office, with their own weapon."

Bill stared at Henry. Blinked. "Say, what?"

"Hey, Bill, you said nothing surprises you," Henry reminded him, index finger extended in Bill's direction.

"That's a bizarre set of circumstances," said Bill with a shake of his head.

"No kidding."

"A person would have to possess the worst luck in the world to be surrounded by that much sad news."

"My thought exactly." Henry explained that the coincidence idea had grown ripe. "Now let me back up. Remember the guest at the casino? She knew the guy. Not only did they know the guy, but the dead man was also her former boss. He was their boss at the time of the chemical exposure."

"The exposure that might have caused the cancer," Bill said. "The exposure that was due to negligence."

"You got it," Henry confirmed. "Police have investigated these deaths. They expect to be ruled accidental overdose and self-inflicted gunshot."

"This woman is ill, correct?" Bill asked. "They were forthcoming throughout the sessions, and so far, the authorities have found nothing suspicious, Henry. Why do you?"

"It's the number of incidents connected to her. Plus, when she told me about running into her former boss, she was angry, irate. She had a hard time calming herself. This was before he died." He checked his surroundings, but their privacy was assured. "Bill, she blurted out that she wanted to kill him." Henry took a deep breath then leaned in close and said, "I think she might have done it."

Bill waved the server over. "I need another damn beer."

"She made considerable progress in our sessions and expressed gratitude for the help," Henry shared. "Then she decided she was done."

"Don't get mad, but I must ask: did that decision wound your ego?"

"No," Henry said, shaking his head, but he had answered too quickly. "It's the timing."

"You could try to talk to her again, maybe one more time," Bill suggested. "You weren't planning to 'end the therapeutic relationship' so abruptly."

"I'll consider it. Maybe I will."

"If you suspect a crime was committed, Henry, you have to report it."

Henry looked at his friend, nodded, tipped back his glass, and drained the last of his beer. They each drank another before they left the bar.

Chapter 41

Driving home from Henry's, I thought about my decisions. I had no regrets, just wanted to assess. Had I acted too soon regarding Davisson? Had I let my own sad news cloud my decision? If Carling was correct, that Davisson was tormented by his role in the laboratory fraud, might he have ended his life as Carling had done? It was too late to question my actions. I had made my choice to seek retribution of the most severe kind.

When I arrived at the house, all I wanted was a nap. As I stretched out on my bed with Avo, I wondered how much longer I'd be able to drive. Other than getting myself to work, my driving had been limited to short trips, early enough in the day that I hadn't yet taken pain meds. With work out of the equation, I could limit my driving even more, to appointments and short errands. At some point, as I became weaker and less aware cognitively due to the disease or the pain meds, I knew I'd have to give up that piece of myself too.

Just before I fell asleep, my phone chimed with a voice mail message. The message was from Detective Stevenson, informing me that the medical examiner had attributed Richard Carling's death to a self-inflicted gunshot. This was not news to me.

After a long nap with Avo, Ed picked me up at the house, requested that I pack an overnight bag so I would have all that I needed to be comfortable, and insisted that I bring Avo along. We discussed dinner, decided to eat in. If I felt up to it on Saturday, we would have an early meal at Jhankar Mahal.

It was difficult to be comfortable. Comfortable often meant experiencing less pain in my back and hips. Changing my position often seemed to help. Ed took this for restlessness at first, until I explained. Once he understood, he began to walk around the apartment with me, or would suggest another way to sit or stand.

My weekend was filled with relaxation. I noticed the way the days seemed to slide into one another, a sensation I had not experienced since college during those brief periods with time off work and no classes due to semester breaks. Our dinner on Saturday at Jhankar Mahal was wonderful. The food, the service, the ambiance, and the company were perfect. I had never enjoyed myself more.

We returned to Ed's apartment after dinner and sprawled comfortably together on the couch. I knew I couldn't stay awake much longer when Ed kissed my hand and said, "I have something to show you."

Ed smiled at my puzzled expression, rose from the couch, and walked toward the bedroom. He returned carrying a flat object, about two feet square in size. Ed sat down and took a deep breath. "If you don't like it, please say so. I'll try again." Ed turned the object around and revealed a sketch. Of me.

I was speechless. The portrait was in black and white, the strokes soft but darker than pencil. I guessed charcoal. The image he had created of me was attractive, the expression content, with a slight smile that rose from the mouth to the eyes. I took in the wisps of hair, the lips, the brows, the way he had defined my features. He had rested my chin on my clasped hands in a very natural pose. Ed made me look happy, more content than I had ever felt.

"What do you think?" Ed asked.

I looked from the sketch to Ed and found my voice. "It's wonderful, Ed. I've never had a drawing of myself. I love it. Absolutely love it." I leaned closer, kissing him.

"I'm so glad. I rarely do facial sketches although I trained in the art form. I wasn't sure I could do you justice."

The comment made me laugh. "When ... when did you do this?" I asked him. I stammered, still in shock.

"After our first dinner at Jhankar. There was a moment when you were looking at me from across the table and the lines of your face struck me as perfect." As Ed spoke, his fingertips delicately stroked the side of my face. It was an intimate gesture that he made often when we were alone. "I decided then to draw your portrait. I asked Joe for a photo of you to study the detail, but the most recent one he had was from high school graduation. It worked for reference, but I mostly used the memory of you at the restaurant."

I stared back and forth between the sketch and Ed. I was amazed by his talent and touched that he saw me in this light. I felt so close to him, and I had never been happier.

***

Amir and Lulu were lazily hanging out on Sunday afternoon when Ed drove me home. Amir had the day off as he usually did on Sunday, but Lulu had to work Sunday evening. Joe stopped over to visit. I had not seen much of my brother as he had been busy dealing with Fred's estate and with his own responsibilities at work.

As we sat around drinking beer, I looked at the caring, supportive people in my life. My heart was full of love and gratitude for them, but I needed to bring up a concern and it wasn't easy for me. "I don't know how much longer I'll be able to drive," I told them, shaking my head as I spoke. "I thought about this on Friday after my appointment with Henry. I'm taking more medication for the pain, and it is hard to sit for very long. I can recline if I'm seated in the passenger seat and take the pressure off my back and hips." I paused for a moment. It was hard for me to give up more of my autonomy.

"My energy level has taken a nose-dive even though I am sleeping better, and my strength is diminishing. I noticed this in a big way when Lulu and I went to Tucson last week. Granted, I had to deal with the shock of what happened, but the progression in symptoms was evident already. If Lulu hadn't been with me..." I could only finish the statement with a shrug.

It was Ed who spoke first. "If it concerns you enough to mention it, Mara, then you probably shouldn't drive. Between the four of us we can help with that," he said, his arm around my shoulder.

"I'll request evening shifts," offered Lulu. "It's easy for me to adjust my schedule. We will coordinate between us."

Joe and Amir sat side by side on the other side of the living room. "Absolutely," they said, in unison as they nodded their assent.

"I don't want you to spend extended amounts of time alone," said Joe. "I don't mean to barge into your business, but I do worry. I worry that you might need something. I feel better knowing that Lulu and Amir are here at the house with you, and I realize that you are spending more time with Ed." My brother was trying to be strong. "I'll help with anything you need. I'd like to visit in the evenings."

Amir reached over and put his hand on Joe's shoulder. "Come over whenever you want, spend as much time as you want here."

Joe looked at Amir and nodded. "Thanks," he said to Amir. I sat on of the couch between Ed and Lulu. Ed pulled me close to him and nuzzled the top of my head. Lulu patted my leg on the other side. I wished I hadn't mentioned the driving issue, but I couldn't have avoided it much longer.

"Of course, Joe," Amir answered, "especially if you bring beer." We laughed and I loved Amir for his humor. We needed a joke.

While I had them together, I brought up my upcoming appointment with the estate attorney. "I want you each to understand my plans," I explained.

"Hey, Mara," said Ed as he pulled me close. "I don't want to intrude. I'll leave this to the rest of you."

"You aren't intruding. You are part of my life. I want you to hear this too," I answered with resolve. "Please stay, okay?" Ed continued to hold me close. He nodded and kissed my cheek.

"I'm going to put the house in your name, Joe, but I want Amir and Lulu to continue to live here. I've talked with each of you about it already, so that's no surprise."

The three of them nodded, affirming that they knew this already. "I'm going to have Lulu assume responsibility as Avo's owner, but he loves all of you and I want him to live here. This is his home." I choked up and Avo must have detected the tone in my voice because he came over and rested his head on my lap. Talking about leaving Avo was hard. Unlike my human loved ones, he didn't know I would soon be gone. Or maybe I wasn't giving my beautiful dog the credit he deserved. Maybe Avo knew and understood better than any of us.

"I'm going to leave the Prius to Lulu. You can keep it if you want or sell it to help with Avo's expenses."

Lulu nodded, looking at Avo to avoid my eyes.

I turned to Ed. "I'm leaving the piano to you. You can keep it, but I know you don't play. I don't know of anyone who does. My grandmother was the only relative who played the piano, and she left it to me. I want you to find a music school or a performance venue that needs it."

"That's a beautiful idea, Mara," said Ed. His eyes were wet as he tightened his arm around my shoulder. The others nodded their agreement. The decision about the piano was very personal and they each knew how important it was to me. Expressing my wish for it eased the emotional tension, at least for me and I managed a deep breath.

Ed followed Lulu out when she left for work. He gave me a big hug and a kiss that nearly made me beg him not to leave. Amir opened another Dos Equis and settled in with Avo on the couch. Before Joe left, he wanted to talk to me privately.

"Mara, I want you to remember that you own half of Fred's estate. The old cuss didn't have much other than the house, but he had no mortgage." When Joe told me the value, I was flabbergasted.

"That would pay off the balance on my mortgage, Joe. Then I can leave the house to you with no debt." My life insurance policy from the resort will cover medical and end of life expenses.

"If that's what you want to do, Mara, but it is your decision. You can leave everything to the animal shelter, you can cover costs of music lessons for kids, or you can start an education fund at the resort. Whatever you want."

"You've been thinking about this," I said with admiration. "Those are all worthy ideas, but I want the people I love to be in my house. I want Avo to be here. It might sound stupid, but it is important to me."

"It's not stupid, Mara," said Joe as he gave me a hug, "But consider leaving the house to the three of us—me, Amir, and Lulu—leave them an interest in it. That way they both know this is their home."

"I'll think about it, and I will ask the attorney what she thinks. That is very thoughtful of you, Joe." I hugged him back. I felt Joe's body shudder.

Chapter 42

Henry was in his office early on Tuesday morning. He checked the time and decided to make a phone call before his first patient arrived. He doubted the person he wanted to reach would be available, but Henry would try, nonetheless. Finding the number on the department website, he tapped on the call option.

"Tucson City Police. How may I direct your call?"

Henry looked through his notes and found the name he had jotted down. "Detective Stevenson, please."

"One moment," said the voice at the other end of the call. "Stevenson is in the office somewhere, but if he is unavailable, would you like his voice mail or to speak with another detective?"

"Voice mail, please. If he's unavailable."

After a few seconds, the call was answered, much to Henry's surprise. "Stevenson," the voice said bluntly. The man sounded busy.

"Detective Stevenson, this is Dr. Henry Maloney. I practice psychology in Phoenix. You interviewed a patient of mine recently regarding an unfortunate experience involving a death. I was wondering if you might have a minute to speak with me."

"Would your patient's name be Mara Cordovan?" asked Stevenson.

Henry was relieved that the detective mentioned Mara's name. He was sure of his responsibility in this situation but would proceed with caution. "Yes, that's right," he replied.

Stevenson was silent for a moment. "Wait a second," he said. "You're a shrink?"

"Well, that's what we are often called, yes," said Henry with a laugh.

"I apologize, Doctor. I meant no disrespect. I knew the woman was ill. I assumed you were a medical doctor."

"No offense taken. Detective, I'm aware of the events that led to your conversation with Mara. It was stressful for her, especially considering her illness. We discussed it at length, and she gave me your name." Henry's statement was true except that he implied having permission to speak with Stevenson, which wasn't the case. All he needed was a means to say what he intended.

"Dr. Maloney, is that right?"

"Yes. Henry Maloney."

"The case in question is closed, Sir. I notified Ms. Cordovan of that. She was helpful, as was her friend. It was fortunate her friend was there. She was able to assist Ms. Cordovan and ensure that she made it home safely."

"I agree. She's a strong woman, but she's been through a lot. To be present at the scene you responded to added to her stress, as I said."

"Honestly, I don't anticipate needing to speak with Ms. Cordovan again."

"Great. Thank you." Henry paused briefly. "I feel for Mara," said Henry, going out on a shaky limb. "It is unusual for a terminal patient to be surrounded by so much death, the deaths of others with whom she was acquainted. Makes it harder."

"I'm sure it would, but Ms. Cordovan talked freely, Doctor. As I said, she was most helpful."

"She sounded competent, aware of her situation, when you spoke?" Henry asked. Stevenson didn't answer right away. Had Henry shared his own seed of doubt?

"Ms. Cordovan was tired. I offered to delay until the next day, but she wanted to complete the interview. She seemed in control of her decision to do so, and Ms. Cordovan's account was verified by her friend and by another person present at the scene."

"That's what I was hoping to hear, Detective. Then she can put this tragic chapter behind her. Thank you for your time."

That was a first, thought Stevenson, as he hung up the phone. He couldn't recall having heard from a psychologist regarding an interview with a patient, but he had not interviewed a person in Ms. Cordovan's situation. He had attempted to interview people suffering from shock, filled with grief or anger, but never a person with a terminal disease. Something Dr. Maloney said bounced around in his brain—*it is unusual for a terminal patient to be surrounded by so much death, the deaths of others with whom she was acquainted.*

Stevenson took a moment to review the notes from his interview of Mara Cordovan. He quickly found the reference he wanted. The name of the other colleague, the one she wanted to talk about with Richard Carling. He pulled up the name Davisson, Paul in the Arizona Law Enforcement Database. He learned that the man died in Scottsdale. Davisson's death was subsequently ruled an accidental overdose due to a combination of alcohol and methamphetamine. Detective Leanna Ochoa with Scottsdale PD was the lead investigator.

***

"This is Ochoa," the detective said as she answered the phone on her desk.

"Detective, my name is Stevenson. I'm with the Tucson PD."

"Hey. How are things down there? What can I do for you?"

"Probably nothing, just checking a couple of things. You recently worked a case, a suspicious death. The deceased's name was Paul Davisson."

"I did," said Ochoa with an abrupt tone. "Closed it. Accidental overdose."

"Yeah, I saw that in the record. The thing is I've discovered a connection to a case I recently closed. A suicide."

"A connection, huh? Okay, Stevenson. You have my attention."

"The deceased's name in my case was Carling, Richard Carling. We concluded that he shot himself moments after a meeting with a woman he had in common with Davisson. Her name is Mara Cordovan."

"I interviewed a woman by that name in the Davisson case. She's an employee of the Anasazi Resort. She tends bar. I interviewed her there along with other employees. Are you saying Cordovan knew Davisson?"

"She did," Stevenson said. "Ms. Cordovan told me she knew him when I interviewed her regarding Carling. Her meeting with Carling ended minutes before he offed himself. Their meeting was about your guy Davisson."

"Davisson was a guest of the Resort when he died. She didn't disclose that she knew him. What was the connection?" Ochoa asked.

"They had known each other professionally, from years back. Chemical labs, research, something like that."

"So ... Cordovan used to work as a chemist?"

"Yes, but this was a long time ago. Anyway, she was in the outer hallway when Carling pulled the trigger. He was in his office. She and a friend were on site when we arrived after the incident. It was her friend that called it in. They were shaken up as you can imagine—in shock."

"Huh. She had a friend with her?" asked Ochoa. "Why?"

"Yes, she did, and it was a good thing. She drove Ms. Cordovan to her meeting with Carling. Did Ms. Cordovan tell you she has a terminal illness?"

"No," answered Ochoa, thinking about what Stevenson was saying. "But her boss was there when I talked with her, and he was very protective. Makes sense now. He said she was dealing with health problems."

"She was in bad shape when I talked with her. I offered to wait but she wanted to get it over with."

"She didn't appear ill when I talked with her. If her boss hadn't said anything I wouldn't have guessed."

"Well, she's not doing so well now. Her condition has progressed."

"That's sad, Stevenson, but why call me about it, other than to tell me she knew Davisson?" Ochoa thought about the question she posed to Stevenson and backtracked. "Don't misunderstand me, it's a big detail. Did you believe her story?"

"Yes, and Carling's assistant confirmed it. Here's the deal: I was contacted by Ms. Cordovan's doctor. He was concerned about the impact of the stress on her condition. He mentioned the situation was unique, a dying woman with people she knows dying around her. But his call was unusual. Just crossing t's, dotting i's, I guess."

"Okay," said Ochoa. "I get that. There was no evidence of foul play regarding Davisson's death. But why didn't she tell me she knew the man?"

"Good question, Ochoa. You'd have to ask her. One more thing: Carling was dying of lung cancer when he killed himself."

"No shit? And Mara Cordovan is dying."

"Exactly."

"The resort had had issues with Davisson—disruptive, bizarre behavior. They cut off his bar privileges," explained Ochoa. "The guy was a big partier, according to the woman who was with him when he died."

"You had a witness?"

"Not exactly. I wasn't that lucky. They had a history of partying together. She was asleep or passed out. Woke up next to a dead Davisson. Cordovan told us that Davisson called the bar about his liquor charges. She offered to bring him a printed copy. We have security video of Cordovan outside Davisson's room. She delivered a room service order, that we know. Video supported her story. Cordovan knocked on the door, but Davisson didn't answer. We see her walk off and seconds later we see him open the door, look around, see the tray, and pick it up. He carries it in and closes the door. She didn't enter the room and she didn't speak to Davisson in person that night."

"Sounds tight to me."

"Except she placed the tray on the floor before she knocked. Now, why do you do that unless you plan to leave it there in the first place?"

Chapter 43

On Wednesday afternoon Lulu drove me to an appointment with Dr. Edmunds. I couldn't make it there on my own and I upped the dosage of my pain meds since I wasn't driving. Maybe I was becoming dependent on them, but I didn't care. I hadn't slept well Tuesday night, my back and hips were in great pain, plus I was experiencing sensations as though I had rolled in ocotillo thorns. Was this new symptom due to the cancer? The meds? Who knew? I could ask, but what difference would it make to know?

And I missed Ed, especially sleeping with Ed, not so much for the sex, as good as that had been, but I craved the intimacy of having him near me. The comfort of his touch relaxed me and helped me rest. When we talked earlier in the day, Ed had promised to stay with me that night. He was sorry that I hadn't slept, sorry for my pain. I was feeling particularly miserable and soaked up his concern. I would rest easier tonight and having him with me was all I wanted to think about.

Physical intimacy had changed because of my condition. When you depend on pain meds like Fentanyl, sensations are squelched, and desire takes a hit. Ed understood and I was amazed that we had developed this harmony so quickly. It had not been within my range of experience ever before with other partners and the knowledge was bittersweet.

Dr. Edmunds had resorted to providing palliative care—pain management—since I had refused the risk of other treatments, like chemo or radiation, at the onset. The only subject left to discuss was hospice. I wasn't yet at the point of having them on notice, but that time would arrive. Dr. Edmunds thought I should know what to expect, as much as was possible anyway. We went over the information she provided to terminal patients. The doctor advised me to talk with the hospice providers and have them answer any questions.

I shared with Dr. Edmunds that I decided to discontinue sessions with Henry. I was clear that he had been helpful, that I had taken his advice about taking control of the time I had left to me, but that I had reached the point where I had dealt with any unfinished tasks. My plans were made. She seemed to understand. Then my oncologist tactfully explained that she would be available to answer any questions or address concerns. I could call and speak with her or with a nurse at any time. What she meant but didn't say was that I didn't need to schedule another appointment.

Lulu and I were in the car, about to make the trip home, when she told me she had received a call from Detective Stevenson while I was with the doctor.

"He asked if he could stop by for a brief visit, that he has loose ends to tie up. I tried to put him off, but he promised to be brief."

I didn't have the energy to care. "Whatever," I said. "I'll try. Maybe you can answer his questions for me."

When Lulu and I returned home from the doctor's office, Ed was there waiting for me. He was sitting in the shade of my driveway with Detective Stevenson. With him was Detective Ochoa.

***

Ed helped me into the house. I ignored our visitors while Lulu took charge. "Detective Stevenson, please come in," she said. "I don't believe we've met your colleague."

"Lulu, this is Detective Ochoa," I told her, deciding to handle introductions myself. "She's with the police here in Scottsdale. Detective, this is my roommate, Lulu Vasquez. I'm guessing you both met Mr. Mancuso while you were waiting for us."

We each took a seat in the living room, except for Ed who went outside with Avo. Ochoa and Stevenson looked like they were afraid I was going to die at any moment. I probably looked sick enough to cause them worry, but too bad.

"What can we do for you, Detectives?" asked Lulu.

Stevenson took the lead. "We need to talk to Ms. Cordovan. If you could give us a minute, Ms. Vasquez?"

"You don't need to talk to me? You did call me, after all."

"Possibly," answered Stevenson, "but we'll talk with Ms. Cordovan first, and I called you, Ms. Vasquez to avoid causing Ms. Cordovan undue concern."

Lulu glanced at me and started to respond, but I stopped her. "It's fine, Lu. Let's get this over with."

"I'll be outside," she told me, then turned to Stevenson. "Come get one of us if you need to." Lulu wasn't happy about being excused, but she walked into the kitchen, grabbed two bottles of water from the refrigerator, then joined Ed and Avo in the backyard.

"First of all, we're sorry to bother you," said Ochoa, "and we won't take more of your time than we need."

"What can I help with?" I asked with a shrug, looking back and forth between them.

"We discovered a connection between our investigations into the deaths of Paul Davisson and Richard Carling," began Stevenson.

"I assumed as much and that connection would be me," I said. I slowly moved my upper body forward into the less painful sitting position. "I can't sit for very long," I explained. "I try to move around when I'm not standing or lying down."

"Why didn't you tell me you knew Davisson?" asked Ochoa calmly, with a touch of care in her tone.

I sighed. "Because he reminded me of a time in my life that I had put behind me."

"When did you realize the guest at the resort was your former employer?" she asked, with less care.

"A friend manages the front desk at the hotel. He called me when he saw the company name on the expense account. It was a heads up. I appreciated it. Davisson was at my bar, ordering a double on the rocks before I even got off the phone," I said with a laugh that contained as much energy as I could put into it. "Davisson didn't seem to have any idea who I was. I'm older and quite a bit thinner now. The last thing I wanted was to talk to him. I even took my name tag off. You know the rest."

"Why did you want to talk to Carling, but not Davisson?" asked Stevenson. "Didn't he remind you of the same period?"

I rested my head in my hands while I thought about the question. It took me but a few moments to answer and I was truthful. "Davisson stepped into my life, the life I lead now, as an imposition," I explained. "I had no choice about seeing him. He just showed up, even though I tried to keep the past and the present separate. When he died, I felt the need to address his death with someone from my past, but on my terms. It was my choice. That's what I needed. It's hard to explain. My therapist might explain it better." I paused for a breath. "Maybe I confronted Carling because I couldn't confront Davisson." *Funny*, I thought, *but it was all true.*

Stevenson and Ochoa glanced at each other briefly then looked back at me. I perceived the slightest of nods from each of them. "I had no idea that Carling was ill. I wasn't prepared for that," I told them.

"Or for what followed," said Stevenson. I shook my head but didn't bother to look up at him.

"One other thing," said Ochoa, her words slowly metered. "When you went to Davisson's room that night, the security video shows you placing the tray on the floor before you knocked on his door. Why didn't you knock first?"

"I didn't want to take a chance that he might recognize me. I brought the printout he wanted. It was easier to leave it there, and honestly, the tray was heavy."

"And you have no idea what happened to the report you printed for him?"

"How would I know? All I know is that I left it on the room service tray."

I was exhausted and must have looked it. "I think I have all I need, Ms. Cordovan," said Stevenson. "Anything else, Ochoa?"

"No," she said shaking her head as she stood, and Stevenson followed her lead. "Thank you, again. We'll see ourselves out."

"Could you ask Lulu and Ed to come in? I might need help getting to the bedroom."

Ochoa and Stevenson appeared embarrassed by my request, but they did as I asked. Then they left my house.

Chapter 44

As the doctor suggested, I talked with hospice workers and while their involvement is not exactly scheduled, they were put on alert that need for their support was imminent.

Fentanyl was no longer sufficient. It was impossible to maintain a manageable level of comfort unless I had enough of the drug in my system to make me sleep. Drug-induced sleep was not the way I wanted to spend the end of my life. I talked with Dr Edmunds' office and switched to morphine, which hospice uses anyway. My home now featured a wheelchair and accommodations in my bathroom. I declined the use of a hospital bed because it wasn't big enough for Ed, Avo and me.

I was never alone. Between Lulu, Amir, Joe, and Ed, one of them was always with me. They might have worked out a schedule of some sort, but I wasn't aware of it. Lulu helped me if I wanted to shower. If she wasn't around, I relied on Ed. I heard them murmuring from time to time, but I was not interested unless they were talking to me directly. I just did not have the energy or strength to care. Meals had reduced to a few small bites each day. I usually felt nauseous with anything in my stomach, but for some reason coffee didn't bother me.

Avo rarely left my side unless I encouraged him to go outside with one of the others while I rested. The highlight of my day had become sitting on the back patio, sipping coffee or beer, watching Avo with one of the others nearby.

The following Monday, I received a call from the law office that the trust documents—I was advised to establish a trust instead of writing a will—were ready for my signature. The assistant offered to bring them to my home, which was considerate of her because I was not venturing out much. She arrived and after Lulu made coffee, we settled at the dining table and reviewed the paperwork. The legal assistant served as witness to my signature. If the end of our meeting was poignant or emotional, it was lost on me. By the time she took her leave, I was exhausted. Even after drinking two cups of Lulu's strong coffee, all I could do was lie down.

That evening, Ed and I took Avo to a park. It would be more accurate to say that Ed and Avo took me along. We stopped for chocolate milkshakes on the way. I couldn't drink much of mine, but the high-caloric, creamy concoction was Ed's attempt to entice me, and I loved him for it.

Ed brought a comfortable camp chair and placed it under an acacia tree. He helped me from the car to the chair and I watched as he threw the frisbee and Avo fetched it. I can't say how long we were there, but dusk was settling in as we left the park.

Chapter 45

It was late Wednesday morning when Henry called Mara's number. A young woman answered. Henry remembered the name of Mara's roommate but didn't want to presume.

"This is Henry Maloney," he stated calmly. "I'm calling to speak with Mara Cordovan."

"Hello Dr. Maloney. This is Lulu Vasquez, Mara's roommate," the woman answered in a quiet voice. "Mara is resting."

"How is she doing?" asked Henry.

"She had a rough night. She's resting easier at least for now. Would you like me to give her a message? I know she'd be disappointed to have missed your call."

"Yes, please tell her I called—that I wondered if she wanted to talk."

"I will let her know as soon as she wakes up," said Lulu. "And thank you, Dr. Maloney, for helping. Mara speaks highly of you. You've been a great help to her."

"That's very kind of you. Thank you for letting her know I called. Goodbye."

***

I returned Henry's call around mid-day, wondering why he would call as he had not done so before. I was surprised that he was available, but he answered rather quickly.

"I know you chose to stop our sessions," said Henry, "but I wonder if I might visit you. If you are hesitant, let me assure you that it is not unusual for a therapist to see certain patients in their home."

"You mean patients who are going to die soon."

"Yes," Henry said with a sigh. "I'd like to help if you feel anxious. Also, I'd like to be available to the people in your life, and I'd like to meet Avo."

"Sure, Henry. I'm sure they would like to meet you," I told him.

"I want to be a resource for you, in case you want to talk, as I said."

"Thanks, Henry. Do me a favor—let's make this a visit between friends. We can both relax and act like it's not weird that one of us has hospice on speed dial."

"The things you say, Mara," said Henry, shaking his head.

"Yeah, yeah, I know. Morbid. That's the way I'm dealing with it. How about later today? I don't mean to put you on the spot, but best not to wait, know what I mean?"

***

Joe and I had a conversation that afternoon about the manila envelope. The envelope was sealed, and I had written contact information for Cameron Rowen on the front. In addition to the copious notes I had previously gathered, I included the following note:

Cameron:

By now you are aware that your dad and I shared the same fate. Please forgive my deception but we each must deal with difficult decisions in our own way. The sad truth for your father and me, as well as for at least a dozen others mentioned herein, is that our lives were taken from us. I'm entrusting you with the information I pieced together, in part, because of your dad, but also because of your proximity to the best in investigative journalism. I am confident the staff reporters at the *Republic* will uncover a great deal more. These wrongs cannot be righted, although I attempted to seek a brand of justice for all of us. I am sure that you will learn more of my efforts at some point but know that I ask neither forgiveness nor understanding from anyone.

With my best for your family,

Mara Cordovan

Without offering much detail, I asked Joe to deliver the envelope to Cameron after I was gone. Joe asked no questions, trusted me, and promised to see the request through. How many others shared my fate with no idea that they'd been deceived was a question I could not answer, but I owed it to the people who had worked for Presson-Hagee to ensure that the story of the company's greed and dishonesty would be exposed.

Chapter 46

When Henry arrived shortly after six p.m., Lula greeted him at the front door. "You must be Henry," she said as she extended her hand. "I'm Lulu. Please come in."

"Henry Maloney," he said as he shook Lulu's hand and stepped into the foyer. Henry's eye found the baby grand across the living room and saw a man sitting on the couch to the right of the piano. Another fellow took steps in their direction from the kitchen at Henry's left.

The man on the couch rose to his feet and stepped toward Henry. "Joe Cordovan," he said as he shook Henry's hand. "Thank you for coming." The man who had joined them from the kitchen introduced himself as Amir, Mara's other roommate.

"Is someone with Mara?" asked Henry.

"Yes, Ed is with her in her room," answered Lulu. "She only left her room once today. Avo is with her too."

"I've heard a lot about Avo, and I look forward to meeting Ed," Henry said as he turned to Joe. "I believe Ed is a friend of yours, am I right?"

"Yes," answered Joe with a nod. "A good friend. We work together."

Henry watched the threesome in their shared grief. He had witnessed the scenario countless times.

"Let's tell them you're here," said Lulu.

Henry followed her down a hallway to the right of the foyer. She stopped at a door that was slightly ajar and knocked on the door frame with her knuckle. "Mara? Ed? May we come in? Henry is here."

"Henry Maloney," he said, as he offered his hand to Ed. The two men shook hands as Ed murmured a faint hello. The awkward introductions were now complete.

It was a pleasant bedroom, large enough in size to hold a large bed and other furnishings without crowding. Nightstands were situated at each bedside. A long dresser was against a wall with a doorway at the other end that Henry assumed led to a bathroom. An upholstered chair and ottoman were near the foot of the bed, the closet to their side.

"Henry," Mara said, waving him in with one hand. She was lying on the bed, her shoulders and head supported by pillows. Her dark hair was pulled up into a messy bun on the top of her head. Her color was not bad, except for the dark circles under her eyes. Her voice sounded stronger in person than it had by phone earlier. Mara was draped by a sheet from the waist down with one knee sticking out at an angle. She wore a black camisole top with straps, the kind his partner Mona wore around the house in the evening. Smack dab in the middle of the huge bed stretched a blond Labrador retriever that looked as big as Mara. Avo.

"Hello," offered Henry as a greeting. "Do you feel like talking for a bit?"

"Sure," said Mara. "But don't be offended if I fall asleep."

"You won't fall asleep," Ed told her. He turned to Henry. "She insisted she wait for a dose of morphine until after she spoke with you."

"We won't talk long. I promise," Henry assured Ed. "It's better for her to stay on schedule."

Ed turned to Mara. "Are you sure you're up to this?"

Mara nodded and gave Ed a smile. "Maybe you can get Avo to go outside. He's been in here with me for hours."

"No problem." Ed walked over and kissed her. "Come on, Avo. Outside time and then Amir and I are cooking dinner."

Avo ambled up from Mara's bed. Bounding to the floor, he stopped briefly to check out Henry and receive his attentive petting. "What a gorgeous dog, Mara. You weren't kidding—he's amazing."

"Yes, he is, like Avogadro's Constant," she said as she watched Ed and Avo leave the room. Henry noticed that Ed closed the door behind them. Had Mara set the stage? Was she wanting to talk privately with Henry as much as he intended to speak to her?

"Do you mind if I sit?" asked Henry as he pointed to the chair.

"Please do," said Mara, as Henry sat down. "I wanted to tell you that I've had a trust created, Henry, for my estate. It was the final item on a list of chores that I needed to complete. I thank you for the encouragement and the direction."

"You're welcome. I'm glad to hear it. How are you feeling about the decisions you made, about your estate?"

"Fine, all fine," she answered waving away any thought of concern.

Henry nodded. "Mara, you mentioned other decisions, other chores. You feel that you've finished what you needed to do. You're not leaving things undone." It wasn't phrased as a question, but an answer was expected, nonetheless.

Mara looked Henry in the eye. "No. I'm quite content, to be honest."

"Then I need to ask you—was Paul Davisson's death one of those decisions?"

Mara took a deep breath, exhaled slowly and with ease. She smiled at Henry. "You are a smart man."

"It wasn't a stretch. You are a trained chemist. He died from a combination of drugs and alcohol. You know the reactions, combinations," explained Henry. "The circumstances were in your favor. You worked there. He was staying at the resort."

"In truth, it was surprisingly easy, Henry."

"Then you admit it?"

"To you, Henry? Of course, I admit it. The man was responsible for my cancer, my exposure to chemicals!" Mara's speech was labored, but the emotion behind her words was crystal. "He deserved to die.

He deserved to die for what he did to my friend, Evan, to his family. To me! Davisson was killing himself anyway. A pathetic sad man, drowning his guilt in drugs and whiskey according to his colleague, Richard Carling. I merely helped him along," Mara said with a shrug of her thin shoulders. "You could almost say it was what he wanted."

"Were you not worried about being found out? You committed a murder, after all."

"Why so judgmental, Henry?" asked Mara. "Out of character for you, and not appropriate for a therapist."

"I'm asking as a human being. A morally obligated human being."

Mara folded her arms across her chest. She tipped her head backed and looked at Henry with derision. "I never really cared if I was found out, Henry, but I was determined to finish what I started, complete my tasks, before I became unable to continue—and I did. And you can shove your moral obligation up your ass."

"Point taken. Mara. I apologize."

"Thank you, Henry."

Henry waited a moment before he asked his next question. "Was it worth it? Do you feel a sense of relief?"

"Profound relief, Henry! You explained in our first session that accepting that you have nothing to lose is a feeling of great freedom! That we often have an epiphany when faced with our own mortality."

"That's not what I meant, Mara."

"But that's what it meant to me! My lifespan was abruptly cut in half! I was sacrificed for greed and didn't know it until it was too late. Now, only now, at the end of my life I've finally stood up for myself. I am happy, fulfilled—at peace."

"I never meant to suggest ..."

"Please don't feel badly, Henry. You aren't responsible for my decisions. If you feel the urge as a professional to alert the authorities, go ahead," Mara laughed, "but I'll be dead before they can charge me, and they can't charge me without evidence. Apparently, there is none because it was ruled an accidental overdose." Mara thought of Detective Ochoa. If she'd had cause, Mara would have been placed under arrest.

"That's true," said Henry with a shrug. "And you feel justice has prevailed?"

"Hell, no. I don't think so at all! Where's my justice?" Mara asked, her breathing stilted, her voice full of agony. "You met my friends, you met Joe. You met Ed and Avo. I must leave them soon, Henry. Where's the justice in that?"

Henry watched as Mara slowly sat upright. It was a struggle, but one that she could still manage. She reached for a small bottle from the nightstand, unscrewed the lid and drew drops of liquid up into the dropper. Mara placed the tip of the dropper under her tongue and squeezed the rubber cap. She closed the small bottle and returned it to the nightstand. Mara resumed her reclined position and took a deep breath, waiting for the sublingual dose of morphine to hit. A few moments later, Henry saw her swallow.

Henry could only respond with a nod. "I'm glad we talked, Mara. I think you should rest now." He stood and walked toward the bedroom door.

"Goodbye, Henry." Mara's eyes were closed. She looked peaceful, indeed. Henry stepped from Mara's bedroom into the hallway and closed the door behind him.

Lulu and Joe were in the living room. Avo was on the floor nearby. Amir and Ed were in the kitchen as predicted, whipping up a meal with an aroma that would have enticed Henry except he had no appetite. Lulu turned her head and upon seeing Henry, she looked concerned. "Is she okay?"

"She's resting," he shared. Amir followed Ed into the living room. Henry looked at Ed and said, "She just took that dose of morphine." Ed nodded.

"How does she seem?" asked Joe.

"I would say ... that she's prepared. I doubt she'll have to wait long."

Henry said his goodbyes and left. He took no consolation from knowing his instincts had been correct.

***

After Henry's visit, I slipped in and out of naps for the rest of the evening. I gave little thought to the conversation we'd had even though I had confessed to the murder of Paul Davisson. In truth, I didn't like Henry's holier-than-thou attitude, but in a weird way, it was freeing to admit to my deed, and I decided to focus on that, dismissing the irritation. I simply didn't care anymore about anything other than my friends, my brother and Ed. And, of course, Avo.

My sweet dog refused to leave me for more than a few minutes at a time. When Ed or Lulu helped me to the bathroom, he insisted on accompanying us. He didn't lie on the floor of the bedroom anymore. He stayed with me on the bed, and we occasionally made room for Ed. When we were awake, Avo gazed intently into my eyes. He was communicating to me. I'm certain he was telling me that he loved me, he knew my time was near, and he would stay close to me until the end. I slept in a morphine fog between Avo and Ed, cocooned in their love for me—and this became my paradise.

***

Two days later, Henry received a call at his office. "Dr. Maloney, this is Lulu Vasquez. Mara passed away early this morning. We wanted you to know."

Coda: a concluding passage of a movement or composition

Chapter 47

"Stevenson," he barked as he answered his desk phone. It had been a busy morning.

"Hey. It's Leanna Ochoa in Scottsdale. You got a minute?"

"I got about one. What's up?"

"In case you hadn't heard, I saw an obit for Mara Cordovan. She died a few days ago."

Stevenson was silent for a moment. Finally, he said, "Okay, I appreciate the update."

"I have one other detail for you—sometimes a detail gets stuck in your head like an earworm, you know how it is. Anyway, I reviewed more video from the resort, watched for Davisson to bring that bottle of JW Red into his room. Never saw him bring it in. I gave up and tried a different angle. I finally accessed video from the store and looked through hours of it to find out when he purchased it."

"Oh yeah? What did you find?"

"A clear shot of Mara Cordovan buying a bottle of Johnny Walker Red."

"Well. I'll be damned," said Stevenson.

"Those were my thoughts exactly. It's all circumstantial, of course. Any rookie defense attorney worth the price of a cheap briefcase would know that."

"But the whiskey alone didn't kill him. It was a combo of booze and drugs." Stevenson reasoned.

"It was ... and a video of her purchasing the bottle is inconclusive. By itself it doesn't implicate her in his death. Davisson got the drugs somewhere."

"Right," Stevenson agreed, figuring the conversation was over. He started to ask why he needed to know any of this, but Ochoa wasn't finished.

"Stevenson, I got a call from Dr. Henry Maloney. He claimed that a couple of days before Ms. Cordovan died, she told Maloney that she caused the overdose. Told him she spiked his drinks because she blamed Davisson for causing her cancer. Maloney claimed he didn't believe her, thought she imagined it, or was confused due to her pain medications. He said he went through his notes from therapy sessions to assess her level of competence. Maloney said he was obligated to report what she had disclosed even if he didn't believe her."

The detective recalled the phone call he received from Dr. Maloney, how it caught him off guard. Maloney might have suspected something but there was no way to prove it.

"He contacted me too, Ochoa, as a therapist concerned for his terminally ill patient who had been through a traumatic incident. That phone call connected Mara Cordovan to both Davisson and Carling."

"Yes, and you called me, and we talked with her. Together. We had no evidence to charge her with anything at that time. The woman died before we put it all together. If she hadn't confessed to her shrink, we still wouldn't know that Mara Cordovan got away with murder.

"You're wrong, Ochoa," Stevenson told her, shaking his head. "The woman is dead. The way I see it, she didn't get away with anything.

***

As requested, Mara's remains were cremated. Her ashes were placed in an urn and the urn rests on the center of the dresser top in her bedroom. Her estate was well organized and there were no surprises as to her bequests. Mara had made her wishes known and there was no detail out of the ordinary. The portrait of Mara that Ed sketched hangs on the wall in the living room near her beloved piano.

Mara requested there be no service in her memory. Instead, her friends sat around the table for hours, drinking beer and eating snacks much the way they had the night Mara came home with the news that she was dying, except that the small group now included Joe and Ed. Toasts were offered up to Mara and countless bottles were tapped together in her memory as Avo stretched out on the floor nearby.

Avo, Mara's beautiful dog, still sleeps on the floor of her room, but he searches the house for her less often. At least that's what Lulu is determined to believe.

THE END

Acknowledgements

Writing fiction can be a community effort. The finished work may contain the effort of many people and this book is no different. There are a host of people I must thank because without their willingness to assist, the telling of Mara's tale would never have happened.

I was fortunate to have four incredible beta-readers who agreed to read an early, unedited draft. Each of the four assisted in very specific ways. Their help and their honesty were essential and working with these four as beta-readers was a pleasure: T.K. Toppin, a gifted author of fiction in her own right, offered unabashed, honest critique and much appreciated encouragement. Lynn Keaveney provided expertise in grammar and diction, reading questionable paragraphs many times over without complaining, for which I am most grateful. Cheryl Hamilton reviewed aspects of the plot regarding cancer diagnoses and treatment and to my knowledge, did not flinch once. In addition, Cheryl shared her expertise of Human Resources, advising on the support an ill employee might expect as well as the rights to which they might be entitled. Dr. Markus McDowell, an accomplished author and editor, caught so many hiccups in the early draft and served as research consultant with regards to estate law.

Thanks go to Shrutidora P. Mohor, my "cosmic sister" and fellow December for helping make the Jhankar Mahal as authentically Indian as possible, providing Mara and Ed with a favorite restaurant. We both became famished while working on that scene. Thanks also to Terri Kitts at Fiverr, for designing the amazing cover and not once screaming "Enough!" no matter how many times I requested a change of one more, tiny detail. Terri is a true professional as well as an incredible graphic artist.

To Edde Rolstad and Carolyn Livingston, thanks for proofreading the final draft with precision while I anxiously lurked. Thanks are due to the members of Write On ..., the writers' group at Robson

Ranch for keeping up as I shared each disjointed excerpt for their review.

I am eternally thankful that my husband, Dave (please see dedication in the front matter) liked the story idea, provided all the chemistry and lab details, and once again, sat through a read-aloud of the manuscript.

Once again, I am grateful to Matt Love at Nestucca Spit Press for serving as editor. Swan Song is our fourth collaboration. Matt asks the right questions, doesn't mince words when I need the truth, and refuses to demand less than my best. And Matt loves a good story—a valuable trait in an editor. You can reach him at necstuccaspitpress@gmail.com.

Discussion Guide for Book Clubs:

1. This novel involves an ethical dilemma. Do you think Mara's actions are justified?
2. Mara seems to disdain some of Henry's advice. If you've had an experience with a therapist or counselor, what was your opinion of that process?
3. What of Mara's new friend, Ed—did he need to know of her diagnosis, or should Mara have kept that to herself?
4. Mara decides against available forms of treatment. Can you see yourself making that decision or would you go for it, no holds barred?
5. Can you relate to Mara's closeness with her dog, Avo? Have you had a similar experience with a pet who brought you great comfort?
6. Mara mentions the stark difference in working for Tomas, the bar manager at the resort and Paul Davisson, her ill-fated former employer. Have you had more experiences with good bosses or terrible ones?
7. Have you had the opportunity to engage with hospice services as Mara did, either as a friend, a family member or as a volunteer? What was your experience?

Don't miss out!

Visit the website below and you can sign up to receive emails whenever Susanne Perry publishes a new book. There's no charge and no obligation.

https://books2read.com/r/B-A-TQXL-XQQEC

BOOKS2READ

Connecting independent readers to independent writers.

Did you love *Swan Song*? Then you should read *Runaway*[1] by Susanne Perry!

[2]

Runaway: a runaway is found dead in an alley. Who is she? Why is she living on the street? The answers lie deep within the community of street dwellers, often ignored or invisible. To find the young woman's killer, Sergeant Liz Jordan and Officer Kyle Connors must earn the trust of people without permanent addresses, who do not trust the establishment. Delving deep into a world of uncertainty and danger, the investigation uncovers a web of deceit and exploitation that preys on the most vulnerable. Runaway is the first novel in the City Streets Trilogy.

---

1. https://books2read.com/u/m2Z89k

2. https://books2read.com/u/m2Z89k

Also by Susanne Perry

City Streets Trilogy
Runaway
Veteran
Gutter Punk

Standalone
Swan Song

About the Author

Susanne Perry is the author of the City Streets Trilogy, a series of crime mysteries set in a fictional urban area in southwest Washington. Previous to writing novels, Perry worked with public programs serving children and families. Future writing projects include short stories, children's books, and of course, mysteries. A voracious reader of who-done-its and historical fiction, Perry resides in Arizona and Washington.

About the Publisher